BLOOD QUEEN

BLOOD DESTINY SERIES BOOK SIX

CONNIE SUTTLE

Subtle Demon
subtledemon.com

Print Second Edition (2018)
Print ISBN: 1-63478-051-5
Print ISBN-13: 978-1-63478-051-3
ISBN: 1-939759-19-6
ISBN-13: 978-1-939759-19-1

Published by:
SubtleDemon Publishing, LLC
PO Box 95696
Oklahoma City, OK 73143

Cover art by Renee Barratt @ The Cover Counts

To Walter, Joe, Larry, Lee, Dianne, Sarah and Mark.
Thank you.

ACKNOWLEDGMENTS

As always, this book is the result of collaboration. If it weren't for the support of my editor, my cover artist and my beta readers, it would be less than it is. All mistakes, as usual, are mine and no other's.

About the Author:
Connie Suttle lives in Oklahoma with her husband and a conglomerate of cats. They have finally banded together to make their demands, which has proven disconcerting to all humans involved.

You may find Connie in the following ways:
Facebook: Connie Suttle Author
Twitter: @subtledemon
Website and Blog: subtledemon.com

High Demon Series:
Demon Lost
Demon Revealed
Demon's King
Demon's Quest
Demon's Revenge
Demon's Dream

God Wars Series:
Blood Double
Blood Trouble
Blood Revolution
Blood Love
Blood Finale

Saa Thalarr Series:
Hope and Vengeance
Wyvern and Company
Observe and Protect*

First Ordinance Series:
Finder
Keeper
BlackWing
SpellBreaker
WhiteWing

R-D Series:

Cloud Dust

Cloud Invasion

Cloud Rebel

Latter Day Demons Series:

Hot Demon in the City

A Demon's Work is Never Done

A Demon's Due

Seattle Elementals Series:

Your Money's Worth

Worth Your While*

BlackWing Pirates Series

MindSighted

MindMage

MindRogue

MindMaster*

Black Rose Sorceress Series

The Rose Mark

Rose and Thorn

Black Rose Queen

Queen of Thorns and Roses

Future Wars Series

Buffer Zone

Black Zone*

Other Titles from SubtleDemon Publishing:

Malefactor

Transgressor

Underhanded*

by Joe Scholes

*Forthcoming

BLOOD QUEEN

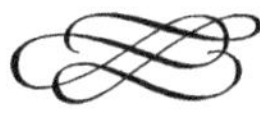

BLOOD DESTINY SERIES, BOOK SIX

CHAPTER 1

Griffin and I stood upon the streets of Veshtul, on the planet named after a god. I recognized the streets and narrow lanes with their multicolored bricks, colorful shops and vending stands run by the comesuli. When I'd seen it before with Kifirin at my side, it had been a peaceful scene in early twilight. Comesuli had called out to one another as businesses were shut down for the evening.

Now, instead of the tranquil city I'd visited before, the shops were deserted and chaos, noise and destruction reigned. Smoke billowed from fires burning throughout Veshtul, and the scent of death was everywhere. I cringed as an explosion rocked the ground beneath my feet and shops collapsed around us.

Thousands of Copper Ra'Ak fought throughout Veshtul, killing many as they lashed out, or crushing others as they crawled along. Screaming comesuli ran before them, desperate to escape the deadly creatures. In the distance, Dragon's roar sounded as he fought off one of the monsters.

Three other Dragons fought beside him; I saw them as they charged their prey—a Black Dragon, a Silver Dragon and a Gold

Dragon. Others were fighting Ra'Ak as well; a Black Gryphon fought alongside a huge Snow Leopard. Giant birds swept the sky, screaming in anger as Ra'Ak leapt at them, attempting to sink rows of deadly teeth into feathered flesh.

A separate battle raged between High Demons—thousands of them warred with one another and from a distance, it was difficult to tell who might be friend or foe. They were all in Full Thifilathi and a single confrontation between any two of them was fierce and terrible to witness.

Griffin set me down in one of the few remaining areas of Veshtul that hadn't been touched by copper-scaled monsters or battles between High Demons. "You can make this right, Lissa," Griffin whispered in my ear as I gazed in horror at the war before us.

I turned to him, then—he was still frightened, his voice urgent. "It isn't just the Ra'Ak; the two largest High Demon Houses have allied with them. They will kill the Saa Thalarr and all who live here if you do not stop them."

Griffin's words shocked me—this was connected to the dream I'd had about the High Demon King and his Queen. All of it was coming true before me. There was more to this story, too; I could see it in Griffin's eyes. He just wasn't telling me the full tale. Nevertheless, what he'd told me was truth; he couldn't lie, just as Merrill said. If I didn't do something, Kifirin would fall.

"All right." I nodded at Griffin, took a deep breath, turned to mist and threw myself into the battle.

There are too many of them, Adam shouted mentally to Lynx, who fought nearby, his giant cat ripping into a Ra'Ak with his claws.

I never thought our last stand would be like this, Lynx replied before cutting off mental communication. The Ra'Ak he fought commanded his full attention.

Xenides' death had given me the weapon I needed—I no longer had to come in contact with poisoned outer scales to defeat the Ra'Ak. I could mist inside their heads and blow my mist outward. They exploded, just as anything else might.

It was a chain reaction, after a while. I found a Ra'Ak, he died. I found the next one and he died—as quickly as I could mist from one to the other. I soon lost count, so many were destroyed. The High Demons I found that held taint? They died just as easily as the Ra'Ak did.

The High Demons, good and bad, all fought in Full Thifilathi. They were at least seventeen feet tall in that form; all of them horned, black-scaled, winged, terrible to look upon and fought to the death. Most fought with other High Demons, but some were targeted by Ra'Ak.

It took many Ra'Ak to bring down even one High Demon. A High Demon I misted past was in trouble, fighting off six Ra'Ak at once, so I gave him a little help. He would probably never know what had come to save him there at the end, just as he was about to fall.

The other High Demons battled one another, their roars deafening as they ripped flesh and limbs away with powerful hands and deadly claws. Nearly half the High Demons fighting held taint, and with the thousands of Ra'Ak helping those rogues, the battle was certainly weighted in their favor.

Until I showed up, that is.

The comesuli, though, had been caught off guard in their city and had no defense against those attacking them. They ran from the Ra'Ak, some of which were eating the comesuli they could reach and allowing their poisonous scales and crushing weight to destroy others.

I wanted to weep in frustration as I misted toward those Ra'Ak. They died, but a sad side effect of killing Ra'Ak is that they dust, blasting fist-sized chunks in all directions and killing anything in their path. I found myself praying that the comesuli casualties would be light and that Roff and Giff would be safe. Shoving my anger at so many comesuli deaths aside, I became a killing machine.

Four seconds passed, a Ra'Ak died. Another four seconds, another Ra'Ak blasted outward. Eventually, though, my timing stretched out. I was tiring. The battle with Xenides earlier, combined with the taking of my blood by the Council, wearied me.

It took longer to pull my mist together. Ten seconds it took. And then twenty. Forty. More than a minute. Five minutes. Until the moment came when I reached exhaustion. I didn't have enough energy to kill anything past that point. Not without killing myself.

The noise and destruction continued in the distance, but I found myself kneeling amid a pile of debris, surrounded by a relative sea of calm—if you call crushed shops, dead comesuli and Ra'Ak chunks littering the ground a sea of calm. I panted as I gazed about me—devastation and the scent of spilled blood was everywhere.

"I'm sorry I didn't get here sooner," I had trouble gasping out the words. I saw a hand stretched from beneath a collapsed wall. A severed leg nearby. A head, matted with blood. All dead. I didn't hear a heartbeat anywhere around me.

The worst thing? Just to my left lay a comesula, his tiny, lifeless child still clutched in his arms. They'd been crushed to death while attempting to flee. I hugged my arms tightly around myself, wanting to weep when there was no moisture left in my body to make the tears. Still struggling for breath, I wished for a drink of water on a world I couldn't find on a star map anywhere.

Where had Griffin gone? Was he lost, like so many others? These thoughts ran through my mind while I knelt there, working to catch my breath, trying to muster enough strength to stand.

Kifirin—this was his world. Where was he? Why wasn't he helping? Griffin—was this one of those things for which I'd been the answer? Was this the ultimate reason he'd searched out my mother to create a child? Kifirin and Griffin—how did those two know each other, and why? They'd engineered this somehow; I was sure of it.

While I pondered those scattered thoughts, something crunched nearby. A noise of scales, scraping across colored bricks came, and then more crunching as an enormous, copper body crawled over wrecked shops and the bodies of the dead.

Lifting my eyes, I watched as the largest Ra'Ak I'd ever seen approached, and I'd killed plenty that were quite large. At least seventy feet in length he was; his copper body wide and gleaming in the late afternoon light. His mouth was open, revealing rows of lengthy, needle-sharp teeth. His eyes, too, were darting quickly, searching his surroundings as he crawled along. He was hunting someone.

He was hunting me.

I only had to turn my body to mist before he caught sight of me, and I would be invisible to him. He would crawl right past me, never knowing his target was mere feet away. This was the Ra'Ak Prince—I knew it. He was searching for whatever had killed so many of his kind.

It was easy; I'd made it easy. The killing had stopped right where I was. Should I go to mist and let him slide past, or should I spend my last breath and destroy him?

When I killed Xenides, I knew his machinations would stop with his death. He'd been the puppet-master, pulling all the other's strings. His goal of destroying life on Earth had died with him.

Sounds of fighting, screaming and roaring still reached me from a distance; the Copper Prince's remaining subjects continued to wage his battle. The worst sounds that came to my ears, however, were the screams of the comesuli as they died. Were more children dying with them? Would it stop, if this one crawling toward me died? Would it stop, if I died with him?

This would take my life. I knew that. I didn't have enough strength to pull my mist together if I blew it outward again. I almost hadn't done it the last time. If I did this, it would be a calculated decision on my part. One I'm sure Griffin had seen. He'd seen all the other things, hadn't he? He'd known I wouldn't be able to stop until I'd done everything I could.

I struggled to stand, making myself visible to the Ra'Ak, who hissed immediately and prepared to strike. I might have been a blink or two slower to turn to mist, but the momentum of the Ra'Ak's thrust as he lashed out, carried my mist right through his head and allowed it

to lodge inside his brain. Working as quickly as I could, I wound my
mist tightly before loosing it for the last time.

CHAPTER 2

An explosion rocked the ground beneath Dragon's clawed feet as he snapped the head from the Ra'Ak he'd been fighting. His three sons fought nearby, all desperate to take the monsters down. All other Saa Thalarr fought the Ra'Ak, some in teams, others alone.

The High Demons loyal to the crown fought beside the Saa Thalarr, along with a handful of Black Ra'Ak, who'd allied themselves with the Saa Thalarr in an attempt to take down the renegade copper monsters.

When the explosion came, however, the Copper Ra'Ak had already been reduced to a more reasonable number. There was now hope, whereas before, the task had been impossible. None knew what had killed so many Copper Ra'ak or their High Demon allies; they only knew that they'd died and in the strangest of ways.

Now, many of the copper monsters were attempting to fold away from Kifirin, rather than staying to fight. The Larentii, who'd come to do what they could, quickly placed a shield around the planet to prevent escape. Once the Copper Prince died and any avenue of escape disappeared, the few remaining Copper Ra'Ak lost their will to fight and were easily destroyed.

"What just happened?" Merrill changed from his Snow Leopard form and stood panting on the steps of the High Demons' palace. Adam Chessman, the Black Gryphon, appeared at Merrill's side, the same question on his lips.

"My darling, are you well?" Merrill reached out to Kiarra, who materialized on the steps between him and Adam. Adam was already running his hands over her, searching for injuries. Kiarra was mated to both Adam and Merrill, in addition to Pheligar the Larentii, who as yet hadn't made an appearance.

"What's that?" Merrill turned swiftly as Griffin appeared nearby. The retired Saa Thalarr wept and fell to his knees on the palace steps.

"Griffin? What's wrong?" Kiarra went immediately to Griffin's side, Merrill and Adam close behind her.

"Brother, what is it?" Merrill dropped to his knees beside Griffin, who was sobbing.

"I had to do it," Griffin wept. "I had to."

"Do what, brother?" Merrill asked gently.

"Bring her forward in time. She was the answer, Merrill. The only one. I killed her."

"Who? Who died?" Kiarra knelt to stroke Griffin's hair.

"Lissa," Griffin's voice held pain. "It was Lissa."

"Why didn't we remember?" Merrill paced angrily before Pheligar. Pheligar looked tired and out of sorts, and Larentii never looked tired and out of sorts.

"The memories were removed after she was brought forward in time," Pheligar replied stiffly. "None were allowed to remember her, so none could interfere. Kifirin made a mistake when he gave the ability to travel through time to the Ra'Ak. Three of those creatures managed to escape before our shield was placed. They will certainly carry tales back to the others—the four thousand Ra'Ak that died here today are only a small portion of their total population. Had the little Vampire Queen lived, they would hunt her through the timeline and destroy her for killing their Prince." Pheligar's gaze traveled over the devastation of Veshtul. Many had died, but Lissa had managed to save most.

"Had anyone remembered her in the past," Pheligar added, "she would have become a target while she lived. Many would have sought her death and it would have been meaningless when she died at their hands on Earth, just to prevent this from happening." Pheligar stretched out a hand—he and Merrill stood on the uppermost dome of the High Demon's palace to hold their private conversation.

"So, the memories were removed to prevent her from becoming a target—until today," Merrill muttered.

"Sadly, that is truth," Pheligar agreed. "The vampires on Earth no longer remember her—the memory was only given back to the Saa Thalarr and a few others."

"Yes, I remembered as soon as I heard her name, as did Wlodek, Radomir, Russell, Will, Weldon, Charles, Brock and the others who are now Saa Thalarr or Spawn Hunters."

"As she is now dead, it no longer matters that the others do not recall her. It is an injustice to the little Queen, I know," Pheligar admitted, raising a hand before Merrill could protest. "All her deeds wiped away and attributed to others."

"It wasn't only this world she saved," Merrill muttered. "Kifirin is the balance for all the worlds. Those copper idiots were about to destroy everything if they took it down."

"I know that well," Pheligar nodded. "It is the only reason the Larentii came."

Earth—Past

Merrill turned Kiarra's written message in his hands. A note coming from her surprised him greatly. Not that Adam and Kiarra didn't contact him often—they did. He'd expected to hear from

Griffin, though; Merrill was waiting for his old friend to bring Lissa home.

The grounds surrounding the manor were wet from a brief rain and weak sunlight shone down as Merrill gazed through his study window. For fifteen hundred years, Merrill had walked in daylight; it was a gift that came with Griffin's blood.

Merrill was powerful before as a King Vampire, but after receiving Griffin's blood, he'd become legend. Many hunted him through the centuries, and he'd taken all of them down. It was easy—Griffin made it possible, and all because Merrill helped Griffin kill spawn fifteen hundred years in the past. Merrill sighed and turned away from the window.

Wlodek also waited for Lissa's return—the Head of the Vampire Council was eager to make an official announcement to the Council that Lissa would be joining them (although they already knew; they'd seen the evidence for themselves). Lissa would sit with Wlodek at Council meetings as a Queen, and not just any Queen—the strongest and most talented that any of them had ever seen.

Instead of Griffin, however, Kiarra had contacted Merrill, asking for a meeting in the afternoon. It was three days after Griffin snatched Lissa away, claiming he needed her help. Merrill sighed—he and Wlodek had both attempted to stop Griffin. Who knew where he'd taken Lissa and why?

Wlodek worried that she'd be offered a place with the Saa Thalarr, just as they'd offered with Adam Chessman. Chessman had accepted the invitation without a backward glance. The vampires needed Lissa on Earth—the Saa Thalarr could find someone else, Wlodek insisted. A knock came on Merrill's study door, interrupting his thoughts.

"What is it, Franklin?" Merrill had to tread carefully with his human child; Franklin lost his mate three weeks earlier and had wandered about the house listlessly since. Merrill had some making up to do with Lissa when she returned; he and Wlodek had made the decision not to give her news of Greg's death.

Wlodek wanted her to remain focused on Xenides and the rest of his and Saxom's turns instead of grieving for a lost friend. Anthony was also fragile; Gavin had taken over Tony's teaching as his surrogate sire after the death of his cousin René. René's loss was a grievous one. He'd gone on many special assignments for Wlodek over the years and Wlodek certainly felt his absence.

"Kiarra, Adam and Dragon are here, Father." Franklin opened the door to Merrill's study quietly, making sure Merrill was prepared to receive guests.

"Please, bring them in." Merrill was happy to see Kiarra anytime. Kiarra was ushered inside Merrill's study, followed by Adam Chessman and the former Falchani Warlord, Dragon. Merrill had seen Dragon once before, prior to Saxom's death in Corpus Christi four years earlier. Merrill's eyebrows lifted when Kiarra walked in; there was something different about her—she seemed sad and troubled.

"You're right," Kiarra sighed heavily. "I am from the future, Merrill. Three hundred years in the future." There were tears in her eyes. Merrill quickly pulled a silk handkerchief from a desk drawer and handed it to her. Kiarra accepted it gratefully.

"Griffin was unable to come," Adam stated bluntly. Merrill went still.

"Is he all right?" Griffin and Merrill had been as close as brothers for more than fifteen hundred years. There shouldn't be any reason for Griffin not to come. Merrill held his breath.

"Griffin is well—physically," Dragon replied. He'd allowed Adam and Kiarra to sit in the two chairs before Merrill's desk. He remained standing, his expression shuttered and his dark eyes enigmatic.

Merrill didn't show his concern, but it was mounting. "What do you mean, physically?"

"What we mean is that Griffin is an emotional wreck," Adam said, his gray eyes revealing nothing. He could wear the vampire mask if he wanted; he'd been vampire before being chosen by the Saa Thalarr, after all.

"Tell me," Merrill whispered.

~

Wlodek's fingers shook slightly as he toyed with his favorite gold pen. He and Merrill had held a private meeting; Adam Chessman, the former Chief of Enforcers stayed to verify the information. Dragon transported Kiarra away; she'd been visibly upset and unable to stay.

Merrill was completely numb over the news brought to him; he and Wlodek now waited to pass that news to Gavin and Anthony. Charles and Radomir were also brought in—this news would be a terrible blow to Charles, and Merrill waited to place compulsion on Gavin and Tony. Wlodek feared it would be required should they become violent.

"You asked to see us, Honored One?" Gavin walked inside Wlodek's temporary office, followed by Tony. He'd taken Tony as his child and was training him as best he could. Gavin waited for Lissa's return, however, to teach some of their lessons simultaneously.

"Please, sit," Wlodek pointed to the chairs before his desk. He was still working out of Merrill's basement, but would return to his manor soon. Lissa had managed to eliminate Xenides and the remaining threat that he'd presented, so it was safe to return home.

But that was before. Wlodek heaved a shaky sigh, making Gavin's head jerk up in alarm. Tony heard it as well and turned to his surrogate sire, fear crossing his features.

"Child, we will wait for the news," Gavin's mask dropped into place. Wlodek knew Gavin was afraid; he merely refused to show it. It was only going to get worse.

"I do not have good news," Wlodek announced. "You know what Griffin is. He took Lissa into the future with him; her help was needed three hundred years from now on a very distant world," Wlodek looked at his gold pen and not at the others in the room.

"He knew, as did Kifirin, that something terrible would happen. We fear, too, that he also knew the price to be paid in order to make things come out right in the end." Wlodek found it difficult to understand Griffin's actions. How had Griffin made this sacrifice? Had he ever truly loved Lissa? It was beyond Wlodek's comprehension.

"You have never seen the Ra'Ak," Wlodek went on, glancing at

Gavin and Tony. "I have only heard them described. They are terrible monsters resembling giant serpents, and carry the deadliest of poisons. Adam Chessman informed me that more than four thousand of these attacked a world simultaneously, along with other creatures that held a might of their own. Griffin knew there was only one who might hold them at bay and keep that world from falling. Adam tells me that had that particular world fallen, all the other worlds would fall like dominoes stacked in a line."

Wlodek wanted to shake his head in disbelief; he still could not bring himself to accept the news. This was the greatest blow to the vampire race—they'd gained a Queen, only to lose her again.

"Lissa killed more than thirty-five hundred of the giant serpents by misting inside their heads and blowing them apart," Wlodek continued. "She also destroyed many of the other creatures in the same fashion. The final monster she killed required the last of her strength. When she blew her mist outward that time, she no longer held the power to call her mist together again. She, along with her enemy, is now scattered across the universe. Lissa is gone and will not return to us."

Charles wept as he dropped to the floor against the far wall. Tony blinked at Wlodek in shock. He couldn't be hearing the Head of the Council properly. This information could not be truth.

Gavin, however, rose shakily from his seat and began keening wildly, his grief evident in the high-pitched wail that came from his throat. Radomir joined with Gavin, his own keening forcing Wlodek to wipe tears away.

Merrill strode silently from the room. Compulsion wasn't needed and he had grieving to do in private.

Kifirin—Future

"Wait! Here's another one!" The search had gone on for four days after the attempted coup. Mostly the search and rescue teams were finding bodies of common demons. Few in this sector were found alive, and those were discovered within the first two days.

"Dead?" Wendevik, High Demon of the House of Greth, led the search detail of common demons through the streets of Veshtul. He rode the ox cart beside his common demon driver, while a dozen commons walked around it, searching through the debris for bodies.

Horoth, his uniform covered in blood, dust and debris from a lengthy search, knelt beside the body he'd uncovered to check for signs of life. Trooper Horoth normally worked with Wendevik's guards in one of two common demon cohorts, and it was his duty to police the marketplace and the residential sections of Veshtul.

Horoth didn't expect to find anything—this one was pale and unmoving. Dutifully he held a small mirror to the mouth and nostrils, blinking in shock when he saw the faintest misting on the reflective surface.

"Alive!" Horoth shouted and six common demons rushed to help.

"There is some swelling at the base of the skull," Darvul pointed out the injury to his assistant. The unconscious common lay on a bed shoved inside a small room; they'd placed other patients together to give this one a quiet space.

Darvul, stooped slightly from years of service and his once dark hair threaded liberally with silver, had lived more than five hundred years and worked as a physician in the city of Veshtul. He and sixteen other common physicians had been working nonstop since the attack and near takeover of Kifirin—the High Demons' planet.

"Has the common regained consciousness?" Nedil, another common physician, walked over to confer with Darvul. Nedil was showing signs of aging, just as Darvul was, and the attack had placed a heavy load on a small and already overburdened health care community.

"Not yet," Darvul sighed. "We are giving fluids as you can see, but there are no signs of waking. We remain hopeful."

"What are the other injuries?" Nedil was giving the small common a cursory examination as well, placing his hands on the head injury.

"Some bruising and swelling in the chest area, two broken ribs, a fractured wrist and twisted right leg. I'm sure the building collapsed on this one while he was hiding from the attackers."

"There was no place for these to run and no safe place to hide," Nedil said softly. "We have the heaviest losses from that section of the city. If my information is correct, we lost more than eight thousand in that area alone. They are still finding bodies. Who knows where the count will end?"

"We will do our best to keep this one alive, then," Darvul nodded. He'd already made that vow to himself, but he wanted Nedil to know he was seeing to this one personally. "What word on the Drith and Croth captives?" The rogue High Demons that still lived were now imprisoned and waiting judgment.

"They are being held in makeshift stockades outside the city; the Larentii helped erect them," Nedil's voice held wonder. He'd never seen a Larentii before, and the tales he'd heard of them said they never intervened in the troubles of any world. Yet he'd seen two in the past four days, and they were helping to gather and contain rogue High Demons.

"When the Raoni and Raona finish with them, Croth and Drith will wish they'd never been birthed," Darvul muttered.

"Has there been any word on those who came to help us?" Nedil witnessed the taking down of four thousand Ra'Ak, along with many rogue High Demons by an unseen hand. Most had exploded—or at least their heads did.

The Ra'Ak had all dusted afterward, and he'd tended many injuries from flying Ra'Ak debris. The High Demons who'd died had splattered bits and pieces of bone and tissue everywhere, leaving the rest of their Thifilathi to fall headless to the ground. Before the attack four days earlier, Nedil would have said the only thing capable of killing a High Demon was another High Demon. He knew better now, he just couldn't explain it.

"Keep cold compresses on the head injury," Darvul instructed his assistant, who barked orders to other common demons waiting to help. "This one doesn't look to be completely mature; I would guess the age at seventeen turns or so. He has not gotten his full height, yet," Darvul estimated. The bones were still small, the hands and feet slender and fragile-looking. "I hope his parent survived and comes looking for him." He leaned down and stroked the reddish-gold hair. "Wake to us," he said softly. "We will care for you."

~

Earth—Past

William Winkler sat in his kitchen, having a cup of coffee with his Second, Trajan, as they waited for Director Bill Jennings to arrive. Winkler knew at least one of the vampire agents was coming, in addition to a werewolf agent he'd met once before—James Renfro. Bill said he had news that should be delivered in person.

Winkler sighed—he couldn't imagine what Director Jennings might say, and worried about it. He and Trajan had both been up with the twins the night before—he'd hired a nanny, but he and his Second were always up and awake quickly whenever the babies cried to be fed.

They'd fed Wynter while the nanny took care of Wayne; Winkler decided to call his son by his middle name. Kellee, well, she was packing to go to her mother—she'd refused to stay and breastfeed the twins. Winkler growled low, just thinking about it.

Winkler might have felt sympathy for Kellee if she hadn't collaborated with her father to plot his death and the subsequent takeover of the Dallas Pack. Only Lissa's intervention had saved him and his Pack.

Karl Johnson would have taken over had things gone the other way; Weldon informed Winkler afterward that he would have split the Dallas Pack—it was much too large for Karl Johnson to handle. Some of Winkler's wolves would have torn their new Packmaster apart at the earliest opportunity, and Trajan might have been one of them.

Winkler answered the doorbell when it rang, inviting Bill, Ken White and James Renfro inside. He offered coffee, soft drinks or juice to his guests when he led them into the kitchen; Bill asked for coffee, the werewolf asked for a soda.

"We've already spoken with the Grand Master," Bill ran hands through his hair. Winkler noticed the Director's face looked older and more worn, although his biggest terrorist threat, Rahim Alif, had been eliminated weeks earlier. Some new worry now rested on Director Bill Jennings' shoulders.

"Is there a problem?" Winkler asked, staring into his cold cup of coffee.

"It's not a problem," Ken White said. "It's just the worst possible news." Winkler's head jerked up at the vampire agent's statement, his dark eyes searching Ken White's face for clues. In the usual vampiric convention, it contained nothing helpful.

"What news?" he asked.

"We offered to deliver it in person, in case, well, just in case," Bill sighed.

"What he's trying to tell you is that the female vampire is dead." James Renfro wanted it out in the open quickly. Open the wound and let it bleed out, that was his philosophy. Even he wasn't prepared for the howling and grieving that came as soon as the words left his mouth.

"Child, there is nothing we can do; they're both gone from us now." Merrill rocked Franklin against him while Franklin wept. This had gone on for days and Merrill was beginning to think he'd be forced to place compulsion on his human child.

Kyle was flying to London as quickly as he could; Merrill placed a call, asking him to come. Of Merrill's two remaining vampire children, Kyle had the closest bond with Franklin. He was hoping Kyle's presence would help; otherwise, it would be compulsion or medical intervention.

Gavin moved out of the manor the day after he'd received the news, taking Tony with him. Tony seemed lost and helpless as he'd loaded bags into Gavin's car. Lissa's things had been left inside her bedroom; Merrill closed the door on all of it and neither he nor Franklin had the strength to walk in there, now.

Charles wandered through the manor like a ghost, only doing what was necessary to keep Wlodek's office running smoothly. Radomir had taken the news harder than anyone suspected he might; Wlodek hadn't heard from him for three days and that worried his vampire sire. Flavio arrived and was now making sure important things were attended to so his sire could have time alone.

Bill Jennings, Director of the Joint NSA/Homeland Security Department, stood with Weldon Harper, Thomas Williams Jr. and William Winkler, next to a grave in Oklahoma City on a sunny October afternoon. The casket was empty, except for a few letters and a dozen red roses. The President had asked for a twenty-one gun salute.

Normally, that honor was reserved for a president, but it could also be performed for a foreign head of state or a member of a reigning royal family. Lissa, as a Queen Vampire, was given the honor. Bill, Winkler, Thomas and Weldon stood straight and still while the ranking officer barked the order and seven soldiers, in perfect unison, fired their rifles three times to honor the fallen.

Four weeks after Greg's death, Franklin walked into the empty second floor bedroom to clean it. He couldn't recall when he'd last been inside it to dust and straighten. It appeared sterile to his eyes; not even a mote of dust remained on the nightstand or the dresser. The closet inside the spacious bath held empty hangers and nothing else. Franklin hadn't recalled that Merrill had it decorated in a feminine style—the pillows and shams on the bed weren't suitable for a male.

It didn't matter; Franklin had nothing to do, here. He'd gone to this bedroom first, putting off going through Greg's personal belongings. That was pain waiting to happen. Franklin sighed as he closed the bedroom door behind him and walked toward the suite he'd shared with Greg. It was time to say a final goodbye.

"Fortune smiled upon us when we managed to destroy Xenides so easily," Merrill pushed a wineglass toward Wlodek. Wlodek was moving out of Merrill's basement—Charles, Rolfe, Radomir and Russell had come to help load equipment and records into waiting trailers.

"I find it fortunate that you were able to get close enough to lay compulsion," Wlodek sniffed the wine before tasting. "After that, it was easy to destroy him. I believe I enjoyed handing him his death more than any other."

"We lost many in the battle," Merrill pointed out.

"I have Charles searching the records already, looking for suitable replacements. The Aristocracy will be complete again for next year's meeting."

Kifirin—Future

"I don't know whether he will wake," Darvul was beginning to lose hope that the unconscious common might live. Nine days had passed and still the young common had not moved or wakened. Darvul and his assistant, Noff, had finished bathing the young one.

He might have been older than Darvul thought, Noff decided; the common demon had pubic hair, which normally arrived at age twenty or so. Common demons were slow to mature, since they lived six hundred years or more. Still, they had no genitalia, although they had pubic hair. Should a Vampire Queen ever come to rebuild Le-Ath Veronis, the common demons might have a chance of becoming something other than the comesuli they were.

"The tale is spreading that Kifirin woke from a long sleep and in his grief at seeing his planet nearly destroyed, he caused Baetrah to erupt. Thousands from the Southern Continent are fleeing northward," Darvul said softly at Noff's side. Noff heard that rumor as well and nodded at his master, his dandelion-fluff hair shining in the early morning sunlight.

"Raoni Jaydevik and his eldest brother, Gardevik, are already executing rogue High Demons," Noff offered information he'd gleaned earlier while searching for herbs and other medicines in what remained of the marketing district.

The common demons were scrambling to rebuild, but so much of their city was destroyed in the attack. The smaller cities and farms outside Veshtul were shipping in extra supplies as quickly as they could, but it was taking time to collect and transport the items to the capital city.

"What happened to Rorevik?" Darvul asked about the former High Demon monarch. Rorevik had taken the throne after Lendevik's death, while Jaydevik, Lendevik's designated heir, had gone missing for centuries. Once Jaydevik returned to Kifirin, Rorevik had stepped aside in favor of his older brother.

"Rorevik is dead, I hear," Noff sighed.

"He allowed Kifirin to get away from him," Darvul nodded. "He was inexperienced and perhaps too lenient with the High Demons. Jaydevik has not held back in his punishment of the High Demons who have broken the laws. Gardevik too. Garde should have been advising Rorevik all along. Perhaps the oppression of the common demons would have been less."

"Perhaps they realize now what we do for them," Noff snorted softly, his dark-brown eyes narrowing in contempt. "The latest death toll stands at fifteen thousand, and even the palace is short-handed."

"So many of our kind gone," Darvul shook his head sadly.

Glindarok, member of the Saa Thalarr and Raona of Kifirin, sat on a comfortable chair in her suite, absently rubbing her belly—Karzac had already announced she was having twins, something unprecedented in High Demon history. It was too early to determine the babies' gender, however.

"Three more weeks," the Saa Thalarr's chief physician said. She'd been left behind in her suite, feeling useless. She wanted to be with Jayd and Garde while they questioned Drith and Croth rogues. She wanted to question them herself concerning their knowledge of the treason committed by both Houses. Few had been innocent or unknowing of the alliance with the Ra'Ak.

"Raona, you must trust the Raoni in this," Roff came to sit beside her, little Toff in his arms. Toff was a scant four weeks old and slept peacefully in the crook of Roff's elbow. Glinda reached out and gently stroked the child's head—he had the barest bit of fuzz there—a promise of Roff's thick, dark hair, perhaps. Giff, Roff's oldest child, had lighter hair. It often happened that way.

Glinda sighed as she studied her sumptuous prison. That's what it was to her—a prison. Rich hangings on walls and windows, rare marble on the floors, beautiful fabrics covering the chairs and the bed —all hid invisible bars.

Jayd was overjoyed at the news of her pregnancy, and then became an autocrat in his worry to keep her safe. Too many Drith and Croth still lived for his liking. Jayd and Garde left the palace, grim-faced each morning, to question more traitors.

Two High Demon guards were stationed outside Glinda's suite at all times, so she couldn't sneak away. Karzac had already warned her —pregnant Saa Thalarr weren't allowed to use any of their real power; therefore, she couldn't fold outside the palace.

Roff, Giff and a few other commons were assigned to Glinda; they delivered her food, cleaned her suite, carried messages back and forth and did their best to see to her comfort. It did nothing to alleviate her sense of confinement.

"Can they not let me go out to see the damage to the city?" Glinda grumbled softly, shoving a swath of platinum hair over her shoulder. "Roff, will you ask Giff to braid my hair?" The last was spoken in a whisper; she didn't want to wake Toff.

"Of course I will find Giff—he enjoys braiding your hair. As for the damage in the city, it is quite extensive in places," Roff replied.

He'd asked Giff to watch Toff at one point and had gone to survey the devastation for himself. "It is worst on the northwest side, where the weavers and thread-makers were. Few were found alive there, Raona. I hear a request was sent to other villages, asking commons to come who know the trade so that section of the city might be rebuilt."

"Who is rebuilding it?" Glinda asked impatiently, running a hand through her length of white-blonde hair—if left loose, it would continue to fall over a shoulder, irritating Glinda.

"I hear Lord Nedevik Weth and Lord Aldavik Foth have taken that task—they approached Jaydevik with their offers to do this. Supplies and builders are coming in from surrounding areas. Do not fret, Raona, all will be well."

"What about the injured?" Glinda asked. "Are they being cared for? Has someone from the treasury offered assistance where it is needed most?"

"Lady Mayarok and Lord Fredevik Greth are seeing to this," Roff replied. "Lord Fredevik is unable to deny his lady anything she wishes, and this is what she wishes. Her personal comesuli have come to assist her and are tallying the needs in terms of money, space for the wounded, and medicines and herbs to treat them. Lord Fredevik is making sure the money handed out by the treasury is spent wisely."

"Will you see that a message is carried to Lady Mayarok, then?" Glinda begged. Roff smiled at her. She'd saved his life more than once. He would do anything she asked of him.

~

"Brenten, they're still recovering," Amara attempted to catch Griffin's arm as he paced. "It's too soon. Give them a chance to regroup." Amara begged her mate to slow down and consider things carefully. A frown tugged at Amara's pretty mouth while worry troubled her dark eyes. Griffin ignored her pleas.

"They don't have a clue," Griffin tossed a hand out wildly. "My daughter kills their attackers and herself in the process and they're worried about everything else. Do they think Pheligar and Renegar are going to allow those rogue High Demons to escape?"

"I'm sure they have no idea what the Larentii are capable of," Amara attempted to reassure her mate. He'd only now come home from wherever he'd been, going somewhere to grieve in private. Even so, his hair was wild, his countenance angry as he paced.

Amara knew Griffin had bent time and folded space to get back to this moment in time with her, and given his current state of mind, she imagined he'd come back earlier than he should. "There will be a memorial to Lissa. It will come, Brenten. You have to be patient," Amara attempted to slow Griffin's agitated pacing.

"Merrill won't speak to me now," Griffin muttered. "Wlodek either. I'm afraid to contact Gavin and the others—they may never be allowed to remember. If they did remember and were able to kill me, I'm sure they'd try. Why did they remove my memories of her, too?" Griffin tossed up a hand in resignation. He didn't say it, and would never say it, but his memories of Lissa had disappeared before the others' had. He worried, too, over why that was.

"Brenten, you're not thinking. You brought her from our past, only days before we were made to forget. Belen explained that to both of us. I can't help but believe that you somehow discovered you would forget her, back then. Otherwise, why would you take her when she was already weary from destroying Xenides?"

Amara examined Griffin's face; he looked haggard and angry. "I know you had your reasons for sacrificing your daughter, but that doesn't mean I understand it any better than the others do." Amara folded away. She had that ability, just as the rest of them did.

"I don't understand it either, love," Griffin sat heavily on the chair Amara had vacated with a sigh.

"The Raona has visitors already," the High Demon guard insisted.

"She will want to see me," the visitor declared. "Tell her Erland Morphis is here. She'll tear your ears off if you don't let me in."

Erland was in a huff; it wasn't often that a Karathian Warlock was turned away for any reason—if the offending party knew what was good for them, anyway. Erland's magic—or any other kind of magic or power had absolutely no effect on any High Demon—they were immune. Erland could pull the palace down around their ears, however, and he was presently considering that option.

"I will inform her, but be prepared if she sends you away," the High Demon's voice held a long-suffering tone.

"That's all I'm asking," Erland didn't hide his impatience, his beautiful face twisting in an angry frown. The High Demon guard knocked on the Raona's door. A common demon answered.

"Lord Morphis," Roff bowed respectfully to Erland. "Please, follow me." The guard's eyebrows rose slightly as Erland offered him a glare and swept inside the suite. He employed a bit of power to slam the door behind him, too.

"Kiarra, Adam, Merrill," Erland nodded respectfully to each of the visiting Saa Thalarr.

"Erland," Adam and Merrill knew Erland Morphis well; he owned a casino on the Gambling planet of Campiaa, just as they did. Glinda, however, knew Erland better than anyone; she'd worked as his bodyguard for many years before she was invited to join the Saa Thalarr. Erland went to sit beside Glinda; she seemed upset. He'd heard she was pregnant, but didn't want to let her know that.

"Glinda, love, what's wrong?" Erland placed an arm around her. She was one of two women he wouldn't mind bedding. Otherwise, his interests currently ran toward males.

"I thought Kifirin destroyed the Ra'Ak," Glinda turned to Erland, burying her head against his shoulder.

"He didn't? Then who did?" Erland rubbed Glinda's back gently. He knew, as did many others, that Kifirin's planet had been attacked by

Ra'Ak and that somehow they'd been beaten back, even with more than six thousand High Demons in league with them. That's what Erland heard from his sources, anyway. Too bad there weren't vid images of any of it.

Kiarra watched Erland Morphis's face. He was interested now, she could tell. None of them knew. "It was Griffin's daughter, Lissa," Kiarra sighed. "The Vampire Queen. She did this for us. Killed herself for us. She died, taking down the Ra'Ak Prince."

Erland was a blur as he stood, and he began cursing in so many languages Kiarra had difficulty interpreting all of it. Glinda was staring at Kiarra in shock. A Vampire Queen? She'd read the records in the archives. The last Vampire Queen on Le-Ath Veronis had stood against the Ra'Ak long ago, dying to protect her people. She'd been the one to beg the High Demons to take the comesuli; the ones they called common demons, now. She'd also begged the High Demons to take some of her vampires.

The High Demon King at the time—Glinda's father—had refused, choosing only to accept the common demons, as they could be useful to the High Demons. He'd almost destroyed them all with the decision he'd made. Glinda still loved him; he'd been a good father to her. He'd just made a few bad choices during his rule.

"The little Vampire Queen is dead?" Erland looked sad, now. Kiarra had no idea how Erland could have known of Lissa.

"You know her?"

Erland snorted. "Knew of her," he replied, beginning to pace inside Glinda's spacious suite. "I forgot her for a time, as did most others. My memory of her returned only recently. This is the worst of news. I and one other have recalled that she saved Refizan three hundred years ago."

"Oh, no," Merrill muttered.

"She's really dead?" Roff had been listening in and was now breaking out of his stunned silence. "There was a Queen Vampire and she died?" He sounded lost.

Glinda stared at her assistant. She knew what the news of a Queen Vampire would hold for the common demons; a Queen was hope to them. Hope that one day they could return to their home world and perhaps become what they held the promise to be—vampire and whole, in their own right.

"She sacrificed herself for us. And for you," Merrill looked Roff in the eye. "You and I have met before, little comesula. You don't remember it because Kifirin took you from the future. The little Queen loved you, Roff. I believe it was her love for you and for Giff and the others that she died as she did."

Roff wept and would have dropped to the floor had Erland not held him up. "I shouldn't have told him," Merrill muttered, rising from his seat.

"I have to go; the King Vampire on Refizan will be greatly disappointed with this news," Erland settled Roff on Glinda's chaise and folded away.

Glinda was staring, first at Merrill, then at Roff, then at Kiarra. "How did this happen?" she demanded.

"Master!" Noff shook Darvul awake. It was late, the moon was nearly down and dawn was perhaps three clicks away. "Wake, master! Our little common is moaning and moving about!"

"What?" Darvul woke quickly. Noff helped him sit up in bed. "What time is it?" Darvul struggled to see the timepiece beside his bed, something nearly impossible for the newly wakened in semidarkness.

"Fourth click, master," Noff was nervous with impatience and anticipation. He and Darvul had taken rooms inside the infirmary, as did many other physicians and assistants after the battle fifteen days before. All remained close, watching over patients.

Many injured commons had gone home already if their homes remained standing. Others stayed, still nursing wounds. None had remained unconscious as long as Darvul and Noff's patient, however. Several others who'd experienced comas died of their injuries.

The little common moaned softly as Darvul rushed inside the room. Fluids were still being administered intravenously; otherwise, the patient would have died. As it was, the little common was emaciated but alive.

"Are you going to wake for us?" Darvul spoke softly, brushing hair away from the common's face.

"Please wake," Noff begged.

"Bring a lamp," Darvul commanded. Noff ran to obey.

He opened his eyes, trying to bring his surroundings into focus. A blurry face hovered over his and words were spoken; words he failed to understand. A moan escaped him and he frowned at the noise until he realized he was making it himself. More words came; they were just as confusing as the others. They seemed to be questions for which he had no answers.

The room brightened; another being brought something that created the brightness. He squinted; the light hurt his eyes. It was dimmed quickly.

"He doesn't understand us," Noff was upset over this new revelation.

"He suffered a head injury. How can we know how extensive it may have been? Go now—find broth—we must attempt to feed him while he is awake," Darvul ordered. Noff left the room in a rush, intent on finding something to feed the little common.

"Here now, eat this," Noff held the spoon to the common's lips, in an attempt to convince his patient to eat. He and Darvul managed to get the small common upright and sitting in bed, stacking many pillows behind his back to achieve that feat.

It took several tries before the scent of food convinced the little common to try it. After that, it was easy. He was quite hungry as it turned out, and Darvul had to ration the broth so the common wouldn't make himself ill by eating too much too quickly.

"We will feed you again soon," Darvul promised as daybreak came. Noff was settling the little common back in his bed so he might sleep.

"He woke briefly," Darvul explained to another assistant. "Please make sure he eats every two hours. No solid food at first—broth only."

The assistant nodded. "Anything else, master?" he asked.

"The little common doesn't understand anything we say. His head injury must have been severe. Please don't frighten or agitate him. I will go to Lady Mayarok later and tell her this one's convalescence may be extensive."

"She will obtain funds for us if such is the case," the assistant nodded. "The Raona herself has promised to provide funding for any common that needs the care. Do we know what the common's name is?"

"We do not and none have come forward with information. We can only assume his entire family perished," Darvul sighed. "I am going to return to bed and sleep for a click or two. Wake me if there is need." Darvul strode down the long hall toward his room.

The assistant went to see the little miracle himself. His master predicted that this common would die. Fortunately, he had been in error.

Noff held a cup of tea in his hands as he leaned against the outside wall of the infirmary. Built on a single level, the long building had square windows spaced at even intervals down each side.

The infirmary was fashioned of whitewashed brick with fired tile floors and stucco walls that could be cleaned easily. Inside walls were painted a muted green with white trim, designed to be restful for the ones who received treatment within.

Common demons were not susceptible to diseases like so many other races. They were often injured, however, just as anyone else might be. Common physicians and their assistants generally treated broken bones, cuts, sprains, bruises and burns. The multitude of injuries resulting from the battle had taxed their knowledge to the limit.

Noff hadn't gone back to his bed as Darvul had done; he'd been too excited to sleep. Their little common had wakened against all odds. He intended to check on the patient again in only a moment or two, as soon as he finished his tea.

"Has anything changed?" Noff asked his fellow assistant as he walked into the room.

"I was about to get broth for him; it is almost time for the next feeding," Orliff yawned, stretching his arms out. Unlike Noff, Orliff's hair was dark, his eyes blue. "My last charge went home earlier, so my master is happy to allow me to help with this one," Orliff added.

"I'll get the broth, unless you want to do it," Noff offered.

"Go ahead," Orliff nodded.

Noff was back in ticks with a bowl of broth and a spoon on a tray. Darvul removed the IV earlier, fearing the little common might tear it from his hand since he didn't understand what was going on around him.

Noff and Orliff woke the little common, who seemed confused as they attempted to sit him up so he could eat. "Eat," Orliff made an eating motion with his hand. The little common stared for a moment before blinking in what Noff hoped was understanding. He allowed Noff and Orliff to place him in a sitting position after that, and accepted the broth Noff spoon-fed him.

"Noff," Noff pointed to himself. "Orliff," he pointed to Orliff. The little common looked from one to the other but still hadn't attempted speech. "What's your name?" Noff tapped the little common's chest gently.

His ribs were still wrapped because of the breaks and his wrist was also splinted and heavily bandaged for the same reason. The little common blinked and shook his head.

"He still doesn't understand," Orliff sighed. "Can we give him a name? He may not remember anything. Who he was, where he lived —nothing."

"Let's call him Niff," Noff smiled. "A combination of both our names."

"That's good," Orliff grinned. "Niff," he tapped the little common on the shoulder. "Niff."

"We're calling him Niff until he remembers who he is," Noff informed Darvul later. "I believe he understands, now; we keep calling him that every time we feed him, and I think he responded the last time."

"Has he attempted to speak?" Darvul walked down the hall toward Niff's room with Noff.

"No, master. Perhaps it is too early, still. He hasn't attempted speech."

"Niff, how are you feeling?" Darvul sat on the edge of Niff's bed. Niff was awake at least and staring up at him. Niff had blue eyes; Darvul could see them clearly in the light from the window. They watched him with curiosity, but Niff had no reply to Darvul's question.

"Darvul," Noff pointed to his master. Niff blinked at Darvul.

"Do you think he understands?" Darvul asked his assistant.

"I think he knows Orliff and me, now," Noff replied. "It can't hurt to try, can it?"

"No," Darvul smiled at Niff. "We're very happy you're awake," he said.

The news was a heavy blow to Gabron. He remembered the little Queen after three hundred years of forgetting. Forgetting anything was unusual for him—Gabron remembered everything of his nine thousand years as vampire.

Three hundred years earlier, he'd erected a bronze monument in the plaza where the Solar Red temple had once stood. It memorialized all the vampires who died defending Refizan from the Solar Red priests and the Ra'Ak.

The quote at the base of the monument was Lissa's—he

remembered that now. The words were her tribute to his child, Briden, who'd been dragged into sunlight and burned to death. *I will hold your name in my heart as I strike down your enemies,* she'd written on the sidewalk where Briden died. It was now an anthem to vampires across the Reth Alliance.

Erland Morphis, the Karathian Warlock, brought the news of Lissa's death to Gabron. He'd met Erland shortly after the vid images of Lissa fighting off the Ra'Ak on Refizan had gone out to other worlds.

Erland had known where to seek him, somehow. Gabron hadn't been surprised; Karathian Warlocks had their own subtle ways of obtaining information. He also posed no threat to Gabron or his vampires; Erland maintained a high level of secrecy.

"It was a terrible blow to me as well, my friend," Erland sipped the wine that Gabron provided.

Gabron still owned and ran brothels with the Refizani government's blessing, even if the common population had no idea they were run by vampires.

"We had hopes that she would take us all to the vampire world," Gabron muttered. "It was a promise made to us, long ago." He didn't tell Erland, although Erland may have guessed anyway, that he'd loved Lissa when he met her three centuries before. Now his hopes were gone, causing Gabron to sigh deeply.

CHAPTER 3

"Niff, let us see whether you can walk," Noff held both of Niff's hands in his, trying to coax the small common off his bed. Darvul had allowed a small amount of solid food the day before, and the little common was improving in many ways.

Nineteen days had passed since the attacks, and the volcano had slowed down in its eruptions on the Southern Continent. Regardless, common refugees from the southern areas were still trickling into Veshtul looking for work, asking to help rebuild the city.

Niff, however, seemed oblivious to all of it, though Noff and Orliff had begun telling him bits of information each day, hoping that something would spark a memory in their patient.

Niff blinked at Noff, his blue eyes wide, and then turned his attention to the floor, which lay a short space below his bare feet. They'd kept the little common dressed in loose pajamas while he convalesced. Niff seemed to be examining his clothing as well.

"Come," Noff pulled gently on Niff's hands. Niff slid off the bed. Darvul said the leg was better and Noff was gentle with the broken wrist. They planned to remove the bandage around the ribs the following day; Darvul hadn't found evidence that the cracked ribs would be a problem, but he didn't want to take unnecessary risks.

Niff was now standing on the floor, wobbling unsteadily on his feet. "Don't worry, it's normal," Noff assured him. "Now, take a step for me." He backed up a step and Niff followed, watching his own feet while Noff kept a firm grip on his hands.

Noff took another step back; Niff followed, his legs trembling slightly. Noff wanted to hug his patient—he was doing so well. Darvul stepped into the room while Niff was walking and smiled.

"Better than I expected," he nodded happily. "Still no attempt at speech and no indication that he understands us when we speak, but he does seem to know what we mean when we mimic something."

"He still blinks when the light is bright in his window," Noff said, taking another step backward. Niff was following now, doing his best to remain upright as he walked.

"A common effect from a blow to the head. It may clear up with time. We must be content with what we have at the moment," Darvul observed. "Turn him around and only hold one hand. See if he can make his way back to the bed on his own."

Noff turned Niff around slowly, before letting go of the splinted hand. Niff gave him a questioning look before making his unsteady way toward the bed.

"Very good," Noff breathed as Niff awkwardly seated himself on the bed. "Now, we will lift your feet," he placed Niff's feet on the bed and covered them with the light sheet and blanket. "Are you hungry? Would you like something to eat or drink?" He mimed the actions to Niff.

Niff blinked twice and then mimed drinking only. Darvul laughed. "I'd say that deserves some juice at the least."

"He understood me!" Noff was quite happy as he trotted away to find juice for his patient.

⁓

"Wash your hands, Niff, we're going to roll bandages," Orliff was working with the little common today; Noff had been forced to take a day off; Darvul insisted.

Niff obediently washed his hands with soap and water, drying them on the towel Orliff provided. Orliff was quite surprised at how quickly the little common accepted his mimed instructions, although Niff couldn't seem to understand anything anyone said to him.

He wasn't deaf; Darvul determined that earlier. He'd deliberately dropped a pot outside Niff's room, causing their patient to startle and jump in his bed. Orliff and Noff had both witnessed the reaction. Niff hadn't uttered a squeak when he'd jumped, so they'd still had no luck at getting any sounds or words from him.

"Now, begin the roll tightly, like this," Orliff showed Niff how to begin. Niff watched carefully, reproducing Orliff's actions on his own roll. "Very good," Orliff encouraged as he and Niff rolled bandages together until they had a full basket.

All their supplies were depleted, so Orliff brought out bark to boil afterward. He and Niff worked on that most of the afternoon. The comesuli physicians had little of the pain relief left and Orliff was happy to receive the shipment of bark.

He and Niff ground herbs together to use in other medicines; Orliff found that Niff's fingers were strong and nimble as he worked, grinding herbs in a marble bowl with a steel pestle. "You are doing well, Niff," Orliff smiled as the herbs were reduced to usable powder. Niff was quite thorough in his work.

"How is our patient doing?" Lady Mayarok walked into the room. Niff drew in a breath and stopped grinding, staring in surprise at Lady Mayarok instead. She was tall—taller than the commons around her, but most High Demons were tall. Dark hair was intricately braided and piled atop her head and a gentle smile lit her features as she examined the small, injured common that Darvul had described to her.

"Niff, this is Lady Mayarok, Lord Fredevik's mate. She will not harm you." Niff blinked at Orliff for a moment before returning to his task.

"Darvul tells me this one may be mentally damaged from a head injury," Lady Mayarok observed, seating herself beside Niff at the table. Niff ignored the scrutiny and continued his work.

"We aren't completely sure of that; he understands if we show him things—he only has trouble processing information if it is spoken. His hearing is fine; we have checked it. He hasn't attempted speech. Darvul says this can happen."

"I will be staying at the palace until the Raona gives birth," Lady Mayarok sighed. "Fredevik is quite concerned over the Raona's children. She's pregnant with twins and I have never heard of that before. As I have given birth so many times, Lord Fredevik desires that I stay and instruct the Raona on her first."

"I heard the Raona was with child but did not realize it was twins." Orliff was very interested, now.

"We will require physicians. Might you consider helping? Darvul and his assistant have already been invited to come. You may bring this one with you; he can perform menial tasks at the palace, I'm sure."

"I will discuss this with Darvul and my master. Of course, I would be pleased to come and help tend the Raona."

"I will see that she asks for you personally," Lady Mayarok smiled indulgently at Orliff. "Do not delay; I would like you to come in the next two days, before the Raona becomes ill in the mornings."

"We have herbs that will help," Orliff nodded and smiled at Lady Mayarok. "They will settle the stomach without affecting the children."

"Good. My physician at home did the same for me." Lady Mayarok rose to go. She had High Demon guards posted outside the room and they fell in with her the moment she left the infirmary's stillroom.

"Lady Mayarok asked me to come, and my master has already given permission if you will consent to take over my training while we are at the palace," Orliff begged Darvul to take him.

"Of course," Darvul smiled at the young one. Orliff was in his thirties and would come to his full adulthood in three years. He would also receive his physician's certification then if he finished his training. "Pack your clothing and supplies; Lady Mayarok is sending a coach for us tomorrow afternoon. Now, we must go out and find clothing for our patient. He cannot wear bedclothes inside the palace."

"We can remove the splint as well; he used that hand to crush herbs with the pestle and it didn't seem to pain him in the least," Orliff said.

"We will examine him after dinner and I will allow you and Noff to make the decision," Darvul said. "Come, we will find clothing for the little common. We have been given an allowance for this."

~

"Niff, we found clothing for you," Orliff held a pile of clothing in his arms as Noff, Darvul and he strolled into Niff's room later. "We also found shoes; we were guessing at those so I hope they fit."

"I think they will," Noff nodded as he studied Niff's feet. They were small, so they'd bought a young one's shoes for him. Niff noticed Noff staring at his feet and looked down at them as well, frowning slightly.

"Now, let's look at your wrist, Niff. We wish to remove the splint." Orliff came forward after dropping clothing and shoes at the foot of Niff's bed. He and Noff began unwrapping the heavy bandaging.

"Look," Orliff turned the wrist this way and that after the bandages were removed. He carefully felt the bones in the wrist, as did Noff. Niff did not complain or appear to be in pain while they did this.

"I think we can leave it off," Darvul nodded as he watched the two assistants make their examination. "I am pleased with his recovery; he is walking very well now. Although he still cannot understand speech, he has made much progress otherwise."

"I will pack for him," Noff offered. Darvul nodded at his assistant and left the room.

~

Niff stood on the bottom step of the transport, examining the richly appointed interior of the coach with wonder on his face. "Come, we are going to the palace," Noff took his hand and pulled the little common inside the coach.

Darvul watched as his assistant settled Niff on a cushioned seat next to an open window, so he might get fresh air in the stifling heat. Late summer bore down on the capital city of Veshtul, although Darvul had doubts the seasons meant anything to little Niff.

Orliff climbed in last and the coach drove off toward the palace.

Several palace commons came to help them unload the coach; crates of medical supplies, equipment and trunks of clothing were dutifully carried inside.

"The Raona's suite is down the hall," one of the commons spoke to Darvul as he led them inside a guest suite. Their suite was large, with a connecting bath and two bedrooms. "I will take the bedroom on the other side and Niff will come with me," Orliff said, pulling Niff through the bath toward the second bedroom. Niff stared curiously at his surroundings as Orliff led him through the suite.

"Is that one simple?" The palace common asked.

"For now; he was injured in the attack—a blow to the head," Darvul indicated the back of the skull.

"Ah. Is there anything we should know about him?"

"He cannot process speech; doesn't understand it, as yet," Noff replied. "If you show him, however, he understands quite well."

"So, if I mimic polishing the floor?" The common asked.

"Then you'll get the floor polished," Noff said, "although we still have not released him for heavy work. You must consult us before you ask something such as that from him."

"I will let the others know," the common said. "Dinner will be brought to you tonight. You may join the other commons in the kitchens after that for your meals. I am Sariff, should you need anything."

"Thank you, Sariff. Will you arrange a meeting with the Raona for us? We are here to tend her, after all."

"The Raona has been moody recently, but I will ask." Sariff nodded and left the suite, closing the door after him.

"Look, Niff, this is a lovely bath," Orliff point out amenities and fixtures. Scented soap lay beside the wide tub, along with a cork-stoppered bottle of shampoo and many towels and washcloths. Niff picked up the soap and smelled it, putting it down quickly after making a face.

"I don't think he likes the soap; the scent must be too heavy," Orliff called to the others.

"Here, I brought field oat soap," Noff pulled the soap from one of his bags. "I will be happy to use the other."

Orliff accepted the soap and handed it off to Niff. Niff took it, sniffed, and nodded happily, smiling at Orliff. Orliff drew in a breath. "He smiled when I gave him the soap!" Orliff was overjoyed.

"We are making progress," Darvul chuckled.

"Glindarok, I fail to understand why you are so obstinate about this," Jayd paced before his mate. "Let the physicians examine you. It will ease my mind as well as Lady Mayarok's; she is nearly frantic over this as it is."

"Jaydevik, if I am forced to call you autocratic and insufferable again, you will be most sorry, I assure you," Glinda's arms were crossed over her chest and her blue eyes flashed a warning at Jayd.

"I am in no mood to have someone's hands all over me. You and Garde go out every morning and when you return at night, do you tell me what is happening? Of course not. I want to know what is going on with those Drith and Croth filth. How many are left? How many have you executed? Have any been set free? If so, are you positive of their innocence?" Glinda was now pacing before Jayd.

"If you do not stop this, I will ask Karzac and Jeff to come and they may place you in a healing sleep," Jayd displayed signs of growing agitation. "This cannot be good for our children, avilepha. Not good at all."

"Jayd, I am only three months pregnant. Much too early for anything of that sort to happen, I assure you. You are only doing this to vex me," Glinda glared angrily at her High Demon mate.

"I am not doing this to vex you; I am doing this for your own good and for the good of our children. Why won't you understand me in this? A pregnant female has no place in these proceedings, and if I describe the executions to you, well, just be assured I will not be doing that!" Smoke curled from Jayd's nostrils. Even his Thifilathi was upset.

"Jaydevik Rath, you merely wish to impress upon me that I am a weak and pregnant female, when only the pregnant portion of that statement is true. You don't allow me out of my suite unless you are inside the palace; I cannot make any decisions without your approval and even Lady Mayarok is getting more freedom and respect than I am at the moment. This is not the reason I accepted you as a mate. If the truth be known, I am currently having second thoughts!"

"Glindarok, is this going to happen every time we become parents?" Jayd walked slowly toward his mate, unwilling to upset her further. She held herself stiffly while he gently massaged his claiming marks on the back of her neck. "I love you more than anything, m'hala. Do not be angry with me, I beg you. Come, we will have our dinner in the arboretum, if you will consent to this."

"I will come," Glinda agreed grudgingly.

"Good," Jayd replied softly, placing a gentle kiss on Glinda's neck.

"Where is he going?" Orliff followed Niff, with Noff close on his heels. Niff was climbing stairs swiftly inside the palace, as if he knew where he was going.

"The arboretum," Noff breathed as Niff ran through a wide doorway, which opened into the palace garden. A lush expanse of trees and rare plants was enclosed by tall windows. The high glass ceiling overhead allowed starlight to filter down upon the wealth of plant life below. Niff was still walking swiftly, straight toward a section of the glass wall that overlooked the city of Veshtul.

"Niff!" Orliff whispered loudly, attempting to convince the little common to stop. Niff ignored him, continuing on his path until he reached the targeted section of glass. He lifted his hands as if he wanted to place them against the window. There he stopped short, wavered for a moment and then dropped to his knees, where he began to weep.

"What is this?" Jayd was up from the dinner table quickly and striding toward the little common.

"Please, Raoni, he has suffered a head injury and does not know what he is doing," Orliff babbled an apology to the High Demon King while Noff did his best to coax Niff away from the window.

"Jayd, if you harm any of these, I will not speak to you again," Glinda was at Jayd's side, watching as the little common demon wept beside the wall of glass.

"You think I wanted to harm them?" Jayd snorted. "I am merely upset that our dinner was interrupted. It is all right," Jayd gestured with a hand. "Take the young one away. That is all I ask."

~

That was my first memory of the High Demon King—Jaydevik Rath. He seemed pompous and somewhat full of himself—as most kings might, I suppose. Of course, I didn't understand a word he said, or any other words spoken to me then or at any time before that moment.

My memory had returned in a rush, however, and there I was, stuck on the High Demons' planet, surrounded by people who spoke a language I didn't understand. Just as well—I might have started cursing and not stopped until they killed me or I ran out of breath.

I had no memory of how I came to be inside the arboretum; my last memory consisted of blasting my mist outward to kill the Ra'Ak Prince. Griffin, my father, and Kifirin, who called me his mate, had engineered my death. I couldn't come to any other conclusion than that. I'd died. How I came to be alive now, I had no clue.

One of the comesuli was pulling at me now, whispering a desperate spate of words, interspersed with the word Niff. They were calling me Niff. To them, I was another comesula.

On a world where females among the comesuli aren't possible, I would appear to be just another androgynous common. I had no idea what to do about that. If I tried to tell them who I was, they wouldn't understand and would probably lock me up, thinking I was crazy. Most likely, that's just what I had been. For a while, anyway.

I went with my two comesuli escorts—they led me down many flights of stairs until we reached a suite of rooms. The one called Orliff showed me to my bed and gestured for me to stay. I stayed. Where else was I going to go?

Griffin told me when he took me from the Annual Meeting that he was transporting me into the future. Three hundred years into the future, he'd said. How nice for me. I didn't know anyone, here and now.

I had no idea where this planet was, and wasn't likely to get a ride back to Earth, even if I asked politely. These people didn't know who —or what—I was. They also didn't seem to care that their asses had been saved by somebody they didn't know.

What else was I supposed to do? I was going to have to pay attention, learn the language and look for a way out of this mess.

Thanks, Dad. Thanks, Kifirin. You assholes.

With much poking and prodding, I was sent to the kitchens the following morning. I was considered an imbecile, I discovered. Everything was mimed out for me. I nodded when I understood what they wanted.

I was commanded to peel potatoes and I had to ask, as best I could, how they wanted them cut up afterward. I diced one potato and sliced another into rounds before tugging on the sleeve of a nearby comesula. He pointed to the diced pile.

I diced up peeled potatoes after washing them. I sliced carrots. Tore lettuce. Stirred soup, kneaded dough and turned meats. I watched and listened, but High Demon is a difficult language to learn.

Kifirin had let me understand it temporarily, before taking it away. The Larentii had given me other languages on Refizan; why hadn't this one been included? At least I wouldn't be adrift on a shifting ocean with no paddle and a leaking boat.

Thank goodness, I could eat normal food or I would have been in real trouble. Who knows what the High Demons would do if they found a modified vampire feeding off the population?

I washed dishes, too, and cleaned the kitchen with help from two young comesuli. Orliff came for me after that. At least they'd let me eat before I had to clean the kitchen, even if it wasn't the best portion of what they served.

I was a kitchen drudge, now. I promised to remind myself of that the next time they needed saving. Oh, I didn't blame the comesuli. The High Demons? I knew from dreams that one of the kings before this one had fucked up and not sent his High Demons out to control the Ra'Ak. That decision had almost cost them everything.

Of course, dear old Dad had hauled me off to this Godforsaken planet so I could take care of their little problem. Then I'd been left here, like a tool that wasn't needed again—just dropped where it was used last.

That was the story of my life. Conceived purposely, to save the vampire and werewolf races on Earth, kill Xenides and his minions, and finally to save the High Demons.

Well done, Lissa. Fuck off, now. You're no longer needed.

I took my bath when I returned to our suite and did more listening. Mostly what I understood was names. Darvul, Orliff and Noff. At least I had pajamas of a sort, though the cloth wasn't the best and felt rough against my skin.

Beggars can't be choosers, my mother always said. I snorted at the memory. I was pissed at her, too. I certainly was a beggar, now, dependent upon the charity of the comesuli around me, as well as the generosity of the High Demons. Had I been on Earth, I would have told them what they could do with all their generosity. I wasn't on Earth though, and it was unlikely I'd ever get back now.

"Niff is upset," Orliff muttered to Noff while Niff took his bath.

"Did they not treat him well in the kitchens?" Noff asked.

"I do not know, but he is holding himself stiffly. I know not whether I should mention this to Darvul," Orliff said. "I do not know how to deal with this."

"Perhaps it will pass; let us keep watch over this and decide later," Noff suggested. Orliff nodded; Niff was coming out of the bath now, struggling to get loosely fitting pajamas situated on his thin body.

"Niff, you should eat more; you need to gain weight," Orliff sighed, knowing his words would not be understood. Niff studied him for a moment before walking past to climb into bed.

"Should we hold a memorial for Rorevik, brother?" Gardevik asked. They'd been served a midday meal at the stockade, between handing convicted prisoners to the palace guards for execution.

"I'm not sure the commons would appreciate it," Jayd muttered. "They suffered under our brother's rule because he was too weak to protect them properly."

"Perhaps a small service, then?" Garde suggested.

"A small service. We should ask Glindarok how she feels about this. She should have a part in this decision."

"I believe she will agree."

"I hope you are right, brother. I do miss him," Jayd sighed. "And we have a request from Griffin, the retired Saa Thalarr, asking permission to put up a memorial to his daughter."

"We had no idea what was behind the killing of the Ra'Ak—I thought it was Glindarok's associates in the Saa Thalarr. Now we learn that even they were not capable of what a Vampire Queen could do."

"Had she lived, the commons would flock to her. We would be forced to let them go, Gardevik. She would take them to Le-Ath Veronis, and we would have to do for ourselves again."

"Perhaps it is just as well then, brother."

"You rejoice in her death?"

"I did not say that."

"We will have to allow the memorial; I just do not know how the knowledge will affect the commons."

"Then we should put it off for a while."

"I will see what I can do. It sounds ungrateful of us, brother, to do it, though." Jayd regarded his brother, who was finishing a cup of wine.

"The Saa Thalarr are not left with the running of a planet, brother," Gardevik observed.

"No, but they made sure we still had a planet to run afterward. Or at least the little Queen Vampire did. The Croth and Drith she killed convinced the others to surrender."

"Lendevik should have done things differently. This could have been avoided." Gardevik snorted and smoke poured from his nostrils.

"Do not speak ill of Glinda's father in front of her, I beg you," Jayd said. "She still loves him. The little Queen Vampire is past all that. We never knew her and cannot pay our proper respects, I'm afraid."

"Then perhaps in a year, when these other things are behind us, we will allow them to erect a memorial. The commons should be calmed down by then," Gardevik observed. "There were only fifty High Demon deaths, not counting the rogue Croth and Drith. The common demon deaths are nearing twenty thousand, I hear."

"Yes, I hear that too," Jayd sighed. "I haven't informed Glindarok; it will upset her greatly if she learns of it. We are even short-staffed at the palace, now; many servants are away, helping families rebuild homes and businesses."

"Supplies are short as well, and we cannot count on any fruit or vegetable shipments from the Southern Continent; the eruptions of the volcano have destroyed all the crops. I have considered sending a handful of troops down to make assessments on the damage there." Garde watched his brother's face closely.

"Do you think there is any truth to the rumors that Kifirin did indeed wake?" Jayd had never seen the god; not during his long life, but there were records in Lendevik's old library that chronicled sightings of Kifirin, and they spoke of meetings between him and the

Raoni of old. Garde may have seen him—he was older than Jayd, but he never spoke of it.

"The rumors among the commons coming in from the villages there are full of sightings," Garde replied. "Are you ready to go back to work, brother?"

"Yes," Jayd rose. "Perhaps we should send troops to the Southern Continent with a few commons. They won't be able to skip with the commons, but by the time they arrive using coaches or wagons, the eruptions may have subsided."

"Good. We'll discuss this over dinner tonight. Glinda can decide who will go; that should make her feel useful." Garde grinned at his brother, who'd described Glinda's tantrum the previous evening.

"Garde, if she thinks you're patronizing her, I wouldn't want to be in your shoes after the babies are born."

"Perhaps she'll forget it by then," Garde laughed. Jayd blew out a breath and shook his head at his brother.

I now understood the words for potatoes, carrots, snap beans and sugar. Too bad there wasn't any way to write it all down. I hadn't seen any comesuli in the kitchens with paper or writing utensils.

There was no coffee on Kifirin—yeah, the planet was actually named after the asshole. Is that enormous ego or what? I found myself wishing for coffee, especially in the mornings.

I was still adjusting to staying awake during the day and sleeping at night. It was getting better, but my eyes were still glued shut whenever Orliff tried to wake me every morning. Cheedas, chief cook in the palace kitchen, was bringing me all the produce to peel, chop or cut up now, because he liked the way I did it.

The word for cutting potatoes into cubes was *dorthi*. Go figure. Yeah, *The Wizard of Oz* came to my mind, too. Every time.

I ate my bowl of stew later, after everyone else was served. I then set about cleaning the kitchen before going back to my little corner of Darvul's suite. He, Noff and Orliff still kept an eye on me, but didn't worry so much when I was working in the kitchen. I guess the High Demons didn't pay anybody anything, either; I hadn't seen any money and wouldn't know what the word for paycheck would be anyway.

Two High Demons came in just as I was finishing my evening duties. They started babbling to me right away, and none of their words were the words I knew. I blinked at them; they were both six-four and brothers; I could tell by the scent.

I had to shake my head at them, trying to tell them I didn't understand what they were saying. One of them—the older of the two—became angry and smoke curled from his nostrils. I made a cutting off motion with my hands and then pointed to one of my ears and shook my head again.

~

"He's trying to tell you he doesn't understand," Jayd slapped Garde on the shoulder.

"What is going on?" Cheedas walked in. "Raoni, Prime Minister," he bowed slightly to both High Demons.

"We can't seem to make him understand that we're hungry," Garde huffed.

"This one suffered a head injury in the attack and doesn't understand speech now, although if you mimic what you want, he understands that very well," Cheedas replied. "You'll have to forgive him—he is good at what he does, otherwise."

"If you act like a steer, maybe he'll broil a steak," Jayd informed his brother, chuckling.

"Just mimic eating," Cheedas suggested. "I'll be interested to see what he cooks as a result."

~

Thanks to Cheedas, the two High Demons were now making eating motions. I sighed and went to the box that held the cold items. It wasn't a fridge, although it served as one.

There were round steaks inside, so I pulled those out and started pounding them with a meat hammer. Those two High Demons, and Cheedas who stayed to watch, were fascinated as I put chicken-fried steak together for them.

Leftover baked potatoes were heated and mashed with cream and butter, and then I made gravy to go with all of it, setting two plates of food before the High Demons first. Cheedas accepted a plate of food and a glass of the wine I'd opened for the other two.

They liked it. All of them did. Cheedas was staring at me after he'd taken his first bite. I recognized one of the High Demons—he was the King. Wouldn't do to piss the King off, I guess. And, since the other one was his brother, well, same thing, almost. I was cleaning the kitchen again after the mess I'd made fixing them a late dinner. They ate and talked while I worked. I'd gotten flour on my freshly mopped floor, so I had to mop that spot again while I waited for their dishes.

∾

"He understands names if you tell him and point to yourself," Cheedas informed the two High Demons, handing his empty plate and glass to Niff. "His name is Niff, by the way. At least that's what they're calling him, as he doesn't remember who he is and can't speak."

"Niff," Jayd said. He recognized the little common as the one who'd interrupted his dinner in the arboretum. Niff looked up as his name was spoken, a question in his eyes. "Jaydevik," Jayd tapped his chest with a finger. Niff nodded his understanding. "Gardevik," Jayd poked his brother on the arm. The little common's eyebrows rose as he stared at Garde.

"I don't think he likes you," Jayd teased his brother. Niff nodded respectfully to Garde and went back to mopping the floor.

∾

The two High Demons sat in the kitchen, sipping additional glasses of wine while I washed their plates and utensils, putting all of it away.

Cheedas had left again, leaving the two High Demons to finish eating. They were discussing something, I could tell. It didn't concern me that much, until Jayd said Niff again. I looked up, thinking he wanted something. Jayd looked at me and went off on some tangent. I had no idea what he wanted, but he kept going, gesturing now and then.

CHAPTER 4

"*S*ince Glinda wants you to go to the Southern Continent, brother, to check the area, you could take Niff, here, to do your cooking. That way we won't upset Cheedas so much and the kitchen won't suffer as a result," Jayd grinned at his brother.

They'd brought their proposition to Glinda earlier, telling her she could make the decision on who led the task force to the Southern Continent. Garde had blown smoke for ticks afterward when she'd named him immediately.

"We'll finish with the questioning and the sentencing first," Garde huffed. "But Niff can go. I like his cooking," he nibbled on a bit of leftover steak. "And he won't be bothering me over every little thing since he can't speak."

"We only have a hundred Drith and Croth left, brother. You ought to select the guards you wish to take with you now—both High Demon and commons—before you go. If you choose a captain, he can make arrangements for transportation and supplies."

"Fine," Garde muttered. He hated taking trips that used ground transportation. He preferred the normal method all High Demons used—that of skipping from one place to another. The drawback to skipping was that High Demons could only skip themselves from one place to another. If commons went, horses and wagons would be employed instead.

"Larevik is a good choice for captain," Jayd grinned.

"If my brother weren't King, I might thrash him," Garde grumbled, pushing his wineglass toward Niff, who accepted it and took it to wash. Jayd laughed and slapped his brother on the back.

It was quite late when I made my way to bed that night, and I almost fell asleep in the shower. My eyes were closing as I cleaned up and I was afraid to lean against the tiled wall in case I did nod off. Orliff was already asleep and snoring softly when I crawled into bed. He was shaking me awake before the sun came up the following morning, just as he always did.

My life as a kitchen drudge went in a different direction, though, after I cooked for the King and his brother. Cheedas would stay after the late meals were served and the kitchen cleaned, asking me through words and mime to cook something else.

He watched me closely as I made sugar cookies. I hadn't seen anything close to chocolate anywhere and wished for it on more than one occasion. I wanted brownies—had a taste for them, suddenly.

They did have oats, so oatmeal cookies came into being and I knew how to make fresh pasta so Cheedas and I tried our hand at lasagna. It turned out very well, even if the noodles were thicker than usual. I resolved to make them thinner the next time.

Jaydevik and Gardevik both showed up for the lasagna tasting; Jayd was more than happy with what he got.

I showed Cheedas the meat grinder at one point, silently asking him, as best I could if we could get another plate with smaller holes so we could make spaghetti. He finally understood when I drew a rough picture in some flour scattered across the prep table. He had a new plate for me in a couple of days and when I made spaghetti for him the first time, he was in raptures.

Cheeses on the High Demon planet were also very good; the goat cheeses were some of the best, I discovered. We made Alfredo sauce and covered more noodles, sliced half an inch in width. I was getting the High Demons hooked on Italian without really meaning to.

~

"How do we tell him he has a day off?" Orliff consulted Darvul and Noff. Niff, thinking he was supposed to go to the kitchens, was dressed and ready to walk out the door.

"I don't know," Noff shrugged. "What were you planning to do today? Do you think we should take him along and let him spend time with us?"

"I was going to visit my father," Orliff said. "I'll take him with me." Orliff went to grab Niff's hand before he could go out the door.

~

Orliff was telling me to come; I understood that word now. I didn't know what he was saying after he said come, though. I blew out a breath, let him keep his grip on my hand, then followed him out the door and down the long hallway that led to the front entrance.

We walked through the city that day instead of riding; I was able to see more of it that way. Most of the city was rebuilding—I was glad about that, but much of it was still empty space.

The comesuli had been busy—much of the rubble was cleared away already. Some buildings still stood—we passed the occasional open shop and vegetable market, all with goods and wares on display.

Small comesuli were running and chasing one another through the streets, laughing while they did so. That cheered me up, although it did make me wonder how many children died when the Ra'Ak attacked.

Orliff and I walked for an hour before we came to a shop where rugs were sold. It smelled of wool, dye and a brush with Ra'Ak scales.

An older comesula came forward and hugged Orliff when we arrived. I knew by scent that he was Orliff's parent, though they looked nothing alike. Orliff explained that I was handicapped and his parent, whose name was Paraf, motioned for me to follow him and found a chair for me inside his tiny living quarters.

Orliff and I were served tea and small pieces of dried fruit dipped in sugar. Paraf and Orliff had catching up to do; they talked nonstop for two hours, after which we ate a small meal and then the talking began again. It was late afternoon when they finally ran down—Paraf often left us to help a customer.

His rugs were beautifully patterned, and made of colorful, hand-dyed wool. I'd fingered one or two of them while we'd stood inside his shop early on.

Paraf was three hundred years old; I could tell from his scent. He'd also been making rugs for a very long time; that was obvious. Curiously, I watched Paraf as he bargained with a High Demon for two rugs, eventually accepting six gold pieces for both. At least somebody was getting paid for their labor.

Orliff and I made our way back to the palace, returning in time to get dinner in the kitchen. I was served a plate of food and it wasn't the scrapings, this time. Dinner was chicken stew, and it made me want to bake biscuits to go with it—to make a chicken pot pie. I held back though, eating my dinner gratefully.

That was my life for the next six weeks; seven days in the kitchen, followed by a day off. I wanted to go back to the arboretum, but was too afraid I'd run into other High Demons so I didn't risk it.

I also wanted to turn to mist at times and sit on one of the palace domes. That would probably scare Orliff and Noff to death; they kept a close eye on me whenever I wasn't working in the kitchen. I didn't want to frighten them; they were doing their best to take care of me, even if I did appear to be a disabled casualty of war.

I was adding to my vocabulary, too, but I hadn't attempted speech. I wasn't sure I could pronounce the words. I understood everything better, at least—Cheedas didn't have to mime so much. I understood cut up carrots or stir the soup or any number of other cooking-related sentences. I got a few other words out of kitchen gossip; the comesuli did love to gossip. None of it had to do with somebody's daughter or girlfriend getting pregnant or fooling around with anybody. The comesuli didn't have sex and their children were produced autonomously.

A pregnant comesula worked in the kitchen and wore a type of sling over his shoulder to hold up his pouch—it was growing on his lower left side. I found that fascinating.

I also heard the word Baetrah mentioned and discovered that the pregnant comesula was missing a traditional trip to the volcano because it erupted and the Southern Continent wasn't a safe place to visit at the moment. I didn't know that soon I would be headed in that direction myself.

"You're taking a comesula injured during the attacks?" Glinda had hands on her hips as she glared at Jayd's brother.

"He cooks very well and since he can't speak, he can't scold me," Garde smiled. He was irritating Glinda, which suited him very well.

Long ago, more than twelve hundred years, in fact, he'd taught Glinda. She'd learned how to fight from him. He'd also taught her how to skip and write and many other things High Demons were expected to know.

He'd angered her, too, when he told her what her life would be as a High Demon female. She'd skipped right off the planet and had gone missing for a very long time, until his brother found her by accident. She had absolutely no respect for Gardevik or his position as Jayd's Prime Minister. Garde didn't mind in the least.

"You said I could choose my guards and commons; therefore Niff is coming with me. Good luck on getting those mashed potatoes you like so well," Garde grinned.

"I can still throw things at you and I won't miss," Glinda snapped, her blue eyes flashing a warning at Gardevik Rath.

"Then I will leave you now before the projectiles fly," Garde was still grinning. "I will inform Cheedas that Niff is coming with me.

That ought to anger him enough that you'll not get a decent meal for a week."

Gardevik left Glinda's quarters, laughing when he heard her shouting, "Jaydevik, come and kill your brother for me!"

~

Orliff was upset; I could tell immediately, as he gestured for me to fold and pack my clothing into a shapeless bag. I offered him a puzzled glance as he did his best to explain something to me, but my limited vocabulary prevented me from understanding much of it.

He said Niff several times, the word go and somewhere in all that he said Baetrah. Were they sending me to the Southern Continent? To the volcano? I thought it was dangerous there. There was probably ash to be dealt with, and none of my borrowed clothing went well with blackish-gray.

A strange comesula came in, dressed in a palace guard's uniform. He seemed to be asking if I were ready. He also had more clothing and a pair of boots in his hands, which he handed to Orliff. Orliff gestured for me to wear one of the new uniforms, so I went to the bathroom to change.

~

"He'll lose that modesty quickly when we travel through the deserted areas," Veris, captain of the common guard grumbled as Niff walked out of the bathroom, dressed in the uniform and boots Veris supplied.

"He is not whole," Orliff snapped. "If an entire shop had fallen on your head, I would hope others might be sympathetic to your plight. Neither I nor my instructor thinks this is a good idea and your taking of Niff goes against Darvul's better judgment."

"I would not take him," Veris snapped back, "but Gardevik is demanding it. He wants Niff to cook for him and be his valet while we are on this mission for the Queen." Orliff was still grumbling when Niff was instructed to follow Veris out of the suite.

How had things come to this? I was wondering that for at least the tenth time as we loaded things into wagons (the comesuli and me; none of the High Demons thought to lift a finger).

It didn't bother me to lift the heavy bags of flour or any of the crates, though if I caught anyone watching, I pretended to need help. The animals hitched to the wagons resembled oxen, with four short horns instead of two, like the ones I'd always seen.

There were comesuli drivers for the wagons, and they would be tending the oxen. The comesuli in uniform (and that included me), were there to act as backup for the High Demons, especially in their dealings with other comesuli.

Midmorning arrived before we were loaded up and on the road, and as I was now considered Gardevik's private cook and personal servant, I rode in the wagon that carried his things.

Gardevik had a lot of things. I felt confident he'd taken most of his belongings with him. My duffle bag of clothing and personal belongings were lost amid his in a corner of the wagon.

Most of the comesuli troops walked, but they switched off with those who rode from time to time, so everyone could get a rest. The High Demons had horses to ride. Yeah, same old horse-type horses Earth had. I was grateful to learn I didn't have to look after Gardevik's horse; somebody else would do that.

Altogether, there were six High Demons, not counting Gardevik, twenty comesuli troops, six wagon drivers and seven grooms to tend the horses for a total of forty.

We left Veshtul behind after two hours, and the road we traveled outside the city sure needed work. It made me think of the Romans and how they'd built roads as they'd marched along. Somebody sure needed to work on this one as we moved over it.

It also made me think of Gavin, and that made me sad. For him, I'd been gone three hundred years. I was probably a distant memory to him, which made me feel worse. The grief over René and Greg's loss was still fresh for me too, although Franklin was gone as well unless

Merrill had talked him into allowing the turn. I had to force myself to think of other things before I broke down and wept.

The wagon I rode in was enclosed, but the driver didn't mind if I sat up front with him so I could see the country we were passing through. He knew I was recovering and spent the day pointing things out and naming them. I could have hugged him when he did that.

His name was Corin, I learned, and he was a patient soul. When we stopped for the night, it was in the middle of nowhere and Gardevik got a steak grilled over a campfire, along with fresh asparagus I found growing wild near the road. He also got biscuits cooked in an iron skillet, which I served with butter and honey.

Larevik, the High Demon captain, came over and had what was left of the biscuits, drizzling honey over them while he and Gardevik talked.

I cleaned my pans and dishes, made sure Gardevik didn't want anything else to eat and got his bed ready in the wagon. It only hit me then that I didn't know where I was supposed to sleep. I went to ask Corin, as best I could.

He understood quickly when I mimed sleeping, pointing to a spot at the foot of Gardevik's sleeping pad and blankets. I was going to sleep there on a thin mat, with a blanket and small pillow.

I nodded my thanks to Corin, who was bedding down beneath the wagon. I discovered quickly what being a High Demon's personal servant meant. Gardevik stripped, went to bed naked and watched lazily as I brushed dust from his clothing. I wiped his boots off and put everything away before going to bed.

Gardevik was completely uninhibited, parading about as if he were proud of his endowments. I'm not saying he shouldn't feel proud over what he had or how he looked. It was damned embarrassing, however.

I sighed softly, told myself to get used to it and huddled under my blanket inches away from his feet.

We stopped in a small city on the second night and had rooms to sleep in—at least the High Demons did, and since I was Gardevik's personal servant, I slept in a corner of his room on a small cot.

The High Demons were also served dinner by our host, while the comesuli made do for themselves. Garde grumbled about the food afterward, but I didn't understand half his words.

He got a bath (we both did), but his came first and I saw to his clothing before cleaning up afterward. He didn't bother me and was snoring softly when I came out. I had my cotton pajamas on—that's what I slept in, and he never looked at me twice anyway. Just as well; had he paid attention, he might have noticed a few things.

To him, I was a common demon and nothing else.

The following two nights were spent on the road and Larevik invited himself to dinner both nights. I made fried chicken for them the first night and smothered steak the second. Gardevik was begging for biscuits on the second night, but he called them indu nera, or round breads. He got indu nera, which was quite good with the smothered steak.

I don't know how they kept their meats cold on the road but they had some way to do it, and I figured it wasn't local technology. Didn't matter; I was happy to have the cold meat and fresh produce they carried, and each town or city we rode through provided fresh supplies.

Gardevik asked our host in the next village for the run of his kitchen, sending me in to cook for him and the others. Some of the comesuli staff helped, and chicken and dumplings were the result of that collaboration.

Apple pies waited for dessert; our host had apples in a basket he intended to give us for our trip. Many of those were baked into pies and every crumb disappeared.

"It's useless—he can't write or speak to give you the recipe—he only remembers how to cook and we are very thankful for that," Gardevik informed his host, who begged to have instructions for making apple pies written down.

"Will he ever remember, do you think?" Garde's High Demon host asked.

"No idea. He sustained a head injury in the attacks and we have lost hope that he will fully recover. I would like to know from whom he learned his cooking skills and why we never heard of some of these dishes before. Perhaps it was a closely guarded family secret," Garde answered. He was quite proud of his assistant, although he kept that information to himself.

～

We'd been on the road more than a week before I received my first taunt. Honestly, I expected it before then, but I was Garde's chief cook and bottle washer, so that's why it probably took so long. It wasn't one of the High Demons, either, which surprised me. It was a comesula—one of the guards.

"Difik," he muttered, when I showed up to get the evening's ration of meat and vegetables to cook. I was now serving Gardevik, Larevik, and Larevik's next in line.

Difik was one of the words I actually knew. As best I could translate, it meant idiot, or even slow idiot. If I'd known how to call him shithead, I would have. I didn't know how and it would blow my cover anyway. I ignored him, collected my supplies and went back to Garde's camp.

～

"He needs a haircut," Veris's lieutenant declared. "Lord Gardevik has more important things on his mind and does not need to be bothered with this."

Veris carefully weighed Breth's claims about the little common who couldn't speak. "I suppose you intend to correct the situation?" Veris crossed arms over his chest.

"With your permission. His hair is too long and appears untidy. It presents the wrong image for the Raoni's troops."

60

"But that one is not of the Raoni's troops," Veris pointed out. "He is recovering from a head injury."

"A haircut is not harmful in the least," Breth declared. "And he will look better afterward."

"Fine, go and get him," Veris muttered.

The one who'd called me difik came to get me shortly before bedtime that evening. "Come," he demanded. I had no idea how to tell him that I didn't want to come anywhere with him. I watched him warily as he led me through camp.

Veris, the one who'd pulled me away from Orliff at the palace, stood waiting. He mimed cutting hair to me. That stopped me in my tracks. I'd worked so hard to get my hair to the length it was. It barely touched my shoulders and was still quite curly as a result. Most comesuli kept their hair short—it was easier to take care of, I suppose, but I wasn't a comesula. I wanted to keep my hair and grow it longer. I wanted it back to the length it was before I'd tried to give myself to the sun.

I was shaking my head violently at Veris, doing my best to tell him I wanted nothing to do with a haircut. He was motioning for me to come and sit down. I shook my head again and tried to walk away. That's when I was grabbed.

"Don't hurt him!" Veris shouted as Breth and another comesula grabbed Niff's arms, forcing him to a nearby stump. Niff was frightened and struggling in their grasp. Veris was beginning to think the haircut a bad idea, but he'd already given permission.

Niff was resisting and he hadn't expected that. At other times, Niff had cooperated when asked to do something.

"Get shackles!" Breth commanded and another comesula came running with the requested chain bracelets. Niff was still fighting

Breth and Weld, so the third comesula locked the shackles on the small common's wrists, tightening them.

The chain between the bracelets was very short—only a few links—and still the little common had to be held down on the stump. Breth accepted the shears from someone else.

Niff's eyes were wide and tears came when Breth made the first cut. Reddish-blond curls dropped to the ground.

"Cut it well or you'll be chained," Veris growled at Breth. The little common was weeping as Breth kept snipping.

"What happened?" Gardevik demanded as his little common rushed past, weeping and wiping his face on a sleeve. Veris had followed along in case an explanation was needed.

"Breth pointed out that he needed a haircut," Veris stood before Gardevik.

"And did Niff agree to this?" Garde asked.

"He didn't want it," Veris replied, wondering if he shouldn't have thought this through before granting permission.

"And he sat there and let you do it anyway?"

"Well, we did have to shackle him and hold him down," Veris didn't like where the conversation was going.

"You shackled my cook to force him to get a haircut?" Garde didn't like Veris's explanation.

"He didn't present the proper image as your personal servant," Veris mumbled, repeating Breth's words to him.

"Don't you think I should decide what my personal servant's proper image should be?" Smoke curled from Garde's nostrils. Veris recognized that as a warning sign. Any High Demon blowing smoke was angry, and an angry High Demon was never far from their Thifilathi.

"My apologies, High Lord. We made a mistake."

"Do not lay your hands on Niff again without my permission," Garde snarled.

"Yes, High Lord." Veris wanted to run to get away from Gardevik, but he walked away instead, in an effort to retain his dignity.

$\sim$

They'd cut my hair. They'd cut my fucking hair. Just snipped it right off while I was chained and held down. If they'd known I could have snapped those chains with a flick of my wrist, they might not have put them on me in the first place.

I was learning my lesson—not all comesuli were kind. They were just like any other people, I guess. I wiped tears off my face and went to find Garde's mirror—he kept one to groom his hair.

The image that stared back at me made me want to weep again. That asshole had butchered my hair. It was an inch in length now, and looked horribly uneven. I wanted to mist the jackass away and drop him in the nearest lake, harboring hope that it might contain crocodiles or large, comesula-eating fish.

No way could I fix this. I was stuck with the worst haircut imaginable. I could have done a better job if I'd cut it myself. Fuck. Fuck to the twelfth power.

Gardevik climbed into the wagon later; I took his clothes and boots from him, as I always did. Tearstains still showed on my cheeks, but Garde never looked at me anyway.

He could compete with Gavin in looks—dark-brown hair, darker eyes and a handsome enough face, and all that was matched with a body most men on Earth would kill to get. High Demons seemed to have it naturally.

I'm sure Kifirin the asshole had seen to that when he'd made them, all those years ago. Kifirin. If he were here now, I'd slap him into next week, I was so mad. Griffin too. They both had a lot to answer for. Maybe that's why they hadn't gone looking for me; I'd served my purpose and now they had no desire to listen to the vampire whine.

Perhaps I was supposed to be bigger than that and understand how I'd had a higher calling or something—that I was supposed to be one of those long-suffering heroines the books all praised.

I wasn't anything like that. I'd been birthed for a specific reason—to keep the peace between werewolves and vampires, destroy Xenides and then save High Demon and comesuli ass.

One of those comesuli had just chopped off my hair and chained me up to do it. My head looked like someone had taken a weed trimmer to it. I sure hoped his ass didn't need saving again, because I might have second thoughts.

~

"Griffin nearly went crazy when he learned that Lissa's memorial wasn't planned for another year," Kiarra was as tactful as possible while speaking with Jayd.

"But we have no idea how this news will affect the commons; they're only now climbing out of the rubble from the attack," Jayd defended his and Garde's decision. "If we tell them the hope they've prayed and waited for is now dead, who knows what will happen?"

"You mean they might stop serving your dinner for a day or two?" Griffin appeared and he was angry. "My daughter died defending this planet and this is the thanks you give her?" Pheligar folded in, as Griffin might have to be restrained.

"We had no idea that's what happened until after the fact," Jayd snapped, his Thifilathi becoming angry as well. Smoke poured from Jayd's nostrils as he glared at Griffin.

"So now that it's over and your posterior and your planet have survived, she is of no consequence?" Griffin shouted in disbelief.

"I didn't say that," Jayd held out a hand, attempting to calm himself. "I am merely working to keep things running smoothly on the planet your daughter saved for us. Do you want it thrown into chaos? We have refugees from the Southern Continent because the volcano erupted for days. The crops we normally get from those farms will not be delivered. We are facing shortages as a result. What do you think I should do?"

"Not a fucking thing!" Griffin shouted and folded away.

"Lord Demon," Pheligar addressed Jayd quietly, "if one of your daughters sacrificed herself to save your planet, you would be wailing to the heavens over it. I will withdraw my protection around the stockade, as will my son Renegar. You are on your own." Pheligar folded away.

"You heard my Larentii mate," Kiarra said. "I wouldn't look to the Saa Thalarr for help in the future." She also disappeared. Jayd cursed and ran a hand through his hair.

"Jaydevik, why did you not consult with me before making this decision?" Glinda's voice was soft and angry. She stood in the doorway to the King's private study, where the meeting with Kiarra had taken place. Griffin and Pheligar's appearance had come unexpectedly. Now, Jayd knew Glinda had somehow escaped her suite and heard the entire conversation.

"Garde and I thought it would be for the best," Jayd attempted to defend himself.

"You have cut us off, that is what you have done," Glinda's voice was louder now. "I am helpless, because I am pregnant. Saa Thalarr cannot use their power in this condition—it will harm the children. We could have asked for supplies to be brought in; Kiarra would not let the planet starve. Yet you have alienated her and the rest of them as a result. Are you truly so coldhearted, Jaydevik? You disappoint me." Glinda whirled and walked away from him, slamming the study door forcefully.

Larevik reached out to touch my hair while I cooked breakfast the following morning. I ducked away from his hand so fast it startled him. I was still so pissed I couldn't see straight. Larevik didn't reach for me again.

Garde didn't say anything; he merely ignored me as usual, ate like there was no tomorrow and then went to get his horse while I cleaned dishes and loaded them into the wagon.

Neither Breth nor Veris were anywhere around when I'd picked up the food for breakfast earlier, and that was a good thing. I had their scent and from now on, I was staying as far away from them as I could get.

We stopped for three days at the next city on our itinerary—Raona Belarok. It was named after the current Raona's mother. I was getting better at the language and wanted to ask someone for Belarok's story, but talking or attempting to talk now would probably give all of them the shivers. I remained silent, instead.

A large house was provided for Garde and the other High Demons in Raona Belarok; it had plenty of space, with servants' quarters and a large stable. I heard the name Croth spoken; the home had belonged to rogue High Demons. Dead rogue High Demons, unless I missed my guess.

"I wonder what this is called?" Gardevik was eating his second slice of custard pie. I could have told him it was my mother's recipe, if I'd been so inclined. I just set the pan with the last slice in front of him instead and he grinned.

Later, Corin went with me to the local market. Garde had given him money and orders to buy food for the next two days to feed him and the other High Demons. The comesuli troops had their own cooks and helpers among them and they were going off to do the same.

Corin enlisted one of the other drivers to help, and we brought back a load of fresh vegetables and meats. I made sure Corin and the other driver, Foss, got dinner and dessert later. They were more than happy with what they were served; I made stuffed pork chops, sautéed snap beans and squash.

I'd also found preserved peaches at the market and while it wasn't as good as fresh, they all loved the peach cobbler.

The other thing that went well, I suppose, was that I was gaining lost weight back. When I'd first come back to myself on Kifirin, I was skin and bones. No wonder they couldn't tell the difference between me and any other comesula.

Now, though, my shape was coming back and I didn't look quite as gaunt. My hair still looked like crap, though, and I grumbled every time I saw my reflection.

Breth was still taunting me every chance he had, when nobody was watching or listening. I heard plenty of *difik* whispered in my direction, some *af te Jufaleh*, which in High Demon meant go to hell—or their equivalent of hell, anyway. Stupid, dimwitted, malformed and stunted was also aimed at me.

At least he had an adequate vocabulary and I was learning new words. No idea why he felt obligated to target me in this way; I couldn't figure him out at all. He didn't put his hands on me again, though, and I figured Gardevik had said something to Veris.

CHAPTER 5

"We'll be in range of ash in two days," I heard Larevik inform Garde over dinner. We'd been back on the road for six days this time, passing the checkpoint between the Northern and Southern Continents.

The landscape was already giving way to a lusher, tropical variety of plants. Those plants were trying their best to crowd the side of the road, since most of the High Demons and comesuli had gone north after Baetrah's eruption.

"We'll go as far as Baetrah an Hafei and see what's left of it," Gardevik replied. He and Larevik were sipping tea I'd made for them after dinner. They didn't hold back on any of their conversations; they figured I didn't understand any of it anyway and certainly wouldn't repeat it.

"What do you make of the rumors that there are Croth still hiding in the area?" Larevik asked.

"If they're hiding, I have no idea how they're surviving if the damage from the ash is as bad as I've heard," Gardevik replied. "The cane crops in the area are destroyed. I hope we have plenty of stores, because we may not see another crop for a year or two and the fields may have to be moved."

"There are the jungles farther south," Larevik pointed out. "We could plant there."

"Those will have to be cleared, at least in part, and I don't like cutting down the trees. The farming in that area must be kept at a minimum."

"I agree, but who will be running those farms? Croth and Drith did it before, and we have thinned them down to nothing. We found so few of them innocent of treason." Larevik shook his head.

"The fools," Garde growled, holding out his cup so I'd bring more tea. I brought the tea and poured for him. "Niffy," Garde grabbed me and planted a kiss on top of my head. "Go to bed, short one." He motioned toward the wagon. I stared at him in shock for a few seconds before getting my head together and walking toward the wagon.

I lay awake, listening to the rest of the conversation; my hearing was still as sharp as it ever was. Garde and Larevik were kicking around ideas regarding what they should do if they did come across Croth or Drith in the region.

We'd met no comesuli at all after passing the border and there were few animals; they'd fled the area as well. Garde talked about food rations, which concerned me. We'd loaded up as much as we could at the border town, but we had three more days to get to the city below the volcano.

Baetrah an Hafei was the name of that city, and it would take another six days to return to the border, once we turned around to come back. That might get tricky. Larevik talked of sending some of the comesuli troops back to the border town to wait for us. Garde thought it a good idea.

"If we send fifteen back with one of the wagons, we can make do with the others—that will leave the drivers and grooms plus a few handpicked troops," Garde agreed. I was hoping Breth would be among the fifteen sent away.

My hope was short-lived as I watched fifteen comesuli leave us the following morning after breakfast. Breth stayed.

Dammit.

That day we came across volcanic ash and it kept getting deeper the farther south we traveled. It choked the vegetation we now passed on both sides of the road, which was nearly covered in the grayish black stuff.

We stopped midafternoon to inspect a farm not far off the road. Furrows were buried beneath heavy, suffocating ash and the plants were dead when Garde kicked away some of it to check. "Heat from the ash and lack of sun," Garde grumbled.

Decomposing corpses of cattle lay nearby and they smelled. I was having difficulty dealing with the stench, but followed Garde and Larevik obediently toward the carcasses when I was instructed to walk behind them.

"Why did the cattle die here?" Larevik asked. "This was a cane farm. The cattle farms were south of here."

"They were running away from the eruption when they were poisoned from eating ash covered plants," I said, and then clapped a hand over my mouth.

"Niffy, how long have you been able to speak?" Gardevik was now frowning at me. Larevik stared in shock—he'd never expected me to speak at all. My eyes were wide as I gaped at both of them.

"Not until now," I squeaked an answer to Garde's question. "It just happened."

"Well, barring future miracles, I think we've seen enough here," Garde laughed and shook his head as he herded Larevik and me toward the wagons and the others waiting there.

"Difik." Breth was back to his old tricks as I got supplies from the wagon to make dinner that evening.

"Shithead," I replied in High Demon and walked away from him, carrying my small crate of food. I didn't look back, but imagined his mouth may have been hanging open as I left him standing there, ankle-deep in volcanic ash.

The ash was nearly a foot deep the following day and deeper than that when we arrived in the deserted city of Baetrah an Hafei. Located roughly forty miles from the volcano, it had been heavily damaged by the eruptions.

Buildings that hadn't burned had collapsed beneath the weight of ash. I found myself hoping nobody had stayed to get caught in all of that, thinking of Pompeii and Herculaneum.

"Turn back, you will find nothing here."

I knew that voice. It had come from nowhere, accompanied by the sudden appearance of the voice's owner. Kifirin.

I'd slogged along behind the others—the High Demons had the easiest time getting over the thick piles of ash in the town. I didn't waste any time now, though, misting myself right in front of Kifirin.

"You asshole!" I shouted at him in English. "You did this on purpose!" I slapped him as hard as I could. "I hate you! You and Griffin both! I was just a convenience for you, wasn't I? You only wanted to save your High Demons' asses. You didn't give a fuck about me. Never gave a fuck about me."

I was crying by then and I slapped Kifirin again. Slapping a god was probably going to make me very, very dead. But that's what he'd intended to begin with, wasn't it?

Gardevik and the others stared as little Niff somehow appeared before Kifirin, shouted at him, and then slapped him—twice. Gardevik understood the English, but none of the others did.

This wasn't a common. He was staring at the Vampire Queen and she knew Kifirin. Not only that, Kifirin was standing there, taking everything she chose to dish out and she wasn't being kind with her words.

My breaths were sobs as I collapsed in the ash before Kifirin. He hadn't moved the entire time I'd yelled at him and then slapped him. And I'd put most of my strength into those slaps.

"Lissa, how are you alive?" Kifirin sounded sad. He could keep that lie to himself. I wasn't swallowing it. Ever again. He knelt before me as I hugged myself, trying to stop shivering even in the heat of the Southern hemisphere.

"I d-don't kn-know," I stuttered. "Leave me the fuck alone."

"Avilepha, please do not do this. I have loved you from the moment I met you."

"D-don't give me that shit, Kifirin. You sacrificed me. You and Griffin. And I'm just supposed to act like that's okay?" I sobbed again. "Go away."

"How will you get off the planet, m'hala?" Kifirin's voice was soft. "I must do this for you."

"I don't want a fucking thing from you." I stood and walked away from him.

"Very well," he called after me. "I will join your expedition. I will work to bring myself back into your good graces, avilepha." Kifirin stood behind me.

"Fuck," I muttered and passed Gardevik, who was staring—first at me and then at Kifirin as I made my way toward the wagon.

"Don't come anywhere near me," I warned Breth later—he'd come to gape, as had the other comesuli. "You see this," I gripped a handful of my hair. "You fucked up my hair and I waited so long for it to grow out again."

"You are the Vampire Queen?" Veris stood beside Breth, his question whispered reverently.

"Yeah. Sure. Don't I look like a fucking Queen?" I snapped. Kifirin had holed up somewhere with Gardevik and the other High Demons. Figures. They were all he cared about anyway.

"But you walk in daylight," Breth accused.

"Yeah. How about that?" I grumped. "Feel free to ask dear old Dad about that." I turned and slogged my way over more ash. I wanted to get away from all of them right then, but figured if I misted away, I'd still be stuck on the fucking planet with no food, money or clothing.

Some days, I just loved my life.

"Your mate is the Vampire Queen?" Larevik couldn't believe what he was hearing.

"You question me?" Kifirin leveled his gaze at Larevik. Smoke curled from Kifirin's nostrils. "She bears my claiming marks. If you hadn't had you head up your posterior, you would have seen them."

"But she was shouting at you," another of the High Demons ventured to say. He was terrified. Kifirin had stepped out of myth and into reality for him in the space of a few moments.

"Yes, she was." Kifirin smiled. "My little Queen is not frightened of me. Nor do I wish her to be."

"What do you want from us?" Gardevik asked. He'd seen Kifirin before, but that had been long ago, when Gardevik was very young.

"I want nothing from you. I want my mate. I want her love. Therefore, I will be traveling with you. Do you have objections?"

"No," Garde shook his head. This was Kifirin. He could do as he pleased. "But Niff has been working as my personal servant. He—she —has been cooking for us."

"I see you cut her hair." Kifirin wasn't pleased about that.

"Some of the commons did that," Garde huffed. "Without my permission."

"Did you punish them?" Kifirin asked.

"No. I just told them not to put their hands on—her—again, unless I requested it."

"Your brother has upset the Oracle, the Larentii and the Saa Thalarr," Kifirin said. "Because he wanted to wait a year to put up a memorial to my Lissa."

"We may have made a mistake," Garde lowered his eyes, afraid to admit his part in that decision.

"It will not be the first High Demon mistake," smoke curled from Kifirin's nostrils.

"Will you punish us for Lendevik's shortcomings?" Garde asked, raising his eyes to Kifirin again.

"You were all punished for Lendevik's blunders. Had the Oracle not come and shown me a path away from your destruction, your planet would have fallen. My mistake was in trusting Lendevik and the High Demons as a whole. That will not be repeated. I sacrificed my love in order for the High Demons to live."

~

"Yes, we now know how she is alive." Belen of the Nameless Ones had called Kiarra and Griffin to him. "And I admit; neither I nor any of my kind had anything to do with it. An unseen hand has performed this feat. One we do not direct."

"You can't tell us any more than that?" Griffin was an emotional wreck.

"No, but it will be revealed in time," Belen said gently. "I will tell you that at the present, she is very upset with both you and Kifirin. When Kifirin found her, acting as a cook and personal servant to Gardevik Rath on the Southern Continent, she shouted at him and slapped him. Twice, I believe."

"How else did you expect her to react?" Kiarra was standing, now, and angry. "None of these choices were hers. I might have done worse than a couple of slaps." Kiarra was ready to fold away and Belen didn't want her upset, too.

"Kiarra, please be patient with us," Belen said. "The conditions that have been presented to me by those above my kind are such that she cannot be taken back to the time she left. She must stay in this time and go forward from here. Many things depend upon this, and it may be very difficult for her. Kiarra, I would like for you and some of the others to do your best to explain things to her."

"What are we explaining? That she can't go back? That we rooted her out of her life for our convenience, and now friends and loved ones are long dead in the past, and we can't do anything about it?" Kiarra paced, vibrating with power and anger.

"This is the time she would have been reborn," Belen attempted to calm Kiarra. "Her life was given back to her without going through the rebirth. You will all know why, eventually."

"She would have been reborn this quickly?" Griffin was now interested.

"Yes. I cannot tell you more than that. You must do your best to make amends with your daughter, and we send our apologies to Amara; we know how much she wanted to be a mother. She will have to settle for being a stepmother."

"Lissa would have been born to us—to Amara and me?" Griffin was having difficulty breathing.

"Yes. It is better this way." Belen smiled. "Make things right with her, Oracle."

"Easier said than done," Griffin grumbled.

"Trust will never come easy to her again; you must deal with that," Belen agreed.

"Why couldn't we find Lissa by *Looking*?" Kiarra asked the question that bothered her most.

"None can find her by *Looking*. None lesser than myself, anyway," Belen replied. "Go now. You have much work to do."

"I called all of you here because most of you knew Lissa," Kiarra looked over the gathered Saa Thalarr and Spawn Hunters.

Dragon had come, with Karzac. One of his mates, Grace, was also there, although she'd never met Lissa. She was Co-First with Dragon, and that position brought her to the meeting.

Most of the others there had been vampire or werewolf and still retained vampire and werewolf abilities—those enhanced their capabilities as Saa Thalarr and Spawn Hunters.

Wlodek was there. As was Radomir, Will, Russell, Brock, Stephan, Charles, Merrill, Weldon Harper, Martin Walters and his son, Mack.

Pheligar and Adam Chessman had also come. They'd both met Lissa, although contact had been brief. "What is going on?" Merrill and Adam both came to Kiarra. They, along with Pheligar, were Kiarra's mates and had known of her meeting with Belen of the Nameless Ones.

"Lissa has been found and she's alive," Kiarra sighed. "We don't have an explanation; Belen only said that instead of allowing her to be reborn, somebody decided to give her life back to her now. He said we'll all know why in time."

"She's alive?" Charles was standing in Kiarra's kitchen, and now he grabbed a chair at the island and sat down. He was a Spawn Hunter for the Saa Thalarr, but held a seat on the Vampire Council, and also worked as Flavio's Chief of Staff. Flavio was now Head of the Vampire Council; Wlodek resigned when the invitation came to join the Saa Thalarr.

"Where is she?" Wlodek asked.

"On Kifirin. Right now, Kifirin is attempting to repair their relationship. I'm not holding any hope on that at the moment," Kiarra said. "Belen says she can't be found by *Looking*—that none lesser than he can know where she is. I have no idea what that means."

"Is she going to come back and act as Queen again?" Merrill asked. Wlodek also wanted that question answered. He and Merrill were informed of Lissa's death three centuries before, and then the memories of her were removed from all of them. It was as if she hadn't existed, and that remained the same until Kifirin was attacked. The memories were returned to the Saa Thalarr and Spawn Hunters when Lissa gave her life to save all of them.

"Does Gavin remember her, now? Or any of the others?" Radomir's voice was quiet and thoughtful, his dark eyes searching Kiarra's face for answers. He'd cared more for Lissa than any of them realized.

"They don't remember," Kiarra sighed. "Belen did give me these, though." She held Lissa's engagement and wedding rings in her hand. "I have no idea what to do with them."

"I will hold them for now," Wlodek came forward and took the rings.

"So, not only are some of her friends dead and gone; the others don't remember her? What kind of blow do you think that will be?" Russell observed. He'd leaned a hip against Kiarra's kitchen island, arms crossed over his wide chest.

"Perhaps it is an opportunity for her to start fresh with them and only accept the ones she wants without any past history," Adam suggested. "After all, wasn't Gavin forced on her as a mate? Isn't that what happened?" He offered Wlodek a pointed glance.

"Yes," Wlodek nodded. "But she did love him, I think. I will check with Flavio and perhaps arrange a meeting—will Lissa be brought to us? When will we see her? Gavin and Anthony are still employed by the Council as Assassins; if she wishes to see them, I will convince Flavio to bring them in."

"I'd ask her, first," Merrill muttered dryly.

"Perhaps Pheligar knows if Lissa will be brought to us," Kiarra said, turning to Merrill. He pulled her against him and kissed her forehead.

Gavin knocked the attacking vampire away with a vicious blow. Anthony was backing him up, but they'd found four rogue vampires instead of two and now they were in a real fight.

Gavin already had one down and turning to ash, now another of their adversaries was attacking. These four that he and Anthony had tracked were killing in the Seattle area; the murders hadn't come to light until one of them had slipped, killing a relief worker among the indigent, homeless population instead of one of the homeless. Until that time, not many had noted the indigent were disappearing upon occasion.

Tony sliced the head from one of his opponents, slipping in under his guard. Now, the odds were better. Gavin snarled and went after his target again.

"I wish we could go to a bar and get a beer," Tony grumbled as he and Gavin loaded into their hover rental afterward.

"You may go to a bar and get a beer. It will not have any effect unless you drink from a drunken patron," Gavin pointed out.

"Thanks for the reminder." Tony slumped in his seat. He was now three hundred thirty-seven years old and Gavin was nearing two thousand. Something seemed to be missing from both their lives, however, and Tony couldn't put a finger on it.

Wlodek offered Tony a position as Assassin for the Council when he'd been barely six months old as a vampire. Tony continued his training with Gavin as time allowed through the required five years, but he'd been sent on many assignments alone, long before that time was up.

He and Gavin only went out together now if they were hunting a pod of rogues. René's wealth was also his—Tony inherited when René died. He remembered little of René's death, and that troubled him. The memory was hazy in his mind.

"Maybe it's because it was so soon after I was turned," Tony said aloud without meaning to.

"What was so soon after your turning?" Gavin turned to Tony, curious now.

"René's death," Tony said. "I only have vague memories of it."

"It is the same for me; that time is quite blurry in my memory, while all other memories are very clear," Gavin agreed. "It was an emotional time for both of us."

"Do you ever feel as if something is missing from your life, Gavin? Something important?" Tony asked, looking out his window.

Rain was falling in Seattle, as it so often did. Gavin directed the hovercraft between buildings, turning toward their hotel.

"Yes. I feel an emptiness at times. Perhaps it is because René is missing from both our lives."

"Maybe." Tony wasn't sure that was all of it, though. "What do you think about the new blood substitute?" he changed the subject.

"Tasteless, just as the others were, but it does feed us. That is all that is required, I suppose."

Vampire scientists developed the substitute more than one hundred fifty years before and the vampire community was dependent on it for sustenance. Improvements had been made, but it still came no closer to actual blood.

Seldom did they get real blood, and getting blood directly from donors was no longer acceptable unless it was an emergency. Gavin snorted. Gavin was one of the oldest now; he'd been turned in an era when taking from donors was the only option.

"Call Charles and let him know our hunt was successful," Gavin ordered. Tony pulled out his tiny communicator.

"Recording the information," Charles informed Tony from the other end, tapping the button on his personal communicator to insert the information into Flavio's computer. "Anthony, does the name Lissa mean anything to you?" Charles asked while he and Tony waited for the transmission.

"Lissa? Who is that?" Tony asked, curious.

"Nobody. I was wondering if you'd ever met anyone with that name." Charles had the answer to his question, now.

"Not that I recall. Gavin is shaking his head, too," Tony passed off the additional information; Gavin was listening in.

"Transmission done," Charles said.

Tiny cameras, attached to every Enforcer's clothing, made recording data so much easier. The microscopic devices were incorporated into clothing in ingenious ways; front, back, high and low, and were difficult to detect.

Cleaning the clothing failed to harm them, they were built so efficiently. The cameras were also quite expensive; therefore, the Council provided them and had them installed.

Enforcers and Assassins faced a heavy fine if they hunted their quarry without the appropriate clothing, unless it was an emergency. Charles terminated the communication and went to report the successful hunt to Flavio.

❧

"And just where do you intend to take me?" I jerked my arm from Kifirin's grasp. He was attempting to persuade me to come away with him, rather than traveling with the High Demons and the comesuli.

Honestly, I wouldn't mind getting away from the comesuli. They were following me now wherever I went, Breth included, many with pure adoration in their eyes. Breth wasn't high on my good list right then.

My hair still looked like a mess, although Kifirin offered to use his power to grow it out again. I'd refused. Kifirin brought in clothing for me, though, that actually fit. At least he hadn't brought dresses or skirts; we were still traveling over ash and with the rains on the Southern Continent, it was hardening and causing problems.

"Away from here," Kifirin replied to my question. I was getting on his nerves and he was certainly on mine. Of course, he'd already been there before he'd shown up out of the blue.

"You made this mess," I grumbled.

"I thought my mate was dead."

"Yeah, well, whose fault is that?" I snapped.

"Avilepha, I am no good at apologies. I have never made them," Kifirin explained. I almost felt sorry for him.

"Maybe you should have thought about that before sticking your teeth in my neck," I smacked his chest. We were having our latest argument in the middle of camp.

Gardevik had already gotten his food and was eating with Larevik and the others. Well, the High Demons didn't have television, so they were settling for the latest episode of *Lissa is Pissed at Kifirin*.

"Lissa my love, I was attempting to save all the worlds, not just this one," Kifirin said. "They would all have fallen if this one fell. Did I realize how much pain it would cause me? No. Nor the pain it has caused you. It was my hope that I could find you in your next life and make things as easy for you as I could. My arms are empty and my heart will be empty as well if you reject me."

"Are you saying you don't deserve those things? Where were you before, Kifirin? Hanging out with dear old Dad?" I wanted to growl at him. Every High Demon and most of the comesuli were leaning forward to catch Kifirin's next words.

"I was sleeping." Kifirin sounded sad.

"Kifirin, I can't do this anymore," I tossed up a hand in a helpless gesture. "Do I love you? Probably. Do I expect you to hurt me again? Yes. I don't trust you. You didn't tell me anything, did you? How can I trust that? Why am I alive now, Kifirin? Can you explain that, please?" I turned away from him.

The High Demons had now stopped eating, content to watch the soap opera unfolding before them.

"Lissa, you are killing us both." Kifirin's arms were around me, and he was breathing warm air against my neck. We weren't in the camp any longer. "I know I hurt you. I know I was instrumental in your death. I felt you die, love. That's what truly woke me. The Dragon's Teeth require blood. Other blood was offered, but yours was what brought me out of my long sleep. You willingly sacrificed yourself in the end. Tell me you didn't know what you were doing. Tell me you didn't give your life freely, making your own decision that very last time. You could have backed away, yet you did not. You saw the opportunity to leave the Copper Ra'Ak leaderless and fighting among themselves for control. That would give the others a chance to win the battle and save this world, as well as all other worlds."

"You know that's not why I'm angry now, don't you?" I tried to get away from him.

"Shhh, avilepha," Kifirin kissed the back of my neck gently. "I was sleeping when you were birthed. I cannot go back and change any of that for you. What would you have done, love, if I told you that you were created to save the worlds? It would have frightened you. And overshadowed any happiness you might have had afterward. Tell me this is not so."

"What happiness?" I snapped, struggling against him. He wasn't letting me go. Yeah, I wasn't a long-suffering heroine. Far from it. Nobody would be singing my praises in any paperback novel, that's for sure.

"You have the opportunity now, love," Kifirin murmured against my throat. "Take it. Use me. Use your father. He would welcome the chance to make things up to you. Ask us for anything you want and if we can get it for you, it will be yours."

"I don't want things," I muttered, tears beginning to fall. "I just want somebody I can trust. Somebody who doesn't want to use me as a means to an end. I want to make up my own mind instead of having somebody telling me what I can do or where I can go, or with whom." Kifirin let me go then and I walked a short distance away from him, keeping my back to him as I wiped tears away.

"Your father and I will do our best to win your trust from this point forward," Kifirin said softly. "We thought we were saving the universes, little mate. We didn't. Our Lissa did it for us."

"Yeah. Just send your kid out to take the hit. Griffin has never been a parent to me. He just showed up one day, announcing he was my dear old Dad, missing in action all those years. He was only waiting for the right moment to snatch me away and toss me in front of an army of Ra'Ak, knowing I'd do the right thing. Does that sound about right? Would you treat your child like that, Kifirin? Would you?"

"Avilepha, it is over." Kifirin's beautiful face held agony—for both of us. "I know this pain is in you and it will be next to impossible to set it aside. Please try. For your own happiness, if not ours."

I looked around me, then, still wiping tears off my cheeks and seeing my surroundings with blurred vision. We stood in a high mountain meadow, and it was lovely there. Snowcapped peaks surrounded us, while tiny white flowers and long-stemmed grasses bloomed and grew at our feet. I had no way to tell where we were and I wasn't about to ask.

"So now what, Kifirin?" I asked, turning toward him. "You want me to go back and be Gardevik's cook for the rest of my life?" I flung up both arms hopelessly. "Wait on the fucking High Demons like a common servant? Is that what my life is going to be? I save their ass and they still expect me to cook?"

"You do not have to cook again unless that is your desire. If you wish for the High Demons to bow to you, then I will command it."

Kifirin was the god now, standing in a high meadow, his face stern and full of power.

"You know I don't want that. I just want someplace to go where I can be left alone," I muttered. "I'm tired, Kifirin." I looked up at him; he'd come to stand before me. "Just tired. I still look like death warmed over and my haircut doesn't help."

"You are depressed." He lifted fingers to my face. When I didn't pull away from his touch, he reached down and lifted me up, encouraging me to wrap my legs around his waist and my arms around his neck. His hand was gentle as he rubbed light circles on my back while I clung to him. "I am here, avilepha. For you."

We were still connected—Kifirin and I. He was giving me mental words of love while he kissed me and the grass was soft beneath my back when he made my clothing disappear. *My little love, you are so thin*, his inner voice sounded sad. *Have they starved you? I will never let that happen again.* He ran his hands through my hair and it grew in his fingers. He kissed tears away, murmuring tender words. His lovemaking was passionate and gentle at the same time, as if he were afraid he might hurt me. Yes, I'd made love before while I wept, and I was doing it then, too.

"I desire to keep her safe while I tend to things," Kifirin said later. He'd appeared inside Merrill's study, a sleeping Lissa in his arms. She was dressed again, as was he, but he'd placed a healing sleep after he'd loved her. "Do not confine her; that will be too much. Provide companions or guards if you can and I will return soon."

Merrill was shocked—not only to see Kifirin, but to find Lissa in his arms. So much time had passed since she'd been inside his home. He rarely stayed there now; he had a place at Gryphon Hall, Adam Chessman's old family home, where Kiarra and Adam were and Pheligar came upon occasion.

He used his old study for business—to find some time alone, here and there. Griffin and Amara stayed at Merrill's old manor now. "She won't want to stay; Griffin is here," Merrill whispered as if he were afraid she might wake.

"He will have to make his own peace with her," Kifirin said softly. "She is very angry with him. She does not understand why or how a father could sacrifice his child."

"I don't understand it either." Merrill accepted Lissa's sleeping body into his arms. "I will take her to Grace and Dragon and the others. Radomir is there, as is Karzac, so there are three she knows in that house. Perhaps they can help her somehow. We won't ask anything of her that she isn't prepared to give."

"If she needs funds or anything else, I will reimburse you for whatever you spend," Kifirin said, stroking Lissa's cheek. "She is so pale and thin. I beg you to do something about that, too."

"She will never want for money," Merrill huffed. "Wlodek and I kept her assets before; he couldn't bear to take anything else from her, although we thought her dead. The investments were placed in my name when we forgot about her all those years. The accounts sat there, gathering interest. I invested it as well as I could, too. She will not have need for anything else."

"Tell her I will return before long. I have much work to do." Kifirin disappeared.

"Lissa, I want Griffin to see you while you're sleeping," Merrill leaned in and kissed her forehead. "I am sorry for so many things, little girl." Merrill sent mindspeech, and Griffin and Amara both appeared in seconds.

"Careful," Merrill handed her to Griffin, who had tears in his eyes. "She's quite frail," Merrill went on as Griffin cradled Lissa in his arms.

"This is our baby," Griffin smiled sadly at Amara. "She would have been born to us, if they hadn't decided to do this."

"Why didn't they let her be reborn?" Amara wanted to weep over the way things were. "She wouldn't have hated us then."

"This is our punishment," Griffin sighed. "She's beautiful, isn't she?"

"I want to take her to Dragon's; Grace and Devin can help take care of her," Merrill said. Dragon, Grace and the others had a sprawling villa less than a mile away. Grace and Devin shared eleven mates between them, as females among the Saa Thalarr were rare. Not as rare as female vampires, but rare all the same.

"We'll go with you." Griffin nodded at Merrill. "I want Karzac to take a look—she doesn't weigh anything and she looks so pale. What did they do to her?"

"No idea," Merrill shrugged. "Let's see what we can do for her while she's asleep."

CHAPTER 6

"'ll set up a transfusion." Those were Karzac's first words after he'd silently examined Lissa. "The vampire is still alive in her and the blood may help. It's possible they gave her fluids only for days and didn't feed her. The common demons don't have anything in the way of feeding tubes, and have no updated training. If they found her unconscious, they couldn't have done much for her."

"I'll donate," Merrill rolled up a sleeve.

"Let me get Jeff, then," Karzac sent mindspeech to one of Merrill's twin sons. Jeff, the oldest of Merrill's twins, had trained as a physician and worked in that capacity for a very long time. He was also a healer for the Saa Thalarr.

"Dad, you want me to take your blood?" Jeff grinned at Merrill when he folded in. Jeff was the only vampire who'd been born vampire, and looked much like his father. His fraternal twin, Franklin, wasn't vampire, although he also was a healer and resembled Merrill more than Jeff.

"Son, get your tubes and bags out, or I'll take yours," Merrill grumped. Jeff knew his father was teasing.

Griffin sat on the edge of the bed; Amara huddled against him as they watched Karzac and Jeff set up the IV to give Lissa Merrill's

86

blood. Dragon came in during the procedure—Karzac sent mindspeech and he'd folded in from Falchan.

"Do we need to get our warrior Queen some leathers?" Dragon peered over Merrill's shoulder as Lissa was given Merrill's blood.

"Wait until she gains weight back," Merrill said. He was sipping a cup of coffee, though Jeff had told him to eat something after donating blood. Merrill had a coffee addiction and wasn't happy unless he had several cups a day.

"I'm only taking the IV out." The voice and scent were familiar, but I couldn't connect them to where I'd been when I'd gone to sleep. I unglued my eyes and stared up at Karzac. He held my right hand in one of his, removing an IV, just as he said.

"That's great, honey," I said. "Do you want to tell me why the fuck I have an IV to start with?"

"Malnourishment," Karzac muttered, pulling the IV out and placing healing light around the wound. "There, all healed up," he gave my hand back to me. "And I still expect you to come to dinner tonight. If I understood Mike and Jamie correctly, we're having pot roast. It's Kiarra's recipe and very good."

Karzac looked much as he had the last time I'd seen him—three hundred years in the past. Same green-gold eyes, same brown hair that looked a bit rumpled, same slight frown as he visually examined me. Yeah—I knew I was as thin as a stick. I didn't know what to do about it, though.

"Who are Mike and Jamie and where am I, Karzac?" I was rubbing my forehead; a headache threatened.

"We will not allow that," Karzac's fingers were cool and careful on my forehead, kneading away the ache. "Little vampire, I want you to find a way to put the incident upon Kifirin behind you. We want you to be happy instead of dwelling on that tragedy. You have been given back to us and that is an amazing gift. Friends are waiting here, if you want them. And a home also, if you desire it. You are at our home outside London; Mike and Jamie are our cook and housekeeper. Merrill tells me Kifirin brought you to him so we could set you to rights again. Kifirin also said he would return when he finished some work or other."

"Merrill," I grumbled, raising my knees. "He so conveniently forgot to tell me about Greg. And now he's one of the Saa Thalarr, isn't he? How does that work?" I sat up in bed, leaning my forehead on my knees. I wasn't sure how I knew Merrill was Saa Thalarr—I just did.

"Lissa, he has fretted over that, I know. We all have regrets, and that is one of his. Wlodek's too, as he is one of us. You will recognize many Saa Thalarr; you knew them before," Karzac sighed softly.

"Radomir is here, with Russell, Will and Charles. Weldon Harper came to us, as did Martin Walters. Brock and Stephan are here and mated. Merrill's last two vampire children are here—Joey is a healer and Kyle is Saa Thalarr and mated to Selkirk of Grey House; also a healer, by the way."

"Someone mentioned Grey House to me once," I raised my head and looked at Karzac. "He said the Grey House Wizards were the strongest and most talented of their kind."

"He was correct. Who told you that?" A smile tugged at Karzac's mouth.

"Someone named Erland Morphis," I said. "I only met him for a few minutes." I didn't explain to Karzac that I'd met him forty years in the future, when Kifirin had taken me to the High Demons' planet. Kifirin had known then I was going to die, and he hadn't said anything. I wanted to cry again. Whoever had kept me from dying probably shouldn't have.

"We know Erland," Karzac nodded slightly, winding up the IV line and taking the empty blood bag off the pole beside the bed. He did something with Power—the whole thing disappeared from his hand. I found myself wishing I could do that.

"You can do many things we cannot even attempt," Karzac read my mind.

"Karzac, what am I going to do?" I rubbed my forehead. "Three hundred years are gone. I don't fit in, anymore. I don't belong here."

"Lissa," Karzac took my hand and patted it, his eyes filled with concern, "We'll help. My mates and I will do everything we can."

"Mates?" I turned to Karzac. His green-gold eyes held a far-away look.

"Many things are different now," he admitted, rubbing my hand with a thumb. "While multiple mates have always been recognized by the Saa Thalarr and by the Reth Alliance, those laws have changed on Earth in the past century. It is now legal to have multiple husbands or wives, and in some countries, group marriages are also legal and accepted."

"You said mates," I pointed out. He smiled crookedly.

"Grace and Devin," he agreed. "They share eleven husbands in a blended group. Dragon, Dragon's twin, Crane, and I are members of that group. Radomir, too—you know him—is also one of the eleven. Please tell me you do not find this repugnant." Karzac sounded embarrassed, which was unusual for him. He worried that I'd judge him, somehow.

"Karzac," I pulled my hand away and patted his arm, "If you're happy, I'm happy. And as long as everybody involved is a sane, consenting adult, well, more power to you, I guess."

"That is what the Earth law states—that all participants must be of legal age and sign an agreement that they understand the complexity of the situation," Karzac nodded. "Of course, on Earth, it is still tradition for men to marry multiple wives, but many powerful women have more than one husband. Come to dinner now; I am receiving mindspeech that it is ready and the others are waiting for us," he smiled.

"I will introduce you to both my mates—they are eager to meet you. Some of the eleven are away at the moment, so you will not see all of them at once." Karzac rose and helped me off the bed.

"Pot roast, huh?" I hadn't had pot roast in a long time. I hoped it was as good as I remembered it as I followed Karzac downstairs and through a warren of hallways toward the kitchen.

The moment I entered the spacious kitchen, I realized I didn't need my eyes to recognize several seated around the granite island.

"Radomir," I nodded at him. He was grinning at me like a fool, and I'd barely seen him so much as smile before. He looked more relaxed than when I'd seen him last—same dark hair and eyes and same handsome face, but there was something intangible about him that told me he was truly happy. Maybe being Saa Thalarr agreed with him.

"You're Adam Chessman's son, Justin," I nodded to a tall man with sandy blond hair. "And you're Martin Walters, Jr." I nodded to the dark-haired, dark-eyed man sitting beside Justin. Both of them stared at me in surprise.

"She knows by the scent," Dragon helped himself to food. Dragon's twin brother Crane sat next to him. Both looked eerily alike, but their scents were slightly different. Dragon said their tattoos were different too, but those were covered by long-sleeved shirts at the moment. Dragon lifted his head and offered a cheeky grin before going back to his plate.

"You must be Crane," I nodded to Dragon's brother. "Dragon told me about you." He smiled politely at me. There were others around the table and Karzac made introductions while he settled me on a stool at the granite-topped island.

"This is Devin," he introduced me to one of the women. Her red hair was a shade or two darker than mine. I drew in a breath—she had Elemaiyan blood. I didn't say anything as she smiled and greeted me. "This is Grace," Karzac identified the other woman at the table. She had honey blonde hair and also smiled at me. Both were beautiful, no doubt about that.

"It's very nice to meet all of you and I didn't mean to hold up dinner. Please, don't mind me," I made a gesture with my hands.

"How do you know me?" Martin Walters, Jr. spoke while buttering a roll. "They call me Mack, by the way."

"I remember that now," I said. "I met you when you were two years old. I already knew your dad; he brought you and your sister to a wedding. Weldon Harper's son, Daryl, was getting married to Kathy Jo Green in North Dakota. I got to hold you."

"They invited a vampire to a werewolf wedding?" Justin asked.

"I was entitled, since I saved Weldon's ass earlier and he made me a member of the Pack afterward. Who knows, maybe my paperwork is still there, somewhere—it did say living or dead."

"May I join you?" A Larentii folded in and it wasn't Pheligar. He'd been the only Larentii I'd seen up until now. This one looked a bit like Pheligar—the hair and eye color was the same. And I knew he was related to Pheligar by his scent.

"I'd love for you to join us—you smell like Pheligar," I said. "And I loved looking at his blue skin; it made me think of the sky when I couldn't see the sky. Except at night."

"I am Pheligar's son, Renegar," he smiled at me. "My mother is Kiarra." Renegar was as tall as his father—eight and a half feet. That was some accomplishment for Kiarra if she gave birth to a Larentii.

"Giving birth to a Larentii is quite an accomplishment," Renegar's smile widened. "Grace and I have a child. His name is Graegar." Well, I was discovering that one of Grace and Devin's eleven mates was Larentii. I wanted to smile or stand up and cheer or something.

"That's a nice name," I said instead. "How old is Graegar?"

"He was taken back in time; therefore he is three hundred, now."

"Really? You're going to have to be careful around me because I want to pester you with so many questions," I said. "I just want to warn you in advance."

"Lissa, you are talking and not eating," Karzac observed.

"Are we going to go a round or two?" I pointed my fork at him.

"Lissa isn't afraid of Karzac," Dragon chuckled.

"Is Lissa afraid of anything? I saw those Ra'Ak exploding," Justin said. "I had no idea what was causing that."

"I was misting inside their heads," I said, cutting into my pot roast (Karzac was watching). "I blew my mist out, causing them to explode. Not a big deal." I placed a bite of pot roast in my mouth and chewed. It was very good and the gravy was excellent.

"But when I got to that last one, I was exhausted," I explained. "I knew if I did one more, I wouldn't have enough energy to pull my mist together again. That last one was the granddaddy of all of them. He was huge. I made the decision and went to get him. I don't remember anything past that until I came back to myself, standing in the arboretum in the High Demons' palace. Everybody thought I was a brain-damaged comesula."

"When Lissa recovers, brother, you should teach her bladework," Dragon told his brother, Crane.

"I don't need," I didn't get to finish my sentence, Dragon interrupted.

"Just see whether she has any raw talent." Dragon smirked.

Don't make me kick your ass, I sent to him. He ducked his head to hide the smile.

"We'll take you shopping tomorrow," Devin announced. "You don't have any clothing, and several people are already asking if they can come along. The styles now are similar to those popular in the 1930s. Jeans are back in, too. I hope you like what's available." I nodded. Shopping was probably a good idea, since I had nothing in the way of clothing or possessions.

"Radomir, how's Wlodek?" I asked casually. "Is Flavio still around? What about Gavin?" Gavin was the one I wanted to know about. Nobody had mentioned his name and I was worried. My heart thumped with fear as I waited for an answer.

Radomir looked uncomfortable for a moment. "Father is fine and wants to come see you very soon, as do Will, Russell, Martin Walters and Weldon. They are all part of the Saa Thalarr. Flavio is now Head of the Council, and—he does not remember you."

That admission came out in an embarrassed rush. "Neither do Gavin, Anthony Hancock or any of the other vampires. Something took our memories of you, shortly after your demise. The ones who became Saa Thalarr remembered when we saw the Ra'Ak dying by the hundreds, but not until then. The others have no memories at all."

"Fuck," I muttered, dropping my fork. I'd just lost my appetite. "If you'll excuse me," I stood up from my seat. I wanted to cry. Or scream and cry.

"Lissa, please sit down and finish your meal, I beg you." Karzac was begging, and that was something he probably didn't do often. I figured he was used to being obeyed for some reason, as the autocratic and curmudgeonly physician that he was.

I felt cold and shivered. I was also close to tears as I sat down again, staring at my plate. I felt ill, on top of everything else. Karzac rose from his seat.

"Keep your seat, I will deal with this," Renegar informed Karzac. He rose from his seat and came to stand beside me, placing fingers on my face and forehead. "Just relax, little one, things will work out," he said gently as light formed around his hands. A tear slipped out anyway, and dripped along one of his fingers as he attempted to fix me, somehow.

"What is the difficulty?" Two more Larentii folded in and I looked up at them while a couple more tears came.

"Pain and betrayal," Renegar said and lifted me from my seat. "This is Graegar, my son, and his Protector, Barrigar," Renegar handed me to his son.

"Why do you need a protector?" I wiped tears off my cheeks as I gazed into Graegar's face. He certainly resembled his father and grandfather. It wasn't embarrassing or anything to be crying in front of everybody there, including more Larentii.

"I am a Wise One," Graegar smiled.

"Uh-huh," I sniffled. "I thought all Larentii were wise."

"They are, but Wise Ones are special. Like Vampire Queens," Graegar replied. "Something very rare and very precious."

"I don't feel rare and precious. I feel like crap," I muttered. "Who took the memories away so nobody would remember me?" I still wanted to cry and felt awful about that. This was just one more blow on top of the other blows.

"I do not have that specific knowledge," Graegar said. "Grandfather may know. We will attempt to find this out for you. The knowledge may upset you, should we find it."

"How much more upset do you think I can get?" I mumbled. I was still trying to clean up my face but the tears wouldn't stop; Graegar wasn't setting me down and everybody around the island was staring.

"She thinks her mate will not love her if he sees her again,"

Barrigar said softly, his voice a low, calming baritone. He was taller than Renegar and Graegar by a good six inches, and he hadn't spoken until then. He'd hit the nail on the head, though, and I misted out of Graegar's arms. I don't know whether he hadn't expected me to do that or not, and just hadn't done anything to stop it.

Where do you go when you don't know where the hell you are, or when, even? I misted to the top of the huge villa; I'd gone straight up and through the second story to the roof. That's where I sat, wiping tears off my cheeks as the sobs came. Gavin didn't remember me. For him, I'd never existed. What a nice payback for saving people.

Kifirin told me that had the High Demons' world fallen, all the others would have followed. It was the balance, he'd explained, for all the worlds. I'd saved the balance. Now, there wasn't anybody for me to share memories with, because none of them had any memories to share. My knees were up to my chest and I was shaking as I wept.

What was I supposed to do? There wasn't a soul out there I trusted; nobody I felt comfortable going to for help or reassurance. It was as if everything had been taken from me when my life ended. Only somebody, somewhere, had decided that wasn't the end of Lissa —it was just the end of Lissa for everybody else. If I'd known who was responsible for all this, I would have gone straight to them and given them hell for putting me through it.

"I exerted Power and it had no effect," Graegar was staring in confusion at his father and his Protector.

Dragon and Grace, Co-Firsts among the Saa Thalarr, were also very concerned. If the Larentii held no power over Lissa and none could find her by *Looking*, could anyone control her and what had she become?

"Lissa will not harm anyone except those who deserve it," Karzac growled. He imagined finding Lissa would be easy enough; the roof was her refuge, as often as not. "She's probably on the roof," he sighed aloud. "Although I cannot decide whether it would be a good thing to disturb her or not. The news that none from her past remember her was a cruel blow."

"I shouldn't have said anything," Radomir rumbled.

"She'd find out eventually," Devin hugged her vampire mate.

"It could have waited until she was better prepared," Radomir said. "She was always afraid to say things around me, because she was frightened that I carried everything she said straight to Wlodek."

"She was the same with me." Charles folded in and sat down at the island. Devin *Pulled* a plate to the table, causing it to slide in front of Charles. Flatware and a glass followed.

"I always wanted her to tell me how she was feeling—I don't think Wlodek would have asked me personal questions unless it was important. She never cracked, though. I tried to be her friend, but she was too afraid to have any friends." Charles helped himself to pot roast.

"Father made a mistake, not telling her about Greg." Radomir picked up his plate and carried it to the sink.

"Who is Greg?" Justin asked.

"Greg was Franklin's mate, years ago," Charles said. "He died of pneumonia—a complication of the cancer he had. Lissa loved Franklin and Greg if she ever loved anybody. Neither Wlodek nor Merrill informed her of Greg's hospitalization or death. They left her in the U.S. because she was trying to track Xenides and some of his followers. He'd turned many Dark Elemaiya who were shapeshifters, mindspeakers and misters, and he intended to destroy everything, with their help and the help of others. Lissa stopped all that. She was the one who captured Rahim Alif. Not the FBI or Homeland Security, as everyone claimed." Charles dipped into his food. He loved to eat and seldom had blood now, though the vampire side of him was still intact.

"The terrorist? That Rahim Alif?" Grace asked.

"Yes. Lissa captured him—recognized him by his scent. You won't ever fool Lissa; she never forgets what you smell like. She scents your blood, somehow."

"Yeah, we got that already," Mack said. "She remembered both of us because she saw us when we were little." He pointed between himself and Justin.

"Where is she now?" Charles asked.

"Probably on the roof," Karzac tossed his napkin on the island. The Larentii had sat down at the island after enlarging the seats to fit their height and were listening to the conversation.

"She always liked to get on the roof," Charles agreed. "Used to sit on Merrill's roof all the time."

"I'm going to the roof to find her," Karzac said.

"I'll come with you," Charles picked up his plate and glass of wine.

"I will come," Radomir said. All three of them folded to the roof.

If I thought I was going to be alone to cry my eyes out, I was proven wrong after ten minutes.

"Lissa, want something to eat?" Charles plopped down beside me and held out a forkful of pot roast.

"I'm not hungry." I wiped my eyes on a sleeve. I looked like crap, no doubt, but Charles was ignoring that. "It's nice to see you, Charles." I would have hugged him, but he was eating.

"Lissa, you are underweight right now. Are you going to force me to stand over you at mealtimes?" Karzac sat down on my other side.

"That wouldn't be uncomfortable or anything," I mumbled against my knees. I'd let my forehead drop to the tops of my knees so Charles, Karzac and Radomir wouldn't see my blotchy face. Radomir had come, too and settled down next to Charles.

"We can make arrangements for you to meet with Flavio, Gavin and Anthony," Radomir offered. "Just to see whether your presence sparks a memory in them."

"And if it doesn't? That sounds like the most awkward thing ever." I was depressed and couldn't shake it off. I wasn't prepared for Gavin's stone face if he didn't remember me or our time together.

"We can meet in Flavio's study—he took Wlodek's manor after my sire gave up his position as Head of the Council. He had no need of it after coming to the Saa Thalarr. I can convince Flavio to bring Gavin and Anthony in, and I can ask some of the others to come—those who are now Saa Thalarr," Radomir offered, his dark eyes concerned. He wanted me to agree. I felt uncomfortable about the whole thing.

"Gavin and Anthony still remember all of those who became Saa Thalarr," Charles grinned. "They just don't know about Flavio and me. Flavio helped the Saa Thalarr in the past, so he was given blood as payment. He walks in daylight, now. He can fold space too, but only on Earth—he isn't allowed to go off-planet. I'm a Spawn Hunter for the Saa Thalarr, but that doesn't interfere with my duties as Flavio's Chief of Staff."

"This may work, Lissa—we can introduce you to Gavin and Anthony as a friend and if nothing happens, then we'll know for certain," Radomir sighed.

"And it won't be disappointing in the least when they don't recognize me," I muttered. "I'm not sure I can handle that."

"Lissa, you'll want to know, eventually. And this will be your chance to make a decision—on whether you want Gavin back in your life. Come, this could work. And even if they do not recognize you, at least you can build a relationship with them if that is what you want." Karzac rubbed my back gently.

"Fine," I huffed.

"I'll set it up for tomorrow night," Radomir said. "I know Flavio isn't doing anything other than slavedriving, and Gavin and Tony recently returned from the states."

"No pressure," I sighed.

Karzac, Charles and Radomir eventually convinced me to go back to the kitchen. My plate was still sitting at the island and someone had used Power to keep it warm for me.

Karzac sat with me, chatting while I ate as much as I could. Charles and Radomir had gone off to visit Flavio to set up the gathering they planned. Karzac told me all about current events on Refizan.

"Do you ever hear any news of Gabron?" I asked. I was too stuffed to eat another bite, and my plate was still half-full.

"No, but the vampires there continue to retain their secrecy. We can search him out soon if that is what you want."

"I'll think about it, but he may have forgotten about me, too," I said. Yeah, I was depressed. While we sat there, two men folded into the kitchen. They startled me and my heart began to pound in my chest at the sight of them. Karzac had his hands on me quickly, regulating my heartbeat, somehow.

"Anything left for us?" One of the two said when things calmed down after a few moments. I knew the scent—these two were Dragon's twin sons and Devin was their mother.

They had the signature Asian look about them, along with very long, very black braids hanging down their backs. They were dressed in what looked like ski outfits and the long skis and ski poles in their hands weren't a giveaway, either.

Tinted goggles were pushed back on both foreheads; they were identical in looks but I could tell the scents were different. Just their appearance made me smile, once my heart was back to normal.

"You're Dragon's," I said.

"Nah, Crane's," one of them grinned crookedly at me.

"Do not attempt to tease Lissa, Drew, she knows better," Karzac informed the one who'd spoken. "Lissa, this is Drew," Karzac indicated one of the twins, "and this is Drake," he nodded toward the other.

"Nice to meet you," I said. "I wasn't aware that Dragon had children."

"You need to meet our older brother, Dragon Taylor, then," Drake grinned. "Grace is his mother."

"Grace had quadruplets," Karzac sighed. "One child for each of her humanoid mates at the time."

That caused my eyes to pop. "You're kidding? That can happen?"

"Not normally," Drew flopped onto a chair at the island. "Are you going to finish that?" He nodded toward my half-empty plate.

"It's yours if you want it," I said, pushing the plate toward him. He dug right in. I slid my glass of wine over, too, and he accepted it with a muffled thanks; he was already eating.

"Hey, is there any left for me?" Drake sat down next to his brother.

"I'll check," I said and went to the huge bank of refrigerators in the kitchen. I found leftover pot roast and vegetables, heating it in what Karzac called a zap oven. Drake started eating as soon as he got his plate, and I filled a wineglass for him and topped off Drew's glass. "Karzac, do you want tea?"

"Karzac only likes his tea a certain way," Drew said, winking at me. Karzac surprised him greatly.

"Lissa made tea for me long before you were even a thought," Karzac snipped. I made tea for Karzac, just the way he liked it. I remembered; vampires have good memories. He sipped from his cup while I sat next to him again.

"So, who are you?" Drake asked. He was about to scrape up the last of his mashed potatoes and gravy.

"This is Lissa, the Vampire Queen," Karzac informed him. Drew almost choked on his wine. "The one who popped all the heads off the Ra'Ak and the High Demons?" He sounded very surprised.

"If you and your brother would show up for more than food now and then, you might learn a great many things," Karzac scolded.

"Feather, Christi and Kerry wanted to go," Drake defended himself. "So we couldn't turn them down. We're so seldom all home at the same time."

"Which one of you did the time bending?" Karzac asked gruffly.

"Feather," Drake grinned.

"Hmmph," was Karzac's response. I was enjoying myself. These people were family and they were acting like it. That made me happy.

"How was the skiing?" I asked.

"Great. We went to Chleroa. Those mountains are amazing."

"I never tried to ski," I said. "Maybe I'll try it, sometime. If I'm about to hit a tree, I can mist right through it."

"That would be handy," Drew laughed. "Bro here had to fold away from that rock pile he was about to run over."

"That'll get you a thrashing in the dojo tomorrow morning," Drake threatened.

"You're on, dude. Let's see you do it," Drew countered.

"So, did your dad teach you bladework, or did your Uncle Crane?" I was curious.

"They both did, and whacked us around pretty good," Drew admitted.

"They still whack you around pretty good," Karzac huffed.

"Well, we're off to get out of these clothes," Drake stood and stretched. "Dad will haul us out of bed if we're not there on time in the morning." He and Drew folded away.

"They seem like a lot of fun," I said.

"Did you like them?" Karzac smiled at me.

"They're young," I said, although their scents said a hundred years. "Sometimes it's nice to be around youthful exuberance."

"You should go to bed soon, it is getting late," Karzac said. "And I will place you in a healing sleep if you ignore me."

"Is there a picture of you next to the word autocrat in the dictionary?" I asked.

"My picture is also next to the word curmudgeon. With me, the terms are interchangeable."

"Stop it," I smacked his arm lightly. Karzac grinned.

The suite I'd been given had a bedroom, an attached sitting room, a huge bathroom and an empty walk-in closet. Pajamas lay on the bed when I walked inside after telling Karzac I could find my own way. There was also a note lying on the pajamas.

"These are Fox's," the note read. "Fox is mated to Wlodek, Weldon and three others. Her clothes were the closest we could come to something that would fit you—Devin and Grace."

The pajamas consisted of silky pants, coupled with a stretchy top that had thin straps. My kind of pajamas. I gathered them up and took them into the bathroom to take a shower. When I crawled into bed later, feeling much better after bathing and washing my hair, I fell asleep quickly.

"I'm Mike." He held his hand out to me so I took it and shook. "I'm the cook. My mate, Jamie, is the housekeeper for this bunch," Mike informed me as he prepared breakfast the next morning.

"How do you keep up with all of them plus the house?" I asked, mystified. The place was huge with a capital H.

"It isn't easy," Mike laughed. "But Conner sends some of hers over now and then, and they help out if we need it."

Mike was in his early thirties, according to his scent, looked younger than that and knew his way around the kitchen. He had a plate of ham and eggs in front of me in no time.

"Look who's up," Dragon grinned when he and Crane walked into the kitchen. "Want to watch us practice in the dojo? Those sons of mine have been off messing about and not keeping up with their training."

"I met them last night," I said, cutting into my ham. I hadn't had ham in a long time. "This is good, Mike," I said.

"Did they say where they'd been?" Crane asked, pulling up a chair.

"Skiing on Chleroa," I replied. "No idea where that is."

"Then somebody bent time for them," Dragon sighed. "It's summer there, right now."

"They said Feather did."

"Feather is Mack's daughter," Dragon informed me. That's all right, then."

"I also heard you have a third son," I glanced at Dragon, who was getting his plate of food.

"Dragon Taylor," he nodded. "We call him Tay."

"You've been busy since I met you on Refizan," I smiled at him.

"I have, little vampire. It might have been easier for me these past few weeks if I hadn't thought you were dead."

I didn't tell him it might be easier for me if I were dead.

We finished breakfast, Crane listening silently as Dragon and I talked, and then Dragon folded us to a dojo somewhere. "My dojo is behind Adam's garage," Dragon caught me looking around the place. "He built it for my family and me."

The single, spacious room had a large square floor, most of which was covered with a padded mat. A nearby wall was covered in thick cork and held a row of practice blades, both wood and metal, in a rack, with another rack of throwing knives. On the opposite side of the room were weights and other exercise equipment.

Crane and Dragon were stretching and preparing to spar when Drake and Drew showed up. "Dad doesn't look happy," Drake whispered to his brother while he grinned. I snickered.

"Hey, quiet you," Drake pointed a finger at me.

"Hey, don't point at me," I said, letting the claw slide out on my index finger.

"Wow, now that's a fingernail," Drew laughed.

"Get over here," Dragon commanded—he was telling his sons to come and spar. I sat on the floor outside the mat and watched them go after each other. They all fought using two blades each, and it was a dance as they moved and clacked wood practice blades together.

Crane took Drew on; Dragon had Drake. They were all sweating when they finished.

"Impressed?" Drake flexed his muscles; he and his brother were just as broad across the shoulders as Dragon and Crane and they were all tattooed. I'd seen Dragon's tattoos before, but Crane had a dancing crane on his back, a crane with widespread wings on his chest and cranes flying up both arms. Drake had black dragon tattoos; Drew had silver dragons. I don't know how they'd managed to sit still for all that work. They were impressive, though.

"Lissa, how are you feeling?" Dragon asked. "Want to go a round with my brother?"

"I could probably do that," I said.

"Just don't overdo it, all right?" A corner of his mouth quirked in a half-smile.

"I can mist out of the way if I have to," I said, standing up.

"Here," Dragon handed over his wooden practice blades. "Crane, see what you think." Dragon moved aside.

"Parry with the flat of the blade," Crane instructed when I came to stand before him. He'd taught, all right. "I'll go slowly."

"You don't have to—I'm vampire, remember?"

"Then how fast do you want me to come after you?" Crane grinned.

"How fast can you go?" I shrugged.

"I like her," Crane said, and went into the middle position. He did come after me, as fast as he could and as hard as he could. He *Pulled* in a wood replacement blade when I hit one of his hard enough to break it. He hadn't touched me and I was blocking all his blows. When I got the first touch in, we stopped; I was breathing hard and Crane knew not to push it.

"So, brother—black leathers?" Dragon pounded Crane on the back.

"Yeah." Crane grinned at his brother.

"Come on, you," Drake came to me and lifted me over his shoulder in a fireman's carry.

"Hey!" I swatted what I could reach, which turned out to be his ass.

"I can hit you in the same spot," Drake laughed and folded me back to the villa's kitchen.

"Young Falchani, please explain what you are doing with Lissa in such an undignified position." Karzac had fists on his hips while he glared at Drake. Drew had come along, with Dragon and Crane right behind. Drew was laughing out loud.

"We had to haul her out of the dojo; she wore herself out whacking Uncle Crane," Drake grinned at Karzac.

"She is still recovering! Explain yourselves," Karzac demanded.

"Lissa had Crane subdued in a matter of minutes; I doubt she's permanently damaged," Dragon was calming Karzac down. Drake set me down on the floor and I swatted him across the stomach as soon as I was in a position to do so.

"Can we keep her, Dad? We've already touched her, we can't put her back," Drew snickered.

"Lissa may have something to say about that," Dragon said.

"What are you doing today?" Drake caught my arm as I started to walk away; my suite was upstairs and down a lengthy hall.

"Going to find a wardrobe; I have no clothes," I sighed.

"That sounds intriguing," Drew smiled.

"You can go if you behave yourselves," Devin walked in.

"Mom, we're models of decorum," Drake hugged his mother.

"You're not supposed to be able to lie," Devin gave him a kiss on the cheek when he leaned down.

"But we can practice sarcasm until the Falchani sun experiences a carbon flash," Drake laughed.

"Lissa, we have more borrowed clothes on your bed and we'll go as soon as you clean up," Grace walked into the kitchen.

"Sounds good," I said and had a quick hand fight with Drew before I got out of the room. He and Drake were enjoying themselves, I could tell.

"Have you ever seen anything like that?" Drake asked as soon as he knew Lissa was out of hearing. Since she was vampire, he waited quite a while.

"Bro, do you think we have a shot at that?" Drew came to stand next to Drake.

"I think you may have to work for that," Karzac growled.

CHAPTER 7

"Merrill said to give you this," Grace handed a credit chip necklace to me. "Most people have these embedded in their wrist, but a few still wear it like this. He says the money is yours, from long ago."

I slipped the necklace over my head and tucked the chain inside my borrowed blouse. "How much?" I asked. I didn't want to upset Grace by cursing Merrill—she didn't have to know how I felt about him.

"He says there are too many zeros to count," Grace smiled, brushing honey blonde hair back. Karzac and Dragon had to be proud; they had two ladies who were knockouts. Devin came in, her red hair in a clip at her nape and dressed tastefully in a jacket and matching trousers.

The shocking thing came while we were preparing to fold to London—I learned the villa was roughly a mile away from Merrill's old manor. Devin explained things after I finished dressing in more borrowed clothing and misted back to the kitchen.

"Lissa, hello," Amara's musical voice hadn't changed since I met her the last time, and she was just as beautiful as I remembered. Another set of twins were right behind her as she appeared inside Grace and Devin's large kitchen. I drew in a breath when they materialized.

"They're your nieces; Brenten's granddaughters," Amara said as I backed away, shaking my head. I knew from the scent they were related—we had the same bloodline—on one side, anyway. They were also beautiful, with long, auburn hair that fell in waves down their backs.

Nearly-gold eyes studied me as they sized me up. Their scents, though, were vastly different. Both held a great deal of power, but the power signatures weren't close. One held a scent of the Larentii about her, while the other could only be described as otherworldly.

"I found a way to duplicate the Larentii power signature," one stepped forward and held out her hand. "I'm Kyler, and Flavio is one of my mates."

"Kyler," I took her hand. I wanted to cry—I had family I hadn't known about. It made me wonder what else Griffin had kept from me.

"My mother—your half-sister, died long ago," Kyler squeezed my hand and stepped away so her sister could come forward.

"I'm Cleo," the other took my hand. "I'm a healer for the Saa Thalarr. Rhett is one of my mates. Our father," she nodded toward Kyler, "is Glendes, Eldest of Grey House. Our step-nephew, Shadow Grey, should meet you," Cleo said, smiling uncertainly. She wasn't sure how I'd receive her or her sister.

There's nothing to worry about, I sent mentally. "So, you both have multiple mates, too?" I asked aloud. Cleo took another step forward and hugged me.

"It'll work out," Cleo whispered in my ear. "Kyler says so, too."

"I sure hope so," I brushed away a bit of mistiness when Cleo stepped back.

"I'm mated to Dalroy, too, and as Cleo said, she's mated to Rhett," Kyler smiled brightly at me. "We know you know them."

"Yeah, I know them. I'd say they're damn lucky," I nodded to my newly discovered nieces.

"And we tell them how fortunate they are all the time," Cleo snickered.

"We'll sit down and tell you about all our mates soon," Kyler promised. "Our Larentii mates want to meet you."

"You have Larentii mates." I shook my head. How did they all get so lucky?

"Come on, you," Drake walked in with Drew and draped an arm around my shoulders. "We have stuff to buy."

"We're coming," three more people appeared in the kitchen. A short, perky brunette with close-cropped curls was there, flanked by Wlodek and Weldon. Truthfully, I wanted to punch Wlodek and hug Weldon. Both those thoughts flew away when I got the woman's scent —she had Bright Elemaiyan blood.

"I'm Bernadette," she held out a hand, "but that name is embarrassing, so I prefer Fox. And I'm the Ka'Mirai—the one the Elemaiya wish they hadn't rejected."

"I've heard of you," I took her hand. Griffin mentioned her before; said she could turn back time or change things for the Elemaiya. Well, they'd fucked that up, just as he'd said they would.

"I've heard of you—now," Fox smiled brightly. I could see her with Weldon—he doted on her, I could tell that right away. What shocked me was the undiluted love in Wlodek's eyes as he watched her.

"Lissa, we'll talk and I'll grovel later," Wlodek offered. Honestly, I felt a headache coming on. Wlodek looked exactly as he always had— dark eyes and hair; dressed impeccably, still, but his face wasn't as shuttered as it once was. The Saa Thalarr had wrought changes in Radomir and his former vampire sire. It made me wonder what it had done for Merrill and the others.

"And we'll talk about withheld information," I retorted, my voice sharper than I'd intended. Wlodek winced at my words, and that wouldn't have happened before—that was a sure bet. His stone face had cracked—courtesy of the Saa Thalarr.

Lissa, if there were any way to change it, I would, he sent.

"Come on, itty bitty pants, we have shopping to do. There's no time for arguments or depression," Drew leaned down and pecked me on the cheek. I stared up at him. He grinned at me and I blinked, thinking how handsome he and his brother were.

Being able to fold was a special gift. It might have taken me ten or fifteen minutes to get to the shopping mall by misting. Malls were making a comeback, I learned from Grace. They'd fallen in and out of favor many times over the three hundred years I'd been missing.

"You don't know how much we missed you, little girl," Weldon said when we landed in a huge department store. He hugged me tightly, too, before letting me go.

"Weldon, what happened to Winkler?" I asked as we were going through racks of slacks, blouses, jeans, dresses and skirts.

"Lissa, why are you asking about things like that?" Weldon put his arms around me again and kissed my forehead.

"Hey, now," Drake tapped Weldon on the shoulder. Drew was right behind Drake, nodding at his brother's response.

"Winkler did what his father did before him," Weldon sighed, pulling away from me.

"Fuck," I whispered. I wanted to cry.

"Hey, we're here to buy clothes," Drew hugged me. "Dry clothes," he added. Somehow, the twins knew. Winkler's father had forced him to make the challenge, allowing Winkler to take the Dallas Pack and his life. Winkler had given the Pack to one of his children. I'd never get to see him or his beautiful, wolfish grin again.

"I'll be okay," I patted Drew on the back and continued looking through the rack of blouses, though I wanted more than anything to mist away and weep. I forced my thoughts away from Winkler and turned back to the clothing racks.

At least Kifirin had given me my hair back; it hung past my shoulders and I'd French-braided it before going shopping. Drake kept playing with my braid the whole time we looked through clothes, and he and his brother had their hands on me as often as possible, offering silent consolation for the hole left in my heart.

"Get everything a little bigger—you still have weight to gain," Devin suggested as we pulled my normal size off the racks. She, Grace, Amara, Kyler and Cleo were doing their best to take care of me, with help from Fox.

Of course, Dragon's twins were offering their opinion on

everything. Every woman in the store, including the sales clerks, was staring at Drake, Drew, Wlodek and Weldon. Charles showed up after a bit and began pulling things off racks and tossing them into my dressing room. It reminded me of a shopping trip we'd taken so long ago.

Wlodek had sent Charles and me to London, to buy a wardrobe after I'd been allowed to live by a margin of one vote by the Vampire Council. I figured Wlodek had sent mindspeech to Charles, asking him to come now.

Are they still meeting in the cave? I sent to Wlodek. He was Saa Thalarr—he'd have mindspeech now, even if he didn't have it before. Wlodek knew what I meant.

The cave was bombed several years ago, he replied. *By zealots hunting vampire. The Council purchased an old church and excavated beneath it. That's where they meet, now.*

I heaved a shaky sigh. So many things changed, so many people gone. *Moro mou, do not let this upset you*, Wlodek added. *And you were correct about Nestor and Cecil. They are gone, now. Dalroy, Charles and Rhett are on the Council instead.*

Good for them, I returned.

"Oh yeah, keep that," Drake and Drew were both nodding approval at the long black dress Charles found on a rack. It had an empire waist and a halter neckline with thin ties that hung down the back. Most of my back was bare; the back of the dress came down to the small of my back and Drew's fingers touched me there fleetingly as I turned to go back inside the dressing room.

Lunch came after we'd bought a mountain of clothing—someone sent all of it back to the villa using the Power available to them. "This is one of Adam's restaurants," Wlodek informed me when we walked inside.

I sighed—I'd gone to one of Adam's restaurants in the past—with Roff, Giff, Franklin, Greg and several others. I squared my shoulders and forced myself not to think about it. Frank was gone; nobody mentioned him. And the whole time I'd been on Kifirin, I hadn't seen Roff or Giff. I had no idea whether they still lived or not.

I'd been seated at the table between Drake and Drew—they'd arranged that somehow. If they were only looking for a fling, I wasn't their girl. I just didn't know how to tell them that.

"The prime rib is good," Drew leaned over my shoulder, reading my menu instead of his own. "And this is good, too," he pointed out a chicken dish. He was as close as he could get, an arm draped around my shoulders as he tapped my menu.

I knew by scent that he and his brother were a hundred years old. It made me wonder how I should determine my own age. Was I forty-nine or was I three hundred forty-nine? I didn't know what to do about that.

I settled for the chicken dish and it was good, but I couldn't finish it. Drew helped me eat it and Drake fed me a bit of his dessert. We went looking for lingerie and shoes after lunch; Charles, Drake and Drew insisted on coming along.

Charles was the only male who'd ever helped me pick out underwear before, and he wasn't interested romantically. I couldn't say that about the twins, and felt my face go hot several times at the suggestions they made. "No, I hate underwires," I poked Drake in the chest over his choice in bras.

"Then get this one," he picked another in the same color—a fuchsia. I ended up with a pile of underthings I was too embarrassed to put back. The twins were grinning when we were done and Devin and Grace were smiling the whole time they shopped with me.

Charles was the voice of reason in all of it, while Kyler, Cleo and Amara made quiet suggestions and watched me carefully. Amara was afraid I might break and Kyler and Cleo were struggling to get used to an aunt they hadn't known about. I'd bet half the zeros on my credit chip that Griffin hadn't told them anything about me—ever. Until now, that is.

After a while, I had so many pairs of shoes I didn't know what to do with all of them. Those and other accessories were purchased after lengthy consideration. And then everything was sent back to the villa, just like all the other bags.

"Now for jewelry," Wlodek announced. Somebody folded us to an exclusive jewelry store.

"We're wearing our girl out." Somehow, I ended up in Drake's lap, yawning as discreetly as I could while we sat at the jewelry counter. A sales clerk showed us tray after tray of earrings, necklaces, rings and bracelets.

Drake was running gentle fingers down my ribs and that wasn't hot or anything. It was all I could do not to collapse against him and close my eyes with a contented sigh.

"I like this," Drew pointed out a cuff bracelet in hammered gold that held several rows of diamonds. The price on it could have bought me a round-trip ticket to another galaxy. The cuff was placed on my wrist.

"See, that looks good," Drew smiled, leaning forward to kiss me. I blinked at him in a stupor. The sad thing? I wouldn't have minded if he'd gone on kissing me, even while I was sitting on his brother's lap.

"We'll take it," Wlodek announced. There was already a pile of jewelry they'd set aside and we ended up with all of it plus several other items. The total was staggering. I thought I might hyperventilate when Weldon and Wlodek split the ticket.

"We owe you," Weldon whispered near my ear. "And the others are chipping in, too."

"Take her home and let her sleep, she's exhausted," Karzac was suddenly with us, handing out orders.

"I get to hold her on the way home," Drew said softly, and I felt boneless as I was passed from one brother to the other. I was asleep before we ever got home and didn't remember how I got in bed.

"What can we do about her records?" Merrill asked Wlodek. Wlodek sat in Adam's study at Gryphon Hall, Adam's family home for centuries.

"Are all of them gone? How are some of those things she did explained away?" Adam studied both former vampires sitting before his desk. They were having a brandy and discussing the difficulty they currently faced. Flavio would demand to know how and why a Queen Vampire had escaped his notice.

"They were attributed to others," Pheligar folded in and promptly *Pulled* in a rather large, comfortable chair for himself, temporarily enlarging Adam's office to accommodate it. None of the former vampires present so much as lifted an eyebrow. They were used to this and could do it themselves if they wanted.

"The Larentii hand in all this," Wlodek sighed. "I had memories of taking Xenides' head—until recently."

"It was requested, lest she become a target in the past and make the future turn out differently," Pheligar drew in a deep breath. "A few werewolves were allowed to remember, and they wisely kept that information to themselves. Belen and his superiors had to arrange for the vampires and any others to forget. It was the only way."

"Yet we were allowed to remember it all the moment she died," Wlodek pointed out. "This could not be done for the others?"

"You know Belen does not like to interfere in that way—any more than is necessary, as he says," Pheligar replied, a large blue hand rubbing his forehead. Adam knew that gesture—Pheligar didn't agree with the way things were going.

"So Lissa gets no credit whatsoever—somebody else gets it?" Merrill didn't appreciate that.

"We know what she did," Pheligar muttered. "At least that is how it was explained to me."

"Those High Demons should be kissing her feet, and the only word I got was a request from Gardevik, asking if she'd mind coming back and making an apple pie." Merrill tossed up a hand and snorted at the irony. "I talked with Glinda, and now she's threatening to toss Gardevik Rath into Baetrah herself."

"Jayd's Spawn Hunter status has been removed." Pheligar dropped that information in front of the others. "Glinda is still considered auxiliary Saa Thalarr, but hers is the running of Kifirin with Jayd, so she may be giving that up."

"Why was Jayd's status changed?" Adam asked.

"He wasn't using it and recent events were taken into account." Pheligar's face shuttered and Adam knew he wouldn't get any more from the Larentii on the subject.

"Does he know this?" Wlodek asked.

"He has been informed," Pheligar sniffed. Adam knew then that Pheligar had delivered the news himself, rather than one of the other Liaisons. Pheligar's official title was Archivist for the Saa Thalarr, but he still helped the Liaisons from time to time.

"And how did he take it?" Merrill was very curious.

"He said the reason he accepted it in the beginning was to remain close to Glinda. Now that they are mated, he does not care."

"They ought to care," Adam grumbled. "Do they realize how close they came—how close we all came—to destruction?"

"I'm not sure they know," Wlodek agreed. "Glinda may, but the rest of them?" Wlodek frowned at the complexity of the situation.

"They don't have a fucking clue," Griffin folded in. He seldom used profanity, but he'd been using it regularly during recent weeks. Pheligar *Pulled* in another chair and Griffin joined the discussion. "My little girl gets killed, and then put back together by an unseen hand and ends up cooking for those fuckers?"

Pheligar placed a calming hand on Griffin's shoulder, forming light around his fingers. Griffin relaxed noticeably and nodded his thanks to the Larentii.

"Tonight may be difficult for Lissa when she sees those blank expressions on Gavin's and Anthony's faces," Wlodek felt a headache coming on.

"What about Dragon's boys? Are they just playing around?" Merrill asked.

"Bro, what is up with you?" Dragon Taylor had never seen his younger brothers like this. They'd come looking for Tay, just to spend some time, they'd said. Drake and Drew were both restless, however, and

Tay didn't know what to think. Drew paced while Drake sat, rose again and then sat a second time.

"You should have been there this morning," Drew said finally. "Dad and Uncle Crane gave us a beating as usual, when we skip sparring for a few days. Dad got Lissa to come and watch, and then convinced Uncle Crane to go a round with her. She got a touch on Uncle Crane in less than ten minutes."

"And that was after breaking one of his practice blades," Drake agreed.

"The Vampire Queen Lissa?"

"Yeah, dude, where have you been?" Drake sounded indignant.

"I heard she came back somehow, but we haven't been able to figure out how that happened. You don't have a M'Fiyah with her, do you?" Dragon Taylor's eyes narrowed at his younger brothers. Even he didn't expect the coughing and clearing of throats that followed his question.

"You ought to go back to the Southern Continent, brother. You never made it past Baetrah an Hafei." Jayd lifted an eyebrow at Gardevik Rath.

"Jayd, there's nothing there except ash and devastation. The animals are dead, the crops are dead or burned in the fields—nothing can survive in that environment, not even rogue Croth or Drith. Besides, Kifirin never said anything when he was with us."

"Kifirin said long ago that he'd never interfere. Why would he say anything? That would be interfering. I think you should plan another trip and check everything, this time." Smoke escaped Jayd's nostrils.

"Fine. I'll put a team together as soon as the fall rains are over on the Southern Continent," Garde sighed. He didn't look forward to going back a second time, and waiting for the fall rains to cease would give him several weeks in Veshtul before he was expected to return.

"The moment the fall rains are over," Jayd gave his brother a hard look.

"This is not a good idea, my Queen, the H'Morr warns against it."

Friesianna regarded her advisor coldly. "That old thing? If we had the Ka'Mirai, we would not have to concern ourselves with that." Friesianna, Queen of the Bright Elemaiya, had never considered the book of prophecy as anything other than myth and tales for children. She offered a disdainful glare at the mere mention of the book, shaking back thick, brown hair to indicate her displeasure.

"We will not get her back. We know this," Rabis muttered. He knew better than anyone just how accurate the H'Morr was—he'd written it. Only one was better than he at the talent of foresight, and that one none could reach. Rabis was more than happy to keep that information to himself.

"We will gain the Ka'Mirai if I make this alliance," Friesianna snapped, her hazel eyes offering a warning to Rabis. "Then she will be forced to come to us and I will demand she eliminate the consequences. That is how things will be." Friesianna was ignoring her Miriasu advisor, just as she usually did.

Rabis stared at Friesianna in vexed exasperation. "My Queen, the warnings were quite clear. We were advised against making an alliance with either of the two you mentioned. It was foretold that justice will come if we do so. And here you wish to ally your people with both of them. Do you expect the serpents to tell us what their desire is concerning the Ka'Mirai? They are notorious liars."

"Do not annoy me with your constant prattling on this subject. Once we have the Ka'Mirai, the potential for any retribution will be eliminated," Friesianna's voice held a contemptuous, bone-chilling frost. "Go now. We must make preparations to receive the Dark King and the new Ra'Ak Prince." Rabis left her side, muttering. He had no desire to be near either of the two she'd named, and felt the Queen wouldn't remark upon his absence anyway. He walked toward the nearest gate, determined to be far away when the pact was struck. Friesianna would have to do without his services from now on. He'd prepared long ago for this day, and was now washing his hands of the Bright Queen and the fools who blindly followed her.

"This is your fault." Veris snarled at Breth. They'd returned to Veshtul three days earlier, and the news that the Vampire Queen was alive had spread swiftly among the comesuli. Veris had no hope of containing the information. Their Queen had left them, however; she'd vanished with Kifirin and not returned. Veris had no idea whom to ask regarding the Queen's whereabouts, or if she might come back to them.

"I did not know it was the Queen," Breth whined.

"You did not treat her well, Queen or not," Veris hissed. "I have questioned the others; they all say you taunted and insulted her. Now you expect her to come back to us? You are acting like a High Demon and not one of the comesuli. Our code says to treat all as if they were our parent, brother or child. This you did not do and we may all pay for your foolishness."

"I beg you, do not tell the others what I did, they will shun me," Breth whined.

"I will not tell because my part in this was nearly as great," Veris muttered. "I cannot stop the others, however. You may be shunned anyway, and it will be your due if you are."

"What did Lord Gardevik say when you asked him about her?"

"He says he has received no replies to his own queries," Veris snorted. "And if the High Demons receive no replies, what can we hope to do?" Veris stalked away from Breth.

They'd held their private conversation in a corner of the comesuli barracks, next to the eastern palace wall. So many of the commons were beginning to make preparations—they anticipated a move to Le-Ath Veronis. Veris hoped their preparations were not in vain.

"How should I dress?" I'd gone to the kitchen to get something to drink and found Devin and Grace there.

"However you want," Devin said. "Although those vampires will show up dressed to the nines." A pretty dimple appeared when she grinned.

"They always do that," I grumped. "It's to intimidate the rest of us." Grace snickered at my comment. "I watched Wlodek fight a truckload of vampires once while dressed in a silk shirt and tailored pants," I added. "Those shoes he was wearing probably cost a fortune, too. He did remove his coat and tie, though."

That made Devin laugh. "Hey, don't laugh, Radomir did the same thing," I added, smiling at the memory. "Russell and Will dressed casually, but then they weren't as old."

I got some juice and went back to my suite to pick out something to wear. I liked Devin and Grace—they were nice and heaven knew I'd not had any female friends the entire time I'd been vampire. Radomir offered to take me to Flavio—although I could have misted there since I knew where I was.

Grace explained that Adam, Merrill and Wlodek had purchased miles of land in all directions surrounding Merrill's old home, and kept it in a garden state while the lands past that had gone commercial or were covered in sprawling parts of a now-extended London and its suburbs.

The pants and silk blouse I picked out reminded me of what a 1930s film star might wear. The neck was high with buttons at the side and long, full sleeves cuffed with matching buttons. The blouse itself was in a chocolate brown, the linen-look trousers in a natural oatmeal.

Low, dark-brown heels finished everything off except for the earrings. Those were diamond drops. Charles had selected those—at least he remembered what I'd liked. I was beginning to get shaky, too. I didn't think anybody was going to remember me and that made me want to cry again. I was surprised I had any fluid left in my body nowadays.

"A brief hit, days ago. That's all," Kiarra handed a cup of tea to Dragon. Dragon murmured his thanks and sipped the tea. "Pheligar says none of our shields were detected or compromised, and the Ra'Ak didn't stay long. Probably realized he'd made a mistake coming here and got away as quickly as possible."

"As long as they left no spawn behind," Dragon grumbled.

"I've checked—there's nothing," Kiarra nodded. "But I'll let you know if we detect another hit. I just want to make sure this isn't a reconnaissance mission. They'll be breaking the rules if that's the case, and I'll get Merrill and Adam to help me take care of it."

"Let me know if you want our help," Dragon rose from his seat inside Kiarra's library. "Grace, Devin and I will be happy to assist."

"I will. Take the cup with you—Devin will send it back," Kiarra smiled. Dragon nodded and folded away.

"I do not understand why we were ordered to come," Gavin muttered, climbing the steps to the Honored One's manor.

"We'll find out, I'm sure," Tony said, attempting to soothe his surrogate sire. Spring had arrived in Kent, and the night sky was unusually clear, with stars twinkling overhead.

Gavin followed Tony's gaze and looked up at the stars as well. He blew out a sigh and moved to follow Anthony through the door. Rolfe was there, as always, holding the door to allow both Assassins inside.

"Flavio, Merrill and Wlodek are upstairs waiting for you," Rolfe rumbled.

"What do they want?" Tony sighed.

"Anthony, we will learn this soon enough." Gavin jerked his head toward the stairs leading to the second floor and Flavio's study.

This wasn't a good idea. I was shaking and felt ill. For the thousandth time I wished I hadn't agreed to allow Radomir and Charles to haul me to Flavio. I wasn't prepared for blank stares and ridicule—from any of them.

"Ready?" Charles and Radomir appeared at the same moment. They'd both dressed well for this, just as they'd done in the past. I suppose Flavio commanded the same sort of respect Wlodek always did. Charles was offering an encouraging smile, but I was too terrified to answer with one of my own.

"Lissa, things will surely work out," Radomir did his best to soothe my nerves; he hadn't failed to notice my shaking hands or unsteady breaths. I watched his hands—they were steady and he wore two rings —one on each ring finger, for each of his wives. He had someone to lean on—two someones, actually. After three hundred years, even if Gavin remembered me, our marriage, as declared by Wlodek, had been over for two centuries. This was a fiasco, no matter how you looked at it. And my rings—the ones Gavin had given me—were missing when I'd come to myself on Kifirin's planet. I had no idea what happened to them. It no longer mattered, more than likely.

"Charles and Radomir will arrive soon," Flavio offered seats to Tony and Gavin. "I have wine, if you wish it," he added. Merrill and Wlodek were already seated—Flavio had brought in extra seating after Wlodek informed him there would be more coming. Tony accepted a glass of wine; Gavin declined.

"I am also curious as to why we were asked to meet," Flavio nodded as Tony accepted the glass poured out for him. "My sire says it is important—to us and to the race."

"More important than you know," Merrill said softly.

We didn't bother with the front door—Radomir folded us straight to

Wlodek's old study. Only now, it belonged to Flavio. Wlodek's Monet was missing from the wall, as was the portrait of Napoleon I'd given him. Distractedly, I found myself hoping the painting hadn't disappeared, as the memories of me had.

Charles placed a hand on my nape as I studied the wide shoulders and dark hair of one of the four sitting before me; Radomir had dropped us behind a row of seats. Gavin's scent hadn't changed, either—it still exerted a power I couldn't name, and I wanted to weep over what I'd lost.

He'd turned slightly when we appeared, didn't recognize my scent and kept his gaze focused on Flavio, who sat behind a desk, staring at me in shock.

Still the most beautiful man I'd ever seen walking the Earth, Flavio's nose still worked as well—he knew I was vampire. "Father," he muttered, turning his eyes toward Wlodek, "why have I not been informed of this one?"

"Lissa, come and sit." Merrill rose from his chair and swept his hand toward the three remaining chairs—the ones in the center—right before Flavio's desk. He knew from my silence just how angry I was with him.

"Lissa," Charles took my hand and led me to the center seat. I was numb and Tony watched me with curiosity as Charles and Radomir got me seated and comfortable before taking seats on either side of me. There wasn't a glimmer of recognition from Flavio, Tony or Gavin. Gavin took it a step farther, though, choosing to ignore me while Flavio speculated and Tony stared in wonder.

"My sire informs me that you were here, long ago," Flavio began, his dark eyes searching my face for acknowledgement. I reminded myself that one of my newly discovered nieces was married to him—along with several other husbands, including Dalroy.

"I was." My voice quavered and I cleared my throat. I wanted to weep, but I wasn't about to do it in front of Gavin. I'd seen the severe frown on his face—he had no desire to be where he was. Forcing my thoughts away from what the old Gavin might have done upon seeing me after centuries of absence, I turned my gaze to Tony.

He was more than curious, his clear, gray eyes traveling over me from tip to toe. My clothes were fine; I'd spent more than enough money on my wardrobe, but I was still too thin. I felt unattractive under his scrutiny.

"Anthony, it is impolite to stare," Gavin growled softly. Tony turned away.

"My sire also tells me you are a powerful Queen." There was a vague question in Flavio's words, but he didn't insult his vampire sire by expressing blatant disbelief. Wlodek was feeding mindspeech to Flavio, and Flavio was struggling to keep the shock from his voice.

"My sire says," Flavio hesitated, "you were once married to Gavin."

Those words infuriated me. He might have saved me much embarrassment if he'd kept that to himself. It was more than obvious that Gavin didn't remember me. Tony, too. I wanted no more pain at the hands of these, or their charity, either.

Gavin's dark eyes were hard as they bored into mine, and there was nothing but contempt there. He didn't want me. Someone, somewhere, had made sure of that. If their ultimate goal had been to break my heart, well, they'd done a fine job of it.

"I can't kill Xenides again, just to prove what I am," I hissed at Flavio. "Fuck you. Fuck all of you." I turned to mist and got the hell away.

"Honored One, I have never been married," Gavin rose from his seat. "With your permission," Gavin nodded respectfully to Flavio and strode angrily from the study.

"I'll get you home," Radomir motioned for Tony to sit down again —he was prepared to follow his surrogate sire.

"Child, she has always been thus; disregard it," Wlodek calmed Flavio. "She is a Queen, and at times, her tone and her profanity are warranted."

The night was calm and beautiful, until I interrupted it with a sob. The roof of the villa was my perch as I wiped my cheeks and struggled to get the vision of Gavin's contempt out of my mind.

Did I love him? I did. I'd loved him from the moment he'd put his hands on my neck, eons ago, outside a mansion in Oklahoma City. That Gavin had touched me with gentleness, massaging my neck to ease the tension away.

I was preparing for another night of hunting Winkler's kidnappers, and I'd been a failure at it up to that point. I would never forget the feeling of weakness that came over me at Gavin's touch. I'd wanted to melt against him and weep my heart out. I hadn't.

Winkler was gone, now, and that made me wipe more tears away. Gavin was just as gone, though he still lived. Why had I been brought back? Why? My last memory before my death was of the late afternoon sky over Veshtul as my mist floated away. Darkness had come quickly afterward.

"Baby, we just got a message from Turtle." Drew appeared on one side, Drake on the other, and both settled in comfortably beside me.

"Who's Turtle?" I wiped my cheeks, hoping the twins wouldn't comment on the tearstains.

"A Falchani Spawn Hunter, like us," Drake wiped away a tear with a thumb, his touch gentle against my cheek. "He still owns a bar on Falchan, in the border town between the Falchani lands and Reldis."

"Turtle's son runs the bar, but since it's on the border, ruffians come in all the time and they always pick a fight," Drew sounded almost happy about that.

"So, quelling a fight is always good therapy if you're upset about something," Drake picked up the story. "Come on, itty bitty pants; let's go crack a few Reldan heads. Don't kill anybody, we're not allowed," he added, grinning.

"Uh-huh," I muttered. I was about to refuse, but the twins folded me away before I could get the words out.

It wasn't a fight—it was a brawl, with most of the bar involved. Even the bartender was wading into the fray as I stood in the doorway of a square building, fashioned of finely sanded wood, with a carefully crafted stone floor beneath our feet. Gouges were cut into the wood wherever a bare space of wall showed—there'd been plenty of fighting with blades inside this bar.

They serve the best noodles here, Drew sent as a body was tossed in our direction. The body in question rose from the floor and tottered back to the battle. Blades and fists were flying throughout the bar, and the entire room was a seething mass of conflict. I'm not sure if the combatants even knew who was friend and who was foe, they merely concentrated on fighting.

You're watching this and thinking about noodles? I sent. I'm sure my incredulity was sent with my words—I was shaking my head at what was going on all around us.

They're really good noodles, Drake weighed in on the mental conversation. *Mom and Aunt Gracie like to come here and eat with Dad and Uncle Crane.*

And I suppose the fights break out then, too? I questioned Drake.

Yeah. Mom and Aunt Gracie have tossed a few punches and crossed blades a time or two. Dad and Uncle Crane trained them, so they can hold their own. Drake was mentally laughing at me. I shouldn't have been surprised—both women were Saa Thalarr and fought the Ra'Ak. They were warriors, just as the men were.

So, you want noodles, then? I blinked up at Drake's face. His eyes, like his father's were nearly black. I liked them.

We both want noodles. But we can't get any until this is over; Drew nodded toward the continuing battle.

Fine, I sent, and waded into the nearest conflict.

When I was done, a pile of bodies, most unconscious, lay against the far wall of the bar. A neat row of blades were sunk into the thick wood of the bar, most to the hilt. A small crowd of others—those still able to stand, were backed against a wall near the door, nursing split lips, cracked ribs, black eyes and multiple bruises.

Drake and Drew were still standing next to the front door, trying very hard not to laugh. The whole thing, start to finish, took maybe ten minutes.

"Can we get noodles, now?" I almost split the bar with my fist as I pounded the scarred wood. The bartender, who was mostly whole and standing behind the bar again, offered me a grin and began preparing noodles.

"Those really were good noodles," I said as Drake folded us to the villa's kitchen after we'd eaten. The rice wine was good, too—I'd had several cups of that. As a result, I was feeling a bit tipsy.

"Aunt Lissa, thank goodness," Kyler and Cleo greeted me as the twins and I dropped into the kitchen. A man I didn't recognize sat at the island, staring at me.

"Is something wrong?" I handed a worried frown to Kyler.

"Baby, you're covered in blood—not yours," Drake snickered beside me. Only then did I survey the damage to my expensive clothing; the blouse and trousers were ruined.

"She just cleared Turtle's bar on Falchan," Drew chuckled beside me.

"Lissa, we brought Shadow," Cleo was also surveying the clothing disaster. "Are you sure you aren't hurt? I can check you over," she offered.

"She's not hurt—I don't think anybody got a hand on her," Drake said, sounding proud. "Our baby went right in and took care of business."

"Cleo?" A whispered voice came, and I turned swiftly to the male Kyler and Cleo brought with them. "Cleo, I can't get up."

"Just as expected," Kyler muttered cryptically. I watched as Cleo went to the man and put her hands on him. He was handsome, with dark hair, gray eyes and a sensuous mouth.

"Aunt Lissa, this is Shadow Grey, a Master Wizard of Grey House," Kyler took my hand. "I'll take care of the blood," she added. She wasn't kidding about duplicating the Larentii power; the blood and every tiny rip in my clothing disappeared, magically repaired by my niece.

"Wow, remind me to come to you the next time I pull one of my sweaters," I gazed down at my restored outfit.

"He's good to go, now," Cleo announced, and Shadow stood up beside her. What came next shocked the hell out of me. Shadow walked straight toward me, took my face in his hands and kissed me.

"Aunt Lissa, it's the way M'Fiyahs work," Kyler attempted to calm me. Drake and Drew were working on it as well. "If you remove a M'Fiyah, it can harm both parties."

"Baby, they're not so bad," Drew pulled me against him. "We, ah, bro and I, well," he didn't finish.

"They have them, too," Cleo sighed, nodding toward Drake and Drew. Shadow Grey was sleeping a healing sleep somewhere at the villa—he'd collapsed when I backed away from him after he'd kissed me. Cleo placed the sleep quickly, and she and Kyler moved him to a bed. I was shaking over the incident.

"What am I supposed to do?" I was right back where I'd been before the twins hauled me away to Falchan.

"Baby, we'll go slow, we promise," Drew murmured. "It doesn't have to happen overnight."

I wasn't sure whether it was going to happen at all. I didn't say that, though. What was I supposed to do? Damage all of them, because I wasn't feeling up to anything at the moment? Gavin's empty memory and defection hurt. Winkler's death hurt. Franklin, Greg, Tony—it all hurt.

"Lissa, the monthly family dinner at Grey House is in four days. Why don't you come for that?" Cleo suggested. "Maybe you can get to know Shadow better—before you make a rash decision. Removing a M'Fiyah is for life, and the consequences can affect more than you might think."

I stared at my hands for a moment before lifting my eyes to Drew's. He smiled at me as I gazed into those dark depths. "What do you think about Shadow Grey?" I asked him.

"He's a Master Wizard," Drew nuzzled my temple before placing a gentle kiss. "They don't hand that status out to just anybody."

"No, hon, that's not what I meant," I sighed.

"We don't feel jealousy. Can't," Drake nuzzled my other temple. I sat between the twins, in a media room inside the massive villa. "Besides, we like Shadow," Drake went on. "He's in our age group, and achieving Master Wizard status before five hundred is unusual. You have to be very powerful and talented to do it."

"What am I supposed to do?" I tossed a hand helplessly. "I mean, I can think of plenty of people in my past who'd fall on the floor with apoplexy if somebody mentioned multiple mates to them. Didn't seem to matter that human history is filled with multiple wives, or even husbands, in some cases. In their opinion, if a woman goes after more than one man, she's a slut, a trollop and a whore."

"Well," Drew drawled beside me, "the laws are different now, and most of those people are dead. You win."

"Honey, I think I love you," I touched his cheek.

"I know I love you," he said, and kissed my fingers.

~

"Aunt Lissa, trust me. I'll place the sleep and you'll feel better in the morning," Cleo promised. "The villa and all of Merrill, Adam and Wlodek's property is warded. Nobody will need your help while you sleep. You're completely safe, here."

I still wasn't sure, but Cleo sounded convincing. Drake and Drew were gone—they'd offered to get Shadow Grey back to Grey House. Master Wizards were busy people, I learned, and their work was highly sought by, well, everybody. Everybody who could afford it, that is.

Drake and Drew explained that Cleo's Master Wizard mate, Harvel, made their blades, and they'd cost in the millions. They were spelled against nicks, rust and breaking, and nobody except the owners could pick them up and use them. If anyone else tried, they'd trigger a spell and die. That was freaky, to the eighth power.

"Fine," I grumped. Cleo and Kyler had chased me around my borrowed suite, ordering me into pajamas and waiting patiently while I brushed my teeth.

"Get in bed," Cleo said. "This will be the best sleep you've ever had," she promised.

Dutifully I crawled into bed, and Cleo placed fingers against my forehead. Just like that, I was out.

"She doesn't trust anybody," Cleo sighed.

"Yeah. I know," Kyler agreed. "I got mindspeech from Flavio, asking me why the hell I didn't warn him sooner. I had to tell him that Em-pah didn't want it."

"I don't know what I would do, if Harvel or Rhett didn't remember me," Cleo said. "That would break my heart."

"Lissa's was broken, long ago," Kyler said. "That's why she doesn't trust anybody now."

"Gram Amara cried after we went shopping the other day," Cleo nodded. "She says Lissa might not ever consider her and Em-pah as parents."

"At least Mom loved me, and Em-pah loved me when I was little," Kyler said. "And your adoptive parents loved you. A lot."

"I know Em-pah had his reasons for splitting us up, but that doesn't make it easier to deal with now," Cleo observed. "And neither of us had to live with what Aunt Lissa did, when we were little. She must look like her mother," Cleo added. "I don't see much of Em-pah there at all."

"I wonder if Em-pah will ever learn who his father was," Kyler sighed. "He said his mother refused to tell him, and there's a wall of power surrounding the information. He can't get to it."

"It bothers him, but we may never know who our great-grandfather was," Cleo agreed. "Em-pah says he didn't ever *Look* to see who Lissa's Elemaiya grandmother was. He says the wars between Bright and Dark have almost destroyed the race, and she may be dead anyway. Is Flavio still mad?"

"He asked me to spend the night with him, so I guess not," Kyler hid a smile.

"Yeah, he's not pretty or anything," Cleo snickered, bumping her shoulder against her twin's.

Cleo was right; I was well rested after a long sleep—I'd slept right through breakfast and Drake and Drew showed up after sparring with Dragon and Crane, hauling me out of bed, shoving me in the shower and then herding me toward the kitchen.

Mike was waiting, and I had a plate of pancakes and bacon in front of me in very little time.

"Lissa, we heard you had a tough time, last night," Devin walked in, receiving a peck from Drake and Drew as she sat down beside me.

"I still don't know what to do," I muttered, accepting a fresh cup of coffee from Mike. He'd added cream and sugar, just the way I wanted it. I sent mindspeech, telling him he was a god in the kitchen. He snickered and went to make a cup of tea for Devin.

"M'Fiyahs are never easy at first, especially if there are several manifesting at once. Kiarra had an easier time, since Pheligar muted his for thousands of years, and hers with Merrill was muted by Griffin."

"They can be muted?" I stared at Devin in shock.

"Not anymore, Belen has forbidden it," Devin stared at her hands. Mike placed a cup of tea in front of Devin and she thanked him absently. "Belen says there has been too much damage caused by muted and destroyed M'Fiyahs. In the past, some have been muted or destroyed, because one party or the other decided, without consent or knowledge, at times, of the other party. The ability has been removed from all of the Saa Thalarr and only Belen can do it, now. He says he will only consider destroying a M'Fiyah if both parties agree."

Devin's skin was flawless as I studied her face—she was fair-skinned and light red hair framed her delicate, oval face. Her blue eyes were troubled as she focused on me. "Kiarra wants Gracie and me to bring you over this morning. Gryphon Hall, Adam's ancestral home, is only a few miles away. We'll fold you over. Kiarra wants to talk to you. There's something else you should know, too. I'm her daughter. She and Adam are my parents."

"But the scent," I said before I thought.

"I know about that. Mom and Dad aren't my birth parents. But they're still my parents."

"Got it," I said. "Didn't mean to upset you."

"I know, and you didn't," Devin rubbed my back and smiled. "If they were my birth parents, it would make things awkward with Justin. They are his birth parents."

That admission made me blink—I hadn't thought about that. Justin, Adam and Kiarra's son, was one of Devin and Grace's eleven mates.

"M'Fiyahs are usually easier on the guys—the love hits them immediately and they always want to hop in bed right away; that's just the way they are," Devin shrugged. Drake and Drew, sitting beside me, snickered and pretended to look the other way.

Schmucks, I sent to both of them.

We're crushed; Drake sent a smile with his mental words. And it wasn't awkward to be sitting there, discussing sex with the mother of the two who wanted to do the bed hopping.

"So, how should I dress?" I'd slipped into jeans and a pullover earlier.

"You're fine," Devin said.

That's how I ended up at Gryphon Hall later, after I finished eating and brushing my teeth. Devin wouldn't allow Drake and Drew to come along, though I was wishing they might come for moral support.

I had no idea what Kiarra might want, and if my guesses were correct, she was the Queen Bee for the Saa Thalarr, even though Dragon and Grace were now Co-Firsts.

"I just ate," I waved off Kiarra's offer of something to eat or drink. She and Fox were in Adam's library—it was as large as Merrill's had been when I'd lived with him, three centuries ago. It made me wonder what his manor looked like now, and whether it had changed through the years.

Comfortable furniture was scattered in a seating area, surrounding a wide, low table. Everything—from the sofas and chairs to the table and the handmade rugs beneath our feet screamed money—lots of money.

"I wanted to talk to you about several things, before we get to the difficult matters," Kiarra's platinum blonde hair was pulled back in an attractive braid. If she'd left it loose, it would probably hang to her waist.

Her blue eyes held concern and a slight frown tugged at her pretty mouth. She wasn't tall—maybe an inch or two taller than I. I didn't measure her might in her stature, though, and anybody who did might have a real surprise coming their way. Power clouded about her—it was so tangible I could almost see it. If I turned to mist, I would definitely see it.

"What things?" I asked. I felt pain coming, and twisted my fingers together.

"Stop that." Fox sat beside me and pulled one of my hands into hers. I'd sat by myself on a small sofa, while Grace and Devin sat opposite me. Kiarra had been standing the entire time, but she sat, now.

I stared at Fox—she knew I was shaky. "We quarter bloods have to stick together," she offered a perky grin.

"Wlodek must have gone crazy when he first met you," I blurted.

"He did. He had no idea how to handle this," she laughed, her short, black curls bouncing a little. "But we had a M'Fiyah, and he figured out soon enough he couldn't do without me."

"Lissa," Kiarra interrupted us. "I know you loved Franklin. I was with him when he died. He was eighty-three."

I drew in a sharp breath and my mouth was suddenly dry. Frank lived twenty years after I disappeared.

"Sixty years ago, Belen came to Merrill and me," Kiarra went on. I was now staring at her, the pain for Franklin settling in my heart. "Belen said it was time for Franklin and Jeff to be reborn. Jeffrey was one of Merrill's vampire children that he lost before he met you," Kiarra explained. "Belen gave us a choice, Merrill and me. He said both could be reborn to us, as our natural children, or born to others. That decision was an easy one to make. They came to us, as twins. Neither remembers their former lives, although that has a great deal to do with who and what they are, now." Kiarra blew out a sigh. I chewed my lower lip, my heart beating painfully in my chest. Fox squeezed my hand.

"Jeff, before Merrill made him vampire in the early 1900s, was a medical student. He contracted the deadly influenza sweeping the U.S. at the time. Merrill turned him before he died. Jeff is the only vampire born vampire. He now has several medical degrees and does charity work in that field, in addition to being a healer for the Saa Thalarr."

"And he doesn't remember," I muttered, staring at my hand that was gripped tightly by both of Fox's.

"No. Franklin has architecture and engineering degrees, this time," a smile lit Kiarra's face. She was speaking of her children, and proud of them, as any mother might be. "He is also a healer for us, but he could build a house or a bridge or a skyscraper if he wanted. He also knows his way around a kitchen, but one of his mates, Shane, is a better cook than any of us. If Shane makes barbecue, Merrill is first in line."

"One of his mates?" I watched Kiarra closely.

"Both are mated to Tomas."

"Is Frank happy? This time?" I sniffled, I couldn't help it. My Frank was gone. I didn't get to say goodbye to him, either.

"Lissa, Shane is Greg, reborn. Conner, my half-sister says so. And as she's the Guardian, she would know. They're all happy."

"We'll explain about the Guardian some other time," Grace said gently. Fox *Pulled* in a box of tissues and handed it to me. I wiped tears away.

"I gave information to Franklin and Greg, before." Griffin folded into the library, accompanied by Merrill and Adam. Kiarra, Grace and Devin folded away. Fox patted my hand, gave me a watery smile—she was nearly in tears, and folded away.

"What the fuck do you want?" I muttered at Griffin. I wasn't speaking to Merrill.

"$\mathcal{I}$ told Franklin and Greg, more than three hundred years ago, that things would come out better this way, if they refused to allow Merrill to make the turn," Griffin sighed. "Franklin asked back then, so I answered. I said their lives would be all right—but only all right, if they became vampire. But, if they lived their lives and waited for rebirth, then things would be better."

"You did this." I refused to look at Griffin. He'd manipulated so many things, including my death. "But you didn't see me coming back, did you?" I wasn't sure how I knew it, but I did.

"No. You were dead, Lissa. Belen says it. The ones above him say it. Some of them know why you're here now, but they had no hand in making it happen."

"They should have left me dead," I muttered, wiping dampness from my cheeks. My pile of used tissues was growing.

"Belen says I have to make this next admission to you, because what I did—what Merrill and I did, was wrong. You already despise us, and this will only make things worse," Griffin raked fingers through thick, light-brown hair. His hazel eyes darted in my direction —once. Whatever he was about to say—he was ashamed of it. Merrill, too, had arms crossed over his chest and was staring at his shoes.

"I told Merrill, after Wlodek asked him to teach you years ago," Griffin began, "that he—Merrill—would have a M'Fiyah with you." My breath stopped.

"I was obsessed with Kiarra, Lissa," Merrill's voice was rough and he still refused to meet my gaze. Just as well, I was gawping like a fool. "I didn't want anything to interfere with my love for Kiarra," Merrill continued. "So I asked Griffin to destroy the M'Fiyah with you. In his defense, he asked me three times if that was what I wanted. I still insisted. He destroyed the M'Fiyah. Without my seeing you, without our consulting you, or doing anything to help you through it afterward. We allowed that pain to live in you, sweetheart. This is our punishment, for doing that. Belen won't allow the destruction of a M'Fiyah, or even the muting of one, any longer, unless both parties agree."

Well, now I knew why Devin had explained it earlier.

"This is your punishment? Admitting it now?" I was on my feet and stifling a sob. "Fuck both of you. And don't ever say that you care about me. Ever. That's the biggest lie, and you're not supposed to be able to lie." I misted away.

I learned, after misting there, that the cliffs of Dover were now a very protected place, and one might see them best from a hoverboat in the sea. Transportation had certainly changed—I saw that quickly. I was glad I'd kept my credit chip necklace on—that's how I paid to get aboard the tourist boat. Now I stood at the rail, staring at the white cliffs in the distance and wiping away tears.

I'd cared about Merrill once—now I knew why. And he'd sabotaged it, repeatedly. He and Griffin, together, had done terrible harm to me. One of them refused me, sight unseen, and the other manipulated my birth and death. How was I supposed to forgive that? How?

It has become my philosophy, over the years, that anger is a heavy burden, and it is better to let it go than carry it around. Perhaps I'd forgiven too much through my life, but I preferred that to the alternative. Until now, there was only one person who would never have my forgiveness, and that person was Howard Graham. Merrill and Griffin had just joined him.

"Your father and your intended mate never thought things might come to this." He shone beside me. And Power? I'd never felt so much of it. "One of them never expected you to live and remember, the other never thought to admit his deed. Now you know of both. What you do with that information is your choice. I am Belen," he smiled down at me.

He was tall. In corporeal form, he had pale hair and blinding white eyes. I found myself staring at Belen of the Nameless Ones.

"Intended mate," I huffed. Merrill made a choice, shoving me in Gavin's direction. And then he'd never interfered, when I was beaten by the Council or when I suffered from Gavin's bouts of anger. No, Gavin hadn't realized how much that anger had cost me—until he'd caused me to break on a September night at Camp David. Now, he didn't remember me or anything we'd had between us.

"Merrill belonged with you, Lissa. And he had that bond destroyed. It is costing him, now. As much as he might wish to restore it, that wish will not be granted by my kind."

"What about Gavin?" I muttered.

"He also was yours. Neither will that bond be restored by my kind." I dropped to my knees and wept. "I only said it would not be restored by my kind." Belen disappeared.

"What did we damage?" Merrill asked with a sigh. Kiarra had just come from a meeting with Belen.

"A M'Fiyah with you would have meant Lissa's membership in the Saa Thalarr. Now, Belen says another path is opening before her. One he barely understands. She won't ever come to us. She could have done so much, too." Kiarra shook her head. "We could send her after the worst of the worst, Merrill, and it would be child's play to her. There are no rules about bringing natural talent into the Saa Thalarr."

"I didn't know," Merrill muttered.

"Griffin could have said something. He didn't," Kiarra snapped. "Now, Lissa's pissed at both of you, and we have no idea where she is. Belen wouldn't tell me earlier, and Drake and Drew are going crazy. Shadow Grey has sent mindspeech six times. I have no idea what to do about that."

A spring rain poured down as I strode angrily through the fields and grounds near Merrill's old manor. I knew what I searched for, and I walked instead of misting there. The cold rain and exercise would help clear my mind. At least I hoped it would.

The gate was there, and I stared at the spot just outside it, where René died. No memorial had been placed. No flowers. No pile of stones or any other thing to remember him by. He only lived in my memory, now.

"René, what am I supposed to do?" I dropped to my knees. My hair hung in wet strands about my face and my clothing dripped water as I hugged myself and wept.

"Franklin?"

Frank lifted his head—he'd been working at a drafting table inside his workshop. His twin brother, Jeff, asked him to design a charity clinic for the jungles on Ooblerik. The indigent population was growing; the government ignored the poor in the cities as well as the aborigines in their southern jungles. Jeff and Karzac were in those jungles now, immunizing children against a disease destroying their numbers.

Franklin had to design something that would fit with the local architecture, and still hold the examination rooms and spaces for supplies that Jeff requested. Franklin added a few hospital rooms to the structure—he feared they might be needed.

"Conner?" Frank asked, although he should have known better than to say Conner's name—the Guardian was present, and bore little resemblance to Conner's normal form. White, shifting flames regarded him with piercing eyes.

"Go to this place. Now." The Guardian's eyes were filled with light and an image was placed in Franklin's mind.

Frank knew the place—the old gate was there—the one Griffin closed so Merrill's property would remain safe. Only Griffin and the Saa Thalarr ever used it now, and that only sparingly—they could fold space, after all.

"Of course." Franklin dropped his screen stylus—his drafting table was a computer and everything he designed was digital. More instructions filtered into Franklin's mind, even as he folded away.

≈

He was Merrill's son. And Kiarra's—the scent told me that as he knelt beside me. He'd shown up as I sobbed my heart out, rocking on the cold ground outside the gate on his father's property.

"Go away," I stuttered. The rain was cold and I was frozen, my teeth chattering. Did I expect him to look so much like Merrill? No. He wasn't vampire, either. This was Franklin. The one who didn't remember me. And he didn't look or smell like my Frank, either.

"Lissa?" Franklin lifted my face to stare into his.

≈

Flavio studied the electronic reports he'd received from contacts in the U.S. There were increasing numbers of disappearances in California, most concentrated along the coast between Los Angeles and Monterey.

Tourist season had begun; vacationers and instate visitors were flocking to the coastal areas for the beach and cooler temperatures.

Eight humans had disappeared in the last two weeks and there were no clues to be had.

Local authorities were confused—no bodies had been found and the last to disappear was a father and his fourteen-year-old son two days earlier. Normally, Flavio's suspicions wouldn't be raised—humans often went crazy and killed.

There was also a thriving community of vampires in the area—they liked the cooler temperatures and misty nights when they came. There'd been a marked decrease in orders of blood substitute recently—and that fact had not gone unnoticed by the two vampires in charge of distributing supplies to the locals.

"Who do we have?" Flavio looked up at Charles, who'd been tidying up.

"You want to send somebody to the California coast?" Charles asked.

"Yes. And soon."

"Gavin and Anthony are the only ones available. They can go. May I make a suggestion, though?" Charles offered Flavio a hopeful glance.

"I suppose," Flavio looked up at his vampire child, who'd accepted a position as Spawn Hunter for the Saa Thalarr. Flavio didn't understand how Charles kept up with all his duties. Charles claimed it was all worth it to be able to eat normal food and walk in daylight. Of course, being able to fold space anywhere was worth it, too, according to Charles.

"Ask Lissa to go with them. Father, you have no idea how fast she can deal with something like this. If vampires are involved, that's a lot of people they're taking. It needs to stop quickly, if that's what is happening."

"You don't need to tell me that," Flavio held his head. "How do we ask her?" Charles smiled at Flavio's question.

~

"Drink this." I was wrapped in a heated blanket and Franklin and Shane were tending me. Tomas, their third mate, handed over a mug of hot soup. They'd tried to explain, Frank and Shane, that Conner, as the Guardian, had shown them their past years ago. She held that power, Frank said. The Guardian escorted lost souls to the other side —that was one of the things she did.

Franklin looked exactly like Merrill, with black hair and piercing blue eyes. Shane, well, he was shorter than Greg, with sandy blond hair, brown eyes and a quick grin.

"Mom and Dad don't have a clue, and the Guardian said to keep the information to ourselves. She said we'd know someday why it was given to us," Frank's smile could twist anybody's heart.

"Frankie, I missed you," I sniffled. "I'm not sure I can get used to calling you Shane," I turned to the reincarnated Greg.

"I know, baby girl," Frank put his arms around me. "You need to stop shivering. This isn't good for you."

"Crying isn't good for you either," Shane pointed out dryly.

"Does my face look awful?" I worried my lower lip.

"Lissa, you've never looked better to me in my life," Shane grinned.

"How much do you remember?" I searched his face.

"Everything," his grin widened.

"And he doesn't mind talking about it," Tomas interrupted. He was smiling, too, so it wasn't a problem. Tomas had an Asian heritage with a lovely nose, dark eyes and a square jaw.

"We just can't spill the beans with Mom and Dad," Franklin cautioned.

"I won't be talking to your father," I muttered, drinking my soup.

"Yeah. I heard," Frank sighed.

"Baby, we were scared to death." Drew lifted me and almost cracked a rib; he hugged me so hard. Frank, Shane and Tomas had finally gotten me warmed up and convinced me to return to the villa.

I'd learned that Conner, when she looked human, that is, was married to Martin Walters, Russell, Will, Graegar, Barrigar and Lynx, one of the Saa Thalarr I hadn't met. Frank laughed at me as I stared at him in shock—he'd attempted to explain who was mated to whom. It was overwhelming, and I still wanted to know what being married to a Larentii was like.

"Drew, I can't breathe," I wheezed. He kissed me when he set me down, and then Drake moved his brother aside and did exactly the same. I had no idea what to do with both of them. I knew what they wanted to do with me, though—that had been evident when they hugged me.

Frank, Shane and Tomas all got a hug before they left, and Drake and Drew herded me straight into the kitchen for more food.

"No more of this freezing shit," Mike muttered as he thumped a mug of hot tea in front of me. "I got mindspeech from Conner. You don't ignore mindspeech from Conner."

"I didn't mean to get you in trouble," I sighed, staring at my mug of tea.

"You didn't, but Conner has a way of pointing out how you haven't been treated with the proper respect. While she's Conner, that's no problem. If it's the Guardian, she'll scare the holy hell out of you."

"And he's not speaking metaphorically," Drake draped an arm around my shoulders. Plates of food were passed around, Dragon and Crane appeared and we ate. Franklin, Shane and Tomas, followed by Drake and Drew, had helped a bad day turn into a not so bad day.

I was shocked to find Charles sitting on my bed when I came out of the bathroom later, dressed in PJs and brushing my teeth. I'd had to push Drake and Drew out my bedroom door—they wanted to stay.

Hold on, I sent mindspeech to Charles and went back to rinse out my mouth. Charles wouldn't be asking for sex. Not from me. Besides, he was fully dressed. I imagine that Kifirin, or even Drake or Drew, would be either naked or mostly so if they'd been on my bed. And not in a sitting position, either.

"What is it, Charles?" I asked, walking out of the bathroom again. At least I didn't look like a foaming, rabid animal this time.

"We have a problem in California," Charles got right to business. "We can wrap this up quickly if you help."

"What's the problem?" I asked.

"Locals and tourists are disappearing on the coast between L.A. and Monterey. Eight that we know of, in the last two weeks," Charles said, his hazel eyes reflecting the concern in his voice. "People have been warned and they're taking extra precautions, but they're disappearing anyway. We've gotten word from the vampires who run the Council's blood substitute banks. They've seen a drop in orders from the area. Flavio's worried that some of ours have gone rogue."

"You can't do that *Looking* thing to find this out?" I asked, sitting on the bed next to Charles.

"Not allowed to use it for this. It's one of the conditions of keeping my job with the Council. I can't use those abilities; it's unethical. I can only use what I have normally." Charles offered a crooked grin and rubbed my back.

"That's gotta suck. When do you want me to go?" I'd already made up my mind.

"It'll be dark there in another four hours. Can you be packed and ready to go in a few minutes?"

"How are you going to get me there?"

"Hey, three hundred years have passed—we're way more efficient in travel these days," Charles's grin widened. "It'll take little more than an hour, and most of that time will be taken up in getting you to the ship station. After that, you'll just orbit over. The pods don't have windows anyway, so it's a great way for vamps to travel."

"This is a Low Earth Orbit?" I asked.

"Yeah. It's great. The pods dock at stations positioned around the globe and then you're taken down to the ground. Neat, huh?"

"Yeah. Neat. Thank goodness I can mist if I have to," I said.

"You won't need to. It's really safe. You'll be going with Gavin and Tony. I'll wait while you pack."

If I hadn't already said I'd go, I would have said no right then. Tony wouldn't be so bad, but Gavin? He didn't want anything to do with me and I wasn't prepared for contemptuous scowls from my former vampire husband.

"What about the family dinner at Grey House?" I asked, trying to find an excuse to wriggle out of going. "Cleo said she and Kyler would come get me and take me to Grey House." Wherever that was.

"They can come get you wherever you are—just send mindspeech. Don't fret," Charles reassured me. "Do this, Lissa. You can get this over with quickly; I just know it. Anybody else will take twice as long."

"I'll need a bag—I don't have anything," I grumped. I'd said yes; now Charles was holding me to my word.

"Give me a few minutes," Charles said. "Don't go anywhere," he turned, pointing a finger at me and grinning. He folded away. Man, I wanted to do that. I dressed while Charles was gone and he was back in less than five minutes with two bags in his hands.

"Did you get those from Wlodek's basement, too?"

Charles looked at me with a puzzled expression, until he remembered. I'd gotten some expensive luggage from him the first time we'd met. He claimed it came from Wlodek's basement.

"Just pack casual clothes, maybe four or five days' worth," he instructed. I was folding and arranging quickly. Toiletries I'd bought in London were now being packed into a bag. "Good enough," Charles said when everything was loaded in and the bags closed. Zippers still worked, I noticed. Then, before I could change my mind, he folded me to Flavio, who patiently waited in Wlodek's old study.

"Gavin and Anthony will meet you at the London station," Flavio informed me when Charles and I arrived. He still didn't remember me, but the mask was in place. Charles had talked him into this, I could tell.

"I'll take her in," Charles said.

"Are we driving or folding?" I asked. I remembered rides in Charles' car—he always drove like a maniac.

"I'll fold you in," Charles said. "And I have ID for you," he held up a tiny chip. "Unfortunately, this has to be placed beneath the skin. Ren is coming to do this for you."

"I like Renegar," I said. Actually, I'd liked all the Larentii I'd met and

I couldn't explain that. I hadn't seen any more of them, either, since that first night at the villa. I was looking forward to seeing Renegar again.

"This is the little Queen?" A Larentii I hadn't seen before folded in with Renegar.

"Ferrigar," Flavio stood and nodded to the new Larentii. "This is the little Queen; anyway that's what my sources tell me. Charles seems very sure of her, and I trust my child."

"If you had witnessed what she did upon Kifirin, you would have no doubts, Sanguis Rex," Renegar said, taking the microchip from Charles by floating it off his finger with Power. "Little one," he turned to me, "this will not hurt at all." He placed the chip on the inside of my wrist and we both watched as it sank into the skin.

"That's amazing," I breathed.

"I find you amazing, little Queen," Ferrigar the Larentii came to stand beside me. "Seldom have I seen any creature I could not detect by using my Power, yet that is how it is with you. We find you fascinating, little one. We may wish to study you, sometime."

"Don't worry. They'll just stand around looking at you and communicating silently," Charles said. "Unless you get pregnant. Then they'll have their hands on you, but that won't hurt, either."

"I can't get pregnant so that won't happen," I said, examining the smooth skin of my wrist. I couldn't tell where the chip was at all.

"Come on then, I'll take you to the station," Charles said, lifting my bags. He had me folded away in very little time.

"The tracking chip has been placed, along with the identification chip," Renegar informed Griffin later. Griffin breathed a relieved sigh. "Only the Larentii will be able to detect the beacon, so she will be safe, and we will not track her unless it becomes a necessity," Renegar went on.

Griffin nodded. The thought terrified him that none of them could find Lissa anywhere. They'd all been blinded to her, now. At least the

Larentii could find her and that eased his mind. When she'd disappeared earlier, he worried that she'd disappeared for good. The information he and Merrill were forced to deliver guaranteed that Lissa would never forgive either of them.

~

"I do not like this," Gavin grumbled. Tony watched as Gavin fretted, which was completely uncharacteristic of the two thousand-year-old vampire. Gavin had the stone face and non-expression the oldest vampires mastered, but now the façade was beginning to crack.

"You don't have to deal with her if you don't want to—I'll do it," Tony offered. Gavin stared at Tony, unable to decide whether he appreciated that or not. Gavin growled softly. Tony didn't bother him again.

"Here we are," Charles walked in with Lissa, her bags in his hands.

~

Gavin was at his surly best—I could see that right away. I knew the look; I'd dealt with it before. I didn't say anything to him or Tony; I just sighed instead and took a seat on a nearby bank of chairs. Three hundred years had gone past and seating hadn't improved one bit at the airport.

"They'll call your flight and you'll load onto the shuttle, which will take you to the pod station," Charles explained quietly, sitting beside me. "I'll stay until you're called."

"Thanks, Charles," I gave him a weak smile. Yeah, I was going to get this over with quickly—no way I wanted to hang around the grumpy vampire. It made my heart ache to watch him. A part of me had been torn away and nothing could fill the void. Once again, I wondered why I was still alive.

"Here," Charles pulled a handkerchief from his inside jacket pocket and handed it to me. I wore a jacket, so I slipped the square of silk into a pocket. It might be needed soon if I didn't get my mind off Gavin.

144

Our flight was called shortly after; Charles pecked me on the cheek and I followed Gavin and Tony to the door where the passengers were loading into the shuttle.

This was a new experience for me. The shuttle took us to the pod station and we were loaded into a bullet-shaped pod quickly, once we arrived. There were no windows on the pod, but each seat back held a vid screen where we could watch the entire journey (if we wanted). I was mesmerized.

The pod detached and I watched my screen in fascination as we hurtled through space—I saw the Earth curving below us—clouds in swirls across oceans—everything. I'd never held any hope of doing anything like this, yet here I was.

Tony and Gavin were bored—I imagine they'd done this too many times to count and it was old, now. They sat together; I was seated across the aisle, next to an executive who'd been in London, negotiating a contract. Now he was traveling back to L.A. He was also asking me out before the flight was over, and it wasn't that long to begin with.

"No, thanks, I'm working," I told him as gently as I could.

"Well, if you ever need anything," he handed me a business card. He was a lawyer, just as I thought. His recycled, holographic plastic card said so. I smiled and waved as he left the pod ahead of me.

I waited for Gavin and Tony, pulled my own bags out of the overhead bin (the bins were huge and were the only cargo space the pod had) and followed my two vampires.

For me, it had only been a few months since I'd seen them—only a short while since René and Greg died and Xenides breathed his last. For Gavin and Tony, that had been three hundred years ago. It was difficult to wrap my head around.

The rental waiting for us was a hovercraft, with a cruising speed of two hundred fifty miles per hour. That wasn't scary or anything. Gavin drove; I sat in the back. He still hadn't said a word to me; Tony was the one telling me where I needed to go or what I had to do. He used mindspeech a couple of times, too, just to keep me from making mistakes. I was grateful for that.

The usual safe house waited for us, on a hill overlooking Morro Bay. Morro Rock shone in the water below us as I stood on the wide, safe house deck. "This is beautiful," I whispered to myself—Tony and Gavin had already gone to the basement.

Dark clouds hung over the water west of the safe house, but the city twinkled below and I wondered if I could visit sometime when I wasn't working. The old Gavin would have been at my shoulder, calling me cara and kissing my neck.

What had happened and why had they forgotten me? I had no explanation for that or any other part of my recent life. Maybe I'd ask Griffin someday what he was thinking. When I could bring myself to speak to him.

"I haven't been here in a while," Tony said behind me.

"Who will have the records of all the disappearances?" I asked, refusing to turn around.

"Gavin has them," he said, coming to stand beside me.

"You think I'm going to ask him?" I snorted. I was still staring out at the ocean. The moon was a sliver, peeking through shifting clouds and hanging low over the water. I recalled that I didn't know what day it was. Nobody had been standing by with a watch or calendar when I'd come back to myself on Kifirin.

"The local police will have it in their computer records," Tony offered an alternative.

"I'll go find the police station, then," I said. "Maybe they'll have something Gavin doesn't have."

"There's definitely something Gavin doesn't have," Tony said softly.

"His choice," I said and misted away.

"You can pull up all the public records right here if you scan your ID," an officer informed me when I walked into the police station half an hour later. I'd asked a helpful delivery truck driver for directions to the station.

I scanned my new ID and got into all the news and recent records quickly—computers were simple to operate in the future. The only thing I found in common with all the disappearances was that all the victims had been going to the beach. The father and son who'd disappeared last had gone surfing. They'd failed to come home for dinner that evening as they'd promised.

I watched a video interview with two wives, who were pleading for the release of their husband and son. I then watched a video interview with relatives of the next disappearances. "She was only going to Pismo for the day," the distraught father said.

This young woman was nineteen and both the father and mother were weeping in front of the camera. It was heartbreaking to watch. The media wasn't any different from when I'd seen them last—going for every tear and heartrending situation they could.

I was mentally keeping track of the disappearances, too. The three most recent were in the Pismo and Morro Bay area. Before that, the disappearances had occurred north of there—near Monterey and San Luis Obispo. Looked like the killer or kidnapper was heading south.

I wasn't sure all of them happened at night, either. Call it a feeling, but the victims had gone out in daylight and most of them were expected home that night. They'd just never shown up. According to the police and the media reports, no evidence had been collected.

"Find what you need?" The policeman was back, a cup of coffee in his hands.

"Some," I nodded. "I'm visiting the area and want to make sure I'm doing everything I can so this won't happen to me."

"Good idea," he said. His nametag said Sergeant Whitaker. He looked to be in his forties and wore a wedding band. I wasn't interested anyway; I had more angst than I could handle on my emotional plate as it was. "Just get in tonight?"

"Yeah," I nodded. I figured he could check my ID in the computer and find out whether that was true or not.

"There wasn't a bit of evidence," he sighed, settling onto a seat at the kiosk next to mine. "Nothing. Like they were snatched from the air." He fluttered his fingers. "Just—gone," he added. Sergeant Whitaker's words made my skin itch.

"Do you think the victims were on the beach or in the water?" I asked.

"Don't know," he scrubbed his face with a free hand. He had a bit of beard showing.

"Long day?" I asked sympathetically.

"Double shift—we're having trouble with this," he sighed. "There's an average of one disappearance every twenty hours or so. We've got extra patrols on the beaches; nobody is out at night like they used to be."

"How long has it been since they stopped going out at night?" I asked.

"At least a week," he replied, sipping his coffee. There'd been five disappearances since then—the father and son the last ones. "This is the damnedest thing," he muttered. I nodded in agreement—it was the damnedest thing.

"I have a question," I said. Sergeant Whitaker quirked an eyebrow at me. His eyebrows were on the bushy side and his dark hair was threaded with gray. Hazards of the job, I'm sure.

"What's that?" he asked.

"Has anything else been disappearing? Animals or anything?" The more I learned about the disappearances, the more convinced I became that vampires weren't involved. It sounded predatory, but it was much too close to daylight, if not during daylight hours, that these humans were taken.

"A farmer up the coast filed a report because some of his cattle were stolen. We haven't had time to investigate the theft, though— we've been too busy with this. Here," he reached over and tapped a few keys. "Something like this—you can pull up the police report; it hasn't been investigated yet and since it's a theft, it's public record anyway."

I nodded and began to read the report. At least they were electronically recorded now—no hastily scribbled notes to decipher. The address of the cattle ranch was listed, so I committed it to memory. Four cows were missing. That sounded weird—why would they only steal four cows? I even said it out loud.

"I don't have the answer to that; you'd think they'd get as many as they could," Sergeant Whitaker said. I agreed with him. "We don't have time to worry about cows now." He rose stiffly. "Gotta get back to work," he said.

"Thanks for your help," I smiled at him. He had laugh lines around his eyes, I noticed, and he had a nice smile.

"Stay away from the beach if you can," he cautioned and walked away.

CHAPTER 10

"Where the hell have you been?" That part of Gavin hadn't changed, and it was the part I wished was still gone.

"I went to the police station to use the public computer kiosk," I said, walking past him into the dining area of the basement. "I don't think we're dealing with vampires." That statement brought a disbelieving glare from Gavin.

"Think what you like," I shrugged off his annoyance. "I'm going out in the morning to see what I can find. A rancher not far from here lost four cows six days ago and that happened on a day when no humans disappeared. I'm wondering if other cattle or animals have disappeared on days when no humans came up missing."

"What are you saying?" Tony came over as I pulled out a chair and sat at the tiny kitchen table.

"Too many of these disappearances happened too close to daylight. And the officer I talked to said there was no evidence left behind—it seems as though the people were snatched from the air."

"You still do not know it isn't vampires," Gavin growled.

"Not a hundred percent," I conceded. "But I don't think it is. There.

Are you willing to accept that? I'm going to bed. Did you take the bedroom closest to the door, like always?" I asked him.

"Yes, how did you know?" he asked.

"You always take that one," I said. "Do I get a bedroom, or am I sleeping on the sofa?" I got up to get my bags from the small living area.

"You get the third bedroom down the hall on the right," Gavin grumped.

"Thanks, honey," I said as I walked past him. Gavin growled at me in reply. Tony and I shared a bathroom, looked like. I brushed my teeth (again) and went to bed.

Gavin and Tony were sound asleep when I woke around eight the next morning. I showered, dressed and misted right through the ceiling. The café I found served breakfast, and you could read the electronic newspaper or watch the local news on a small screen at the table while you had your meal or coffee. I did both.

The newspaper came first and I went to the lists of calls for burglaries and the like. More cattle were missing; another report had been made after I'd left the police station the night before. The rancher didn't know how long they'd been missing. I got the address off that one, too.

The local news came next, and while I sat there having scrambled eggs and bacon, I learned that two more humans were missing; a teenage couple this time. Their small vehicle was shown on the news, its folding top pushed back, leaving the interior open. It was a convertible hovercraft.

"They left the house early this morning," a relative said. They'd certainly been snatched in daylight and whatever was taking these victims was now grabbing two at a time. How did that figure into the equation? I used my money chip to pay. No tips were accepted nowadays and there wasn't any way to leave a tip. I thanked my waitress anyway, after asking where I could find a map.

I had to buy a small, handheld electronic map that had everything on it you could possibly want. Nobody made paper anything now unless it couldn't be helped.

The first ranch address was entered; the gadget pulled up an image of where I was and where I needed to be. The little map would have given me turn-by-turn directions on how to get where I wanted to go, so I confused the hell out of it when I found a shadowy corner and turned to mist, flying in a straight line toward my destination.

My electronic map informed me that I'd reached my location when I materialized a few minutes later. I was grateful it wasn't cursing me instead. The location was higher in the mountains above the nearby city; fenced pasture lay all about me and there was a sprawling home in the distance. I was standing at the edge of the road outside the ranch itself.

"You lost?" somebody pulled alongside me in a hovercar.

"No, but thanks for asking," I said, shading my eyes against the midmorning glare to study the man. Faded blue eyes examined me from the dim interior of his vehicle. Red hair going to silver and a lined, leathery face told me he'd been ranching for most of his life—he looked as if he'd worked in the outdoors for years.

"This is my ranch," he nodded toward the house in the distance.

"Did you lose cattle recently?" I asked.

"Yeah. You with the police?"

"No," I said. "I'm doing some private investigation on this. I have a theory that the disappearances at the beach and your missing cattle are connected."

"That's a hell of a theory," the rancher said. "I can't say I see any connection, but the cops don't have time to investigate my missing cows and I'll take any help I can get."

"Do you know where your cows were when they disappeared?" I asked.

"Over on the southwest pasture. I can give you a lift if you want; I was going to check it again anyway."

"Sure," I said, climbing in on the passenger side of his vehicle. It was exhilarating to rise above the fences and take off over the pastures.

"Somewhere around here," the rancher said, pointing toward a spot near the fence. His name was John—he'd told me while we drove

—the golden-brown grasses below us whipping beneath the hovercar as we rushed along. I'd given him my first name, too. I couldn't see that it hurt anything.

I climbed out of the hovercar and sniffed around. He'd parked the vehicle near the fence and I headed toward the barbed wire structure. There was a spot near the fence where the grass was beaten down, so I walked in that direction, just to check scents.

John came with me. There were plenty of hoof prints there, as if the cattle had been frightened and churned the ground getting away. John was busy examining the ground, but what hit me when we reached the fence was the smell. Well, stench would be a better word. I wanted to hold my nose to keep from gagging as I moved closer to the barbed wire.

"Do you know what this might be?" I pointed out what looked to be a piece of leather caught on a barbed spike.

"No idea—kinda stinks though, doesn't it? You don't think that's cowhide, do you?"

"Wouldn't it have hair if it was?" I asked, holding my breath.

"Probably. You think the rustlers were wearing leather? Some people still do."

"Don't know, but surely it wouldn't smell like that," I said, making a face. Turning my gaze westward, I could see the ocean in the distance, sparkling in the midday sun. My skin itched.

"If you find anything, will you let me know?" John asked as he set me on the road again.

"Sure," I nodded. "Thanks for the tour." He returned my nod and took off toward his house. As soon as he was out of sight, I misted away, flying straight toward the section of beach where the teenage couple disappeared.

The police had the area blocked off for half a mile in every direction, and there were search boats in the water. I wandered through the crime scene as mist; no way could I have gotten in otherwise without using compulsion. I would have had to use it many times, too; police were everywhere and the FBI was present and involved.

I knew one of them was a werewolf as I misted past him. Hovering around the vehicle the teen couple was snatched from, I detected the slightest bit of stench about it. I wondered if the werewolf had noticed the scent. John had smelled it around his fence, and if a human could smell it, the werewolf had to have it too.

The werewolf was now leaving the scene, striding away and climbing into a vehicle farther down the beach. I was taking a big chance, but there was always compulsion, wasn't there?

Following him swiftly, I materialized in the seat beside him, causing him to jump as he prepared to drive away. "The same stench is on a fence where cattle disappeared two days ago," I said, right off.

The werewolf was so shocked he didn't think about going through the change. "Where the fuck did you come from?" he hissed at me instead. That hiss would have done any vampire proud.

"I was mist," I said. "But that's not important right now. There's a predator out there, and we need to find it. Don't you find it interesting that at first single individuals were disappearing, and now they're disappearing by twos?"

"What the hell are you?" The werewolf demanded. He had red in his dark-brown hair, which curled crisply around his collar. His light-brown eyes and finely shaped mouth frowned at me—he was still trying to determine what I was. I'd guess he was a russet colored wolf when he changed.

"Somebody who knows what you are and that you undoubtedly scented the stench around the vehicle. Do they still have the paranormal division of the FBI, or are you completely undercover?" I asked.

"They still have it and how the hell do you know about that?" I had his curiosity raised, I could tell.

"I knew the guy who started it," I shrugged.

"That was a while back," he huffed and then turned to face me, shock in his eyes. "Tell me what you are," he demanded.

"Something you may never see again," I said. "I'm a Vampire Queen. What does that tell you?"

"I heard that was next to impossible," he turned away from me and stared out the tinted window of his vehicle. "I can't get a scent off you. Why is that?"

"No idea, but ever since I came back from the dead, some people seem to have a problem with that."

"Why do you think two are disappearing now, instead of one?" He was back to a previous question, and I could see he was worried about the increase in victims, just as I was.

"I think that whatever is preying on these people—and cattle—is getting hungrier, somehow." The werewolf growled softly as he jerked his head in a quick nod at my words. He suspected, as did I that all these people were dead— that they'd been consumed in some way.

"It's not a vampire," he muttered, staring through the windshield at the ocean beyond.

"Yeah. I get that too," I said.

"Did the Council send you? I didn't hear anything from our vamp agents."

"The Council sort of sent me—they asked for my help," I replied. "I'm different from other vamps; that's why we're having this conversation in daylight."

"I already figured that out," he said, sarcasm coming through in his voice. I deserved that, so I didn't say anything. "So, what now?" he asked when I remained silent. Light-brown eyes assessed me, determining whether I might be a help or hindrance to him.

"After lunch and a nap since I was up late last night, I may travel up the coast and see what else I can find."

"Take this," he handed a card to me. "Call me if you find anything, all right?"

"Are you going to report me to anybody?" I asked, flipping the thin, plastic card in my fingers. It held a name and phone number only.

"Not yet. Don't give me any reason."

"Oh, don't you worry about that," I said and misted away.

The restaurant near the water had great clam chowder. The bowl was almost empty when I pulled the werewolf's card from my pocket. Joshua Billings was his name, and he was listed as a special agent for the FBI.

I tucked the card into my jacket pocket again and paid for my meal. The temperature outside was in the low sixties with heavy cloud cover coming in over the course of the afternoon, whereas the morning had been bright and sunny.

After misting from the ladies' restroom to the safe house, I turned on the latest version of what passed for television and watched a national news program until I fell asleep on the sofa.

Gavin stood over the little Queen, thinking it would only take a quick swipe with his claws and she'd be ash. He breathed a frustrated sigh and moved into the kitchen, pulling a bottle of blood substitute from the pantry. He twisted the cap off and drank, waiting for Anthony to finish showering.

The sound of a bottle cap hitting the bottom of a wastebasket woke me from a deeper sleep than I'd intended. "Geez, what time is it?" I mumbled, rubbing my eyes as I sat up on the sofa. I hadn't made my trip up the coast as planned—I'd slept the afternoon away instead.

"After eight," Gavin growled. His temper hadn't improved any with his sleep.

"The cattle disappearances are connected to the people disappearances, Gavin," I said. "And two more are gone; two teenagers as of this morning. They were taken in daylight, so if it's a vampire, it's not any vampire I ever imagined; the stench is unbelievable."

"Hey, Lissa," Tony came out of the bathroom freshly showered and smelling nice. He didn't quite come up to Gavin, but he still smelled good.

"Tony," I nodded to him.

"What's on the agenda for tonight?" Tony asked, getting a bottle of something from the pantry and unscrewing the top.

"What is that stuff?" I asked.

"Blood substitute," Tony said, holding the bottle out to me. I got up and went to sniff it. I can't say I liked the scent, but if it fed them, then I didn't have a problem with that.

"How does it taste?" I asked.

"Not so good, but it's food," Tony said. I nodded my understanding.

"Hurry up, Anthony, I wish to question relatives of the missing," Gavin grumbled. I didn't think that was going to help us out in the least, but I didn't say anything.

We went to see the two women who'd lost their husband and son. "They just went surfing," one of the woman wept as Gavin questioned her. "They left right after lunch on Saturday and never came back. They were only supposed to be gone four or five hours." I handed her extra tissues; she wasn't in any shape to be answering questions like this.

"Did the police find anything—clothing or such?" Gavin asked.

"Their wetsuits were still in the car," the woman wiped away more tears. She looked to be in her early forties to me, and stress and loss had made her normally pretty face haggard. I knew that feeling, all right.

"Were the suits wet or dry?" Gavin asked. That was the question I had so we were on the same wavelength about that, anyway.

"Still dry—they never made it into the water." That told me they were taken in daylight. Gavin knew it, too. He thanked the woman for her time and we left quickly. Gavin was on some sort of communicator as soon as we were inside our rental; the communicator looked like a tiny cell phone and Charles was on the other end in seconds.

"Charles, inform the Honored One that this is not the work of a vampire," Gavin said. Charles asked how he knew that. "The last two incidents happened in daylight," Gavin said. Flavio's voice came on, then.

"You may return if you wish," Flavio said.

"I'm not coming back until I get to the bottom of this," I said. Flavio heard.

"Lissa may do as she pleases, we have no control over her," he said.

Nice of him to realize that.

"I will be coming back," Gavin growled, terminating the call.

"You must find your own lodging," Gavin informed me as he and Tony packed to return to London. They could get a pod out that evening, so they were going.

"Be happy to," I snapped. It was one thing to be indifferent, another to be a total dickhead. I went to my bedroom and threw what little I'd unpacked into my bag, including my toiletries in the bathroom.

He can be a bit grumpy, Tony sent.

You don't have to make excuses for him, I returned, slamming my bags in the floor next to the upper floor steps. *I'm well acquainted with Gavin, inside and out.* I lifted my bags and misted the hell out of there. I didn't even bother to say goodbye.

Hotel rooms were plentiful, due to the disappearances. I splurged and booked a luxury suite near the water, with a great view of Morro Rock. I might have wept at Gavin's treatment, but I was out of tears at the moment. I misted to the roof of the hotel instead, draping my arms around my knees as I stared out at the ocean.

Waves slapped against a jetty in the water—the rock structure was placed there to keep the waters calm near the shore. Sailboats and other watercraft were moored there; they bobbed gently upon dark waters that rippled and glinted in the lamplight from the shore.

"I don't know when she'll be back; Lissa said she was staying until she got to the bottom of this," Charles accepted a warm brownie from Devin when he folded into the villa's kitchen. Drake and Drew were questioning Charles over Lissa's disappearance two nights before. Charles realized quickly they weren't happy.

"It might be different, Charles, if we could locate her by *Looking*. We can't. And the Larentii are tighter lipped than clams over this. We know they placed a tracking device." Drake almost growled at his fellow Spawn Hunter. He and Drew were angry and out of sorts after Lissa's abrupt departure; neither she nor Charles had informed anyone that she'd left the villa.

"They did place a tracking device, but Ren says that's only for emergencies, and Lissa doesn't know. This isn't an emergency. Is there any milk?" Charles asked. Brownies were best with a tall glass of cold milk. Devin poured a glass of milk and handed it to Charles.

"Charles, are you trying to stand in our way?" Drew snapped. "We want her, and you take her away at the first opportunity."

Charles's hand stopped halfway to his mouth, the brownie poised in midair. Slowly he lowered it to the plate. "Is that what you think? Damn. No, that wasn't my intention," Charles admitted. "I knew Lissa was upset over Gavin, and I was just trying to get him to loosen up toward her. You don't know how much he loved her before. Now he's like an iceberg. Of course it didn't help any that this investigation turned out like it did—I don't think I've ever seen a time when I hoped so hard that the perpetrators were vampires instead of something else."

"Where is she? Tell us." Drake crossed well-muscled arms over his chest and glared at Charles. "You said Gavin and Tony were coming back without her."

"Morro Bay," Charles went back to his brownie. "Don't go tonight, she'll be upset."

"This is quite amusing." Prince Cridel of the Bright Elemaiya held the gate with his Dark counterpart, Martis. The Ra'Ak had merely asked them to hold gates open on select worlds so the transports might be accomplished with none the wiser.

Cridel hadn't seen what was coming through; none of them had. As long as it caused problems and ultimately brought the Ka'Mirai to them, he had no difficulty with it. The Ra'Ak materialized at the edge of the gate after making his brief delivery. The Ra'Ak was in humanoid form; otherwise, Cridel might have worried. Friesianna instructed him to flee through the gate if he saw the Ra'Ak in any other guise. Even she knew not to trust them, although she'd been more than willing to make the alliance with them and their Dark Elemaiya cousins.

~

I was staring listlessly at my breakfast at the hotel restaurant the next morning when a jacket was tossed onto the booth seat opposite mine. I raised my eyes to see that Joshua, the Werewolf FBI agent, had found me.

"If you'd bothered to tell me where you were staying, I could have gotten here sooner," he said, sliding into the red leatherette booth. It was retro—1950s retro. The tabletop was plastic, made to look like a black and white checkered cloth.

"I only moved here last night," I said, dipping into my scrambled eggs, which were now cold.

"I went to the ranch yesterday afternoon," Joshua said. "Talked to the owner who said he'd talked to you. He took me to the same spot. Thanks for leaving the evidence there; I collected it and we've got people working on it now."

"I didn't want to disturb it in case you guys did think to look into it," I muttered. My toast was the only salvageable thing on my plate now; the rest was too cold and tasteless.

The waitress came to take Joshua's order—ham and eggs, with extra ham. Werewolves were the same, no matter where or when you were. They could still eat more than two normal people. Joshua snacked on my cold bacon while he waited for his food. I pushed my plate toward him and he ate the cold hash browns, too.

I drank my coffee; the waitress had given me a fresh cup that was nice and hot. Joshua didn't even comment on the fact that I was eating toast and drinking coffee. His food came and he ate quickly and efficiently. "How long in your job?" I asked. I knew he was seventy or so.

160

"Thirty years," he stopped eating for a moment and grinned.

"Who is Grand Master, now?" I asked softly.

"Jason Harper," he said.

"Is he related to Weldon and Daryl Harper?"

"Daryl Harper's great-great-great-grandson. I guess that makes him Weldon Harper's great-great-great-great-grandson. I was born long after Daryl's stint as Grand Master. His son, Daryl Harper Jr. was taken down pretty quick and there was another two not so good ones in between, but Jason came along about twenty years ago and took care of that problem."

"I knew Weldon and Daryl. Daryl's wife was pregnant with Daryl Jr. when I saw him last." I wondered how werewolf history had been affected when I'd been removed from the records of that era.

"Want to come to the newest site when I finish breakfast?" Joshua asked.

"Sure, if you don't mind," I said.

"It's the least I can do since you led me to the only evidence we've been able to collect so far," he said. "And you can call me Josh, when nobody's looking. Otherwise it's Agent Billings."

"Sure thing, Agent Billings."

"What can I call you? That was a hint, you know."

"Lissa," I said. "Just Lissa."

"I can track you through your registration at the hotel."

"Then do it," I shrugged.

"You don't seem worried that I can find out all about you," he sipped his coffee.

"Agent Billings, if you threatened me at all, I'd let you know," I muttered.

"You're that confident?" He watched me over the top of his coffee cup.

"No. It's just that I've been dead before. Should still be dead, actually. I don't think you could do any worse to me than what has already been done. How's that for an answer?"

We walked out of the restaurant later and I climbed into Agent Billings' vehicle, flying north with him toward San Luis Obispo. There was another army of police and FBI agents covering an empty stretch of beach when we set down.

"Who's this?" An agent walked up to Josh and me as we made our way toward the biggest knot of investigators on the beach.

"Special consultant," Josh sounded snarly. The other agent backed off. We continued toward the site as the other agents moved aside to let us through. The only things left at this site were a large beach blanket, a cooler, suntan lotion and a few toys. *Fuck.*

"Their vehicle is located on the parking area off the road," someone told Josh as I stood, staring in horror at the toys scattered across the blanket. "It's registered to a Michael Thomas. Married. Wife and six-year-old daughter." I wanted to kneel on the sand and scream.

There was no scent around this area; Josh and I both checked unobtrusively. There hadn't been any contact between what had swept this family away and any of the objects left behind.

"We got something!" Someone shouted just north of us. Josh grabbed my arm and hauled me in that direction. Something turned out to be a small blanket that looked as if it had been carried for years—the kind a child might refuse to turn loose of at night, though it was full of holes and should have been tossed long ago. It also held the stench; the one Josh and I both recognized yards before we reached the scene.

"Going north," I muttered to Josh, who nodded slightly at my side. Someone was saying the blanket looked as if it had been dropped from the sky. There were no footprints, paw prints, claw prints, hoof prints—nothing anywhere around. No beach grasses or plants had been disturbed; the blanket had just magically appeared there. I drew in a huge breath.

"What is it?" Josh demanded, pulling me over to the side so he could talk without being overheard.

"Nobody ever sees anything, do they?" I asked urgently.

"No. Nobody has seen anything. It's like one minute they're there, the next they're not."

"What will people think if you leave for a while?" I asked.

"I'll just say I'm following a lead; they've got more than enough here," he muttered and walked away. I watched him as he talked to somebody who looked to be in charge while the winds off the ocean whipped hair into our faces.

The man Josh spoke with looked grim, but he'd looked grim before Josh approached him. The man nodded and Josh walked back to me. "We can go," he said. We made our way over loose, warm sand toward Josh's vehicle.

"Just get us out of sight; somewhere we can leave this thing behind," I said, meaning the hovercar. Josh nodded, started the thing up and off we went. We traveled two miles north of the crime scene before Josh parked at a lookout over a particularly pretty stretch of beach. There were people below us, either lying in the sun or playing in the water. I sighed.

"Are you afraid of heights?" I asked.

"Not particularly," Josh said.

"Well, Agent Joshua Billings," I said, patting his shoulder, "prepare to be airborne." I turned both of us to mist and followed the coastline, paying special attention to the higher cliff areas. Twenty miles north of the last crime scene, I caught the briefest whiff of stench and zoned in on that.

Have you ever gone looking for something, thinking it might be one thing, and when you find it, discover that it is so much worse than you'd imagined? I remember once when Don and I had a couple of cats, we'd installed a pet door so they could come and go as they pleased.

One day when I was cleaning, I caught a whiff of what might have been a mouse decomposing. Thinking the cats had brought one in and left it in the house; I started moving furniture until I found what I was looking for.

It wasn't a mouse. It was a snake. Dead, thankfully, but a snake, and a poisonous one on top of that. What Josh and I found was something out of nightmares.

A huge nest was situated atop a rocky cliff, built of tree limbs, grasses and anything else available. Some of those tree limbs were thicker than my arm. What lived in that huge nest, though, was the frightening thing. They looked like evil pterodactyls.

There were two of them inside the nest and each was larger than an ultralight aircraft. I could feel Josh's impatience as we misted over the nest. It had to be twenty feet in diameter and the two creatures inside were the source of the stench, along with the regurgitated bones littering the nest itself.

The nestlings were curled up and sleeping after a nice meal of a man, a woman and their six-year-old daughter.

I misted Josh downwind and dropped him on the ground, materializing right beside him. He was cursing softly and hauling out his communicator.

"Not yet," I put a hand over his. "Those are the babies. The parents are still out there somewhere and we don't need to blow this." Under other circumstances, I would never have called them, but I needed help and knowledgeable help on top of that. *Griffin—Pheligar, can you hear me?* I sent, praying that they could.

I hear you, baby, Griffin came in loud and clear. Pheligar's assent was right behind Griffin's.

We have some terrible creatures, here, and they're eating people, I sent. *Please come and look before I try to kill them.*

Griffin and Pheligar were beside me in seconds, frightening Josh half to death. He was used to the extraordinary, but he wasn't prepared for an eight and a half foot blue Larentii who fed on sunlight.

Pheligar was the one who transported us nearer the nest—he shielded us, somehow. "Flakkar," Griffin muttered.

"Yes," Pheligar nodded slightly at Griffin's assessment.

"Flakkar?" Josh was still quaking from Griffin and Pheligar's sudden appearance, but he kept his wits about him enough to ask good questions.

"Giant, flesh-eating, flying reptiles. They bend light around themselves, effectively hiding from any observer," Griffin muttered. "And they have a heavy shield that defies most tracking methods and mutes sounds. The only warning you have is their stench. They are next to impossible to locate."

"I am concerned over how they arrived. Flakkar do not have the ability to transport themselves across the universe," Pheligar observed, frowning at the sleeping young inside the nest.

"Somebody imported those things?" Josh was about to hyperventilate.

"That's exactly what happened," Griffin looked grim. He sent out mindspeech, I guess, because Pheligar's shielded space became crowded quickly. Dragon and Crane arrived, with Adam, Kiarra and Kyler.

"Why don't you let me take care of this?" Kyler stared at the Flakkar.

"Because you will release their particles," Griffin held Kyler off. "Agent Billings here would like bodies and evidence to show to his colleagues." Josh nodded rapidly at Griffin's assessment.

"I'll do it," I said. "We just have to wait for Mom and Pop to get here."

"Get them right behind the head, their necks are thinnest at that point," Dragon was at my side and offering instructions. I didn't think the little ones were going to be a problem; it was the bigger ones that concerned me. I nodded up at Dragon. He grinned and hugged me. "My sons are worried," he leaned down to whisper in my ear.

"Uh-huh," I whispered right back. "About what?"

"That you might not come home," he said, hugging me and kissing the top of my head. Dragon was saying home as if I belonged there or something.

Mom and Pop Flakkar came home right about then, letting their light-bending shields down. They clutched a large cow in each gigantic claw. I'd seen the vibration of the air around them when they first came in, besides smelling the additional stench. *I'm going*, I sent to the others and misted outside Pheligar's shield.

Papa Flakkar was the first to go, but maybe I should have gotten mama first. She was shrieking and flapping, causing quite a stir. And the babies? They weren't nice either. It was going to be a trick, getting close enough to take heads; the whole nest was boiling with Flakkar.

I was fine, getting a good shot at one of the young, but the minute I got one of her kids, mama kicked into a higher gear, thrashing, snapping and clawing like a three-dimensional buzz saw.

When I saw my chance at her, I took it, but as my hands and claws materialized to sever her spine, her remaining child got in a blow of his own. I was shrieking in pain after mama's head was separated from her body, and that's when somebody else stepped in.

Baby Flakkar's body disintegrated into tiny sparks that winked out as they floated away. I was standing in the middle of the nest, hugging my arm to me; it was bleeding all over the place. My flesh had been sliced to the bone.

"We'll take care of this," Karzac was beside me, as was Pheligar, Renegar, another Larentii I didn't recognize and at least three healers. It didn't matter; I fainted in less than two seconds.

CHAPTER 11

"Did you see this?" Flavio handed the microcomputer to Gavin and Tony. The screen displayed the image of an FBI agent, standing beside three large corpses.

"They look like dinosaurs," Tony muttered in disbelief. "Flying dinosaurs."

"The forensic specialists are not releasing particulars," Flavio said. "However, the Larentii say these were brought here from another world. If these hadn't been found, they would have continued to feed off the population. The nest was shielded in some way unless you came very close to it; I'm not sure how that was accomplished. Lissa stayed behind and killed those things, although the authorities are taking credit for eliminating them."

"I still don't remember her," Tony said, sorting through the photographs and text on the small computer.

"None of us remember," Flavio shook his head. "Although Wlodek's memories of her are very clear, now. He wasn't surprised in the least that she was able to do what she did."

Gavin didn't comment; he wanted to leave.

"We can feed you soup," Drake was sitting beside my bed and grinning at me when I woke. I slapped a hand over my face.

"Please don't feed me anything," I muttered through my fingers.

"Tummy upset?" A hand started rubbing my abdomen from the other side, and I found Drew lounging on the bed beside me when I turned my head.

"Who said you could get in my bed?" I asked. Drew gave me a lazy, heart-squeezing smile.

"We did," both said at the same time. Drew hadn't stopped rubbing my belly, either, and just like the lazy lizard I was, I enjoyed it. Those guys weren't hard to look at. Uh-uh. Not hard at all. "I feel like a cougar," I said, closing my eyes in pleasure.

"You're not. Dad says you're officially forty-nine years, eleven months and eight days old. We're a hundred and one. Way older than you, itty bitty pants." Drake was now scooting in on my other side.

"Itty bitty pants?" I frowned at him as he settled on the bed beside me. "Who taught you English?"

"We had a tutor," Drake leaned in to kiss me. "And then we went to college," he kissed me again. "Want to see our resumes and statements of net worth? Grampa Adam takes care of our investments."

"I tell you to sit with her and I come back to find you in her bed?" Karzac came in and swatted Drake on the leg, just when I was beginning to think I might have to throw one of those boys on his back and see how his belt unbuckled.

"Damn," Drake grumped softly, sliding off the bed. Drew came off on the other side.

"Let's see the arm," Karzac said, asking for my right arm. It had been deeply sliced by the Flakkar.

"It looks okay," I said, showing him my scar. There was only the faintest of white lines there, and that was fading fast.

"Baby, don't come back to us like that again," Drake scolded from the foot of the bed. Drew nodded and agreed with his brother. "Karzac gave you three bags of blood this time."

"How long have I been out?" I was trying to sit up. Karzac pushed me down again.

"The best thing about your vampirism is that any blood will do to replenish what you have," he said, ignoring my question.

"You've been down a day and a half," Drew said.

"You didn't wake me?" I knew I felt sluggish, but a day and a half?

"You missed the family dinner at Grey House," Karzac grumbled. "I have informed Wizard Shadow of your condition. He has been upset and irritable ever since, according to my sources."

"That's not awkward or anything," I mumbled. "Have they found out how the big, bad and stinky things got onto the planet?"

"Not yet. Everyone is looking into it, however."

"Maybe they should check other worlds, too, and see if the same thing is happening elsewhere," I suggested.

"I will send mindspeech," Karzac said, folding out of the room.

"Good," Drake smiled. "Now, where were we?" He and Drew climbed right back in bed with me.

When I woke the second time, it was to find a chest bearing a black dragon in front of my face. They'd taken their shirts off while I slept. Now there was a very nice nipple located in a strategic spot within the tattoo. I touched it lightly.

"I'll pay major money if you'll put your mouth on that," Drake said lazily.

"I'll bet you say that to all the girls," I removed my fingers from his chest and rose to a sitting position.

Drew was lying on his stomach on the other side, his long braid in a curve down his back. "How do you guys deal with all this hair?" I lifted Drew's braid and fingered the thickness—it was like black silk.

"I'll give you thirty minutes to stop playing with my hair," Drew turned his face to me and grinned.

"Schmuck," I dropped his braid and considered what might be the best way to get out of bed. Crawling over one Falchani or the other just seemed undignified. In the end, I misted out of bed.

"Need any help?" Drake called as I materialized and walked into the bathroom to clean up.

"You need to stay where you are," I stuck my head through the door and pointed a finger at him.

Kyler and Cleo were waiting for me when I walked out of the bathroom later. "You don't look Falchani," I smiled at my nieces.

"We had to chase them away," Kyler grinned. "How are you feeling?"

"Better, I guess," I said. "My arm isn't split open." I lifted it to show them.

"Shadow almost had a heart attack when he heard, and he hasn't stopped cursing since," Cleo snickered. "He's got it bad. Raffian and Glendes threatened to send him to work with the beginning students after he ruined three spelled jewels. This morning."

"He ruined seven yesterday," Kyler agreed with Cleo, her gold eyes sparkling with mischief.

"I don't know what to do about that," I said, shoving hair behind an ear. I didn't. I had two Falchani who wanted me in the worst way, and now, a Grey House Wizard couldn't function because he heard I'd been injured.

"That's, uh, why we're here," Kyler admitted, refusing to look at me. I saw the dimple in her cheek, though. She was up to something. I knew it, and I hadn't known her very long. It made me want to ask about her mother—my (now deceased) sister.

"We're going to take you to Grey House. Maybe Shadow will calm down when he sees you." An identical dimple showed in Cleo's cheek.

"Uh-huh," I said. At least my sarcasm was alive and well. The rest of me might be walking wounded, but my cynical side was just fine, thanks. I should have kept my mouth shut. My nieces had me whisked away as soon as the unintended assent came out of my mouth.

"I have us shielded," Kyler whispered in my ear. She and Cleo flanked me as I stared at Shadow Grey. We were in a dimly lit workshop and metal, jewelry, raw jewels and jewelry-making tools were scattered across a workbench.

I imagined the workbench might be much neater under normal circumstances—I couldn't imagine a Master Wizard accomplishing anything while surrounded by such clutter.

Shadow held his hands around a floating, diamond cut jewel, and intense light filled the space between his hands. I guess that's why he wore what looked to be welder's goggles. The light intensified and I winced—it was too bright for me to look at it.

Here it comes, Cleo sent mindspeech. Light blasted away from the jewel, the jewel exploded, Shadow flung his goggles away and cursed so fluently and vividly my ears turned pink.

"Ahem." Kyler's single word made Shadow stop in mid-rant, and when he saw I was there with Kyler and Cleo, he walked straight to me, lifted my face in his hands and kissed me. And then kept on kissing me, while Kyler and Cleo deserted us.

"Don't ever," smack, "let me hear," smack, "you're wounded like that," smack, "again." Shadow muttered between kisses.

"That was an unplanned wounding," I tried to step away. Tried. Shadow came right along with me. His gray eyes narrowed as his lips met mine again. Eventually, we were backed against a wall in his workshop, and the only choices I had were to mist away or stay and try to calm Shadow down.

"Shadow, we don't know each other," I held a hand over his mouth (he was preparing for another round of kissing). And while his kisses were getting hotter (I can't begin to describe it—and the tongue part was about to drive me wild) I didn't know him, just as I'd said.

"Fuck." Shadow stepped away and raked a hand through thick, nearly black hair. "I'm sorry. It's just, when Cleo came and said you'd gotten hurt and couldn't come to the dinner, all I could think was you were dying and Dad and Grampa wouldn't let me go to you. I sent mindspeech to Drake and Drew. They sent a few images back, but all I saw was blood." Shadow paced before me. "They said you were fine, but I couldn't fucking be there."

"See, I'm really fine," I held up my arm. "It was just a slice here, that's all." I pointed to the fading white line. "Karzac's really good with this, and Pheligar helped."

"Look, I know you don't feel this as intensely as I do. When a M'Fiyah hits a Grey House Wizard, it's a little consuming. I'm sorry."

Shadow shook his head. He was a handsome man, even with worry lines and his mouth set in a frown.

"How many jewels have you ruined, Shadow?" I asked, watching his face.

"Fourteen, now," he admitted, rubbing the back of his neck and offering an ashamed grin. "Fifty million credits' worth."

"Oh, lord."

"Don't worry," he held out a hand. "It's the spells that are worth so much. The jewels are manufactured, and are relatively inexpensive. It's my power and the complexity of the spells that command such high prices."

"What are you working on?"

"Crown jewels," he said. "For the new King of Parthin."

That's how I spent my day (with a short break for lunch) watching Shadow Grey spell fourteen jewels and place them in a gold and platinum crown. He explained while he worked that he'd gone to school on several worlds, earning three engineering degrees before coming back to Grey House and working spells for a living.

He also explained that the fifty million price tag only covered the jewels he was making—the crown was extra. "It'll kill anybody who attacks the King of Parthin," Shadow sighed as he placed the last jewel in the crown with Power. He was exhausted, I could tell, but he'd made a deadline he might not have made otherwise.

"If you hadn't come," Shadow rubbed my shoulders gently as we walked out of his workshop. "I'll send somebody in to clean up," he added, closing the door behind him.

"You're the one who needs the shoulder rub," I pointed out. "You ought to get that taken care of and go to bed."

"I don't suppose you'd come with me?" His gray eyes held a bit of hope.

"Shadow, I'm trying to come to grips with all this. Can we give it some time?"

"If you promise not to consider removing the M'Fiyah," he muttered, pulling me into an embrace.

"I won't." I knew, first hand, just what that could do to somebody.

Merrill's actions had cost me, and I didn't want anybody else to suffer as I had.

"Good. Please say you'll come back. It was easy to get the work done when you were with me."

"I'll see what I can do." I leaned away from him. He used that as an excuse to kiss me.

"What are your plans for tomorrow?" Shadow asked when he pulled away. I watched his mouth—a lazy grin formed there.

"I'm going to move a boulder," I said.

"Twenty-seven worlds are being attacked by Flakkar," Pheligar gave the information to Griffin, Kiarra, Adam and Merrill. "One world is already devastated; fifty nesting pairs are there and the population is unprepared to handle the onslaught. They do not have the necessary weapons. Thirty pairs were found on another world, where a similar situation is developing. We are at a loss to explain this. When we *Look*, it is as if the reasons slide away from us and we fail to grasp them. We cannot find the Flakkar themselves by *Looking*; their shielding prevents it. We had to *Look* for the killings and then go find the creatures physically. Before, we would have said the Flakkar numbers were small. This defies logic."

"Crap," Kiarra muttered. "What can we do? Somebody has to be putting those things out there, but we aren't getting any hits on the Ra'Ak folding space to those worlds." The Saa Thalarr weren't allowed to interfere unless the Ra'Ak were involved in some way.

"Who has weapons to fight these things?" Adam asked.

"There are only a few worlds that have proper weapons," Pheligar replied. "The Reth Alliance has Ranos technology which will kill the creatures, but they aren't willing to cooperate in defense of non-Alliance worlds. The Flakkar can scent most poisons so that is also not an option."

Griffin was listening to all of them discuss the situation. He wasn't about to interfere this time. Not at all.

I dreamed that night, and I hadn't had one of those dreams since I'd come back from the dead. I was seeing gates. Many gates. On so many worlds and in so many places on those worlds.

Some had several gates. I don't know how I knew that, I just did. I knew I had the power to travel through all of them, and I could have described every one of those gates in detail if I had to. A voice whispered to me about Power. And desperation. And retribution. I jerked awake to find morning light streaming through my window.

I was having an omelette with orange juice later at the kitchen island. Mike and Jamie were off since it was Sunday. Dragon, Crane, Drake and Drew wandered in; they'd been sparring. Drake and Drew had obviously gotten a drubbing from Dragon and Crane, and both looked so pitiful I got up and cooked breakfast for all of them.

"These biscuits are wonderful," Crane was helping himself to another. They'd gotten scrambled eggs, ham, biscuits and gravy. There was plenty of jam and jelly to go with the biscuits, too; I'd made a large pan to feed everybody.

"Why didn't you send mindspeech that food was ready?" Radomir, whom I hadn't seen for days, wandered in, offering a beautiful smile. Mack and Justin came in a few minutes later, followed by Grace and Devin, all of them yawning. Mack slapped Crane on the back. Crane grinned and kept eating. I ended up making more biscuits, wondering while I worked just how things got coordinated with so many mates.

"We have schedules," Mack grinned after reading my mind—he was having another biscuit. Karzac had been up early and out somewhere; he folded in and sat down. I put a plate of food in front of him. He thanked me quietly and started eating.

"I haven't gotten breakfast on Sunday that I didn't have to fix in a long time," Grace heaved a happy sigh. She and Devin, being vegetarian, got scrambled eggs and biscuits with jam.

"So, you have a bulletin board somewhere that just announces who's with whom and when?" I asked, sitting beside Drew to have a biscuit with strawberry jelly and a glass of milk. A published schedule sounded embarrassing; I just didn't say that out loud. Drew rubbed my back gently—he was picking up my thoughts.

"Something like that," Mack laughed. He looked so much like his father.

"What are you doing today?" Drew whispered.

"I have some things to take care of today," I said.

"What about tonight?" he asked. "Come to dinner with Drake and me."

"Okay," I said. "Casual or dressy?"

"Casual," he said. I nodded. "Around eight?"

"I can do that," I said. I left them all at the island, eating and talking while I went back to my bedroom to find my sturdiest jeans, a pullover shirt and athletic shoes.

I knew where the gate was on Merrill's property and I was going there as quickly as I could. Since I didn't want anyone to see me, I misted to the gate straight from my bedroom and focused on the first gate I'd seen in my dream the night before. I had no idea what I would find.

There was no mistaking the stench. This world was under attack by Flakkar, too. At least fifty nesting pairs—most with young, and all of them not far from the gate. If I couldn't take their heads, I misted inside them and caused them to explode. Nearly two hundred died that day, all in the space of two hours or so. I went straight home and napped when I finished.

"That looks nice," Drake complimented my outfit. I'd met up with the twins in the kitchen, dressed in a sleeveless white V-neck top with jeans and low-heeled sandals. Platinum jewelry went nicely with the outfit.

"Where are we going?" I asked.

"You'll find out," Drew grinned. We folded away. It was a pizza place in New York, and with the time difference, it was three in the afternoon there.

"Oh my gosh," I said, after biting into a pizza with everything. It was so good. We finished off the whole, huge pizza. We then folded to Port Aransas; Adam had a beach house there.

"This is where Adam and Kiarra met when Saxom was killed," Drew said when I told him I'd been there long ago. I discovered I was there working for Winkler a scant two years after all that had happened.

We took off our shoes, rolled up pants legs and went wading in the waters of the gulf in front of the massive beach house. Winkler might have been jealous of that beach house, it was so big.

I was splashed with water and I chased after the twins. Drake gave me a piggyback ride while he waded along and we found sand dollars and scallop shells. We sat on the sand after a while, content to watch the water lapping the shore.

The occasional tourist passed by, but we might as well have been there on the beach alone. Drew was lying on a beach towel next to me, smiling when I touched his cheek. His fingers buried themselves in my hair when I leaned down to kiss him.

We went to a bar in Austin after that to listen to jazz and have a few drinks. Yeah, I was a little drunk afterward and somehow let those guys talk me into getting into the hot tub with them when we got home, sans clothing. They undressed me and that wasn't erotic or anything.

"No touching," Drake laughed when he made his clothing disappear. "Karzac says you're still recovering, so no sex for another day." I wanted to find Karzac right then and have a few words with him.

Drake and Drew both would have put just about anyone to shame, and they didn't try to hide their arousal. Yeah, I couldn't look away. It's a good thing they got in the water quickly. I was yawning before long and one of them, I'm not sure which one, lifted me out of the water, folded me to my bedroom, wrapped me in a towel while his brother helped and both of them got me into bed afterward.

~

"Jaydevik, why am I hearing now that there may be Croth and Drith on the Southern Continent and that you may have known about this already?" Glinda poked a finger in Jayd's chest.

"Glindarok, we did not wish to trouble you with this," Jayd said, trying to pull her against him.

"Has anyone been farther south than Baetrah an Hafei to investigate this?" Glinda moved away.

"Not farther south. The area was completely covered in ash and impossible to get the wagons through to check. We found Kifirin there and he disappeared with Niff—I mean Lissa, shortly afterward. The reconnaissance party came home after that."

"Jayd, someone needs to go and soon. I do not trust any Croth or Drith left alive."

"I will send someone," Jayd sighed, successfully pulling her against him this time. He didn't tell her that he'd allowed Garde to wait until after the fall rains were over on the Southern Continent. Rumors were growing, however, and Jayd knew he should have sent a scouting party already.

The second gate from my dream was the objective when I woke Monday morning. I discovered it was Monday, May tenth. As Earth measured time, anyway. I misted away right after eating a quick breakfast.

Mike and Jamie were off on Sundays and Mondays, so I cooked for myself. I figured the twins were out sparring with Dragon and Crane.

The second gate I went through landed me in the middle of a jungle. The animals were all missing when I arrived and it wasn't hard to determine why. More stench. Thirty pairs of Flakkar this time, but they were scattered.

I found deserted villages for hundreds of miles in all directions while I hunted. The predators were becoming prey as I tracked them and their scent. Just for fun, I attempted the Saa Thalarr trick of *Looking*.

No, I hadn't tried it before. I assumed it wasn't possible. What can I say? I was going to have to be more adventurous. I found a few more nests that way; the knowledge just settled into my mind as if it belonged there. Breathing a happy sigh, I went after those Flakkar, ridding the planet of them.

It wouldn't have taken these very long to destroy all life on the planet; they'd already accounted for nearly a third of it. What did those creatures imagine they were going to live on, if no more prey was available to devour?

It made me wonder where they came from, and in such great numbers, too. Did they have natural enemies? What about their homeworld—how had it survived with their predations? I had many questions—all of which I might have to *Look* to find answers.

I gated to the world I'd gone to the day before just so I could double check with my newfound ability, making sure there weren't any other Flakkar to kill. I found one nest and took it out.

"How much longer?" Queen Friesianna demanded of the newly crowned Ra'Ak Prince. "When may we submit our demand for the Ka'Mirai to be given to us?"

"We will give it another week or two to ensure the Flakkar devastation is severe enough," the Ra'Ak Prince smiled.

He had no care for the Elemaiya and what they wanted. He only cared for his own desire, and that involved bringing the High Demons to their knees before destroying them. The Ka'Mirai could help with that. He already held her Dark Elemaiya counterpart, and if he had both, nothing could stop him.

He smiled at his subtlety—the Elemaiya had no idea he planned to ignore the bargain. The Elemaiya would serve him until he had no further use for them, and then they'd be eaten or destroyed.

The creature that saved the High Demon world before was dead. That news was everywhere. There was nothing left to save them a second time, and he'd already made contact with allies remaining on

Kifirin. He looked forward to using them just as his predecessor had, to eliminate others of their kind. Then it would be a simple matter to be rid of them completely.

They would struggle against one another for power and that could kill them all. Prince Narval of the Ra'Ak would become King of the Dark Realm and all would bow to him instead.

"You know the Flakkar cannot be found by *Looking*," King Baltis of the Dark Elemaiya complained. "How will we determine how successful this venture is?"

"By checking the devastation instead," Narval smiled maliciously. "I have already done this only this morning. The first world has lost a quarter of their population already. The second has suffered even more losses." Friesianna and Baltis both *Looked;* they knew which worlds were seeded with Flakkar.

Narval had bent time greatly to gather the nesting pairs from known worlds destroyed by Flakkar. Then, with the help of the Elemaiya, his kind had spread the starving creatures across vulnerable worlds, sending them through gates located on those worlds while the Elemaiya held the gates open.

The creatures were easy enough to capture; starving Flakkar on devastated worlds dropped their shields—they had no strength to maintain them.

"Very nice," Baltis complimented Narval's efforts. Being of the Dark Elemaiya, he reveled in death at times. Friesianna was less comfortable with it, but felt it necessary to accomplish her goals.

"Good," she nodded instead. "The Ka'Mirai should be ours soon. I will draft the demand."

"No, we will draft our demand; we share in this, remember?" Baltis growled at Friesianna, his words causing her to go cold. Baltis had his own designs on the Ka'Mirai. Who knew what he might ask to change with her Power? Friesianna hid her shudder.

∼

"Lissa, we want you to come for dinner," Merrill folded into my bedroom while I was wrapped in a fluffy robe and drying my hair with a towel. A bath had been a necessity after taking out Flakkar earlier.

"No," I snapped, dropping the towel onto a chaise in my sitting area.

"Lissa, are you going to be angry with me forever? I made a terrible mistake. I admit it. I apologize." Piercing blue eyes begged me to accept the offered apology.

"So, an apology is supposed to magically make everything all right?" I glared at Merrill.

"I was hoping to make things up to you, somehow. That you'd consent to give me a chance. Kiarra and Adam both want to thank you for what you did for us on Kifirin—as do I. We'd have died if you hadn't come."

"Merrill, I didn't do it for you." I turned my back on him. I wasn't about to explain the screams of the comesuli, or the dead ones surrounding me when I made the decision to go after the Ra'Ak Prince.

"I know why you did it. That doesn't make the rest of us any less grateful."

"Merrill, we were on a collision course," I sighed, turning toward him and shaking my head. He was still as handsome as ever, and it wrenched my heart. "You're a nice person to most people. Respected and loved. To me, you were the one who agreed to a beating because I tried to save your ass. Also the one who withheld the information that a friend was dying, so I'd keep doing what you wanted me to do. I wanted to love you, Merrill. Truly. Only you sabotaged that at every turn." I shook my head, still confused over the blows life had dealt me.

"And now," I went on, "I know we had a M'Fiyah. You asked Griffin to destroy it. He knew then I was his daughter, and he did it anyway. Both of you have done nothing but cause me pain. How am I supposed to forgive that? How? Why did you agree to teach me in the first place? You could have refused and had me sent off to someone else. Neither you nor Wlodek ever gave me credit for having the sense to come in out of the rain. Explain that to me Merrill. Explain what you want from me now, Merrill." I wanted to cry and beat on Merrill's chest, I felt so hurt and angry.

"I'd allow it," he nodded, reading my mind. "As would Wlodek. I know you don't trust us, Lissa. That you may never trust us. I also know you're not comfortable around us. I hope that bridge can be repaired, someday. We owe you everything, and we haven't repaid our debts very well, have we?" Merrill sighed as he sat on the edge of my bed.

"Merrill, you refused to give the love I needed when I desperately needed it. How do you think that makes me feel?"

"I don't often use the term like shit, but it's appropriate in this case, I believe."

"Got it in one," I said, hugging myself. I still wanted to cry. I just didn't want Merrill to see it.

"I will go to Belen, and ask to have the M'Fiyah reinstated, if that's what you want," Merrill offered.

"Don't bother." I didn't want Merrill's charity, and Belen already said neither he nor any of his kind would consider it.

"Lissa, I know you suffer. I just," Merrill raked a hand through black hair in frustration.

"Merrill, you made a choice. You get to live with that choice. As I have. At least I don't have to answer to the fucking Council anymore," I grumbled.

"Lissa, I've gone over this in my mind for the past few days. I don't look good in any of the scenarios presented." Merrill shook his head. "I made Sarita, did you know that? I couldn't love her either; I held myself away, again because of Kiarra. Perhaps I shouldn't have. Wlodek loved her, and she loved him—as much as she could. She walked into the sun because she couldn't have children and she couldn't have me. Do you think I don't feel guilt over that? Do you? When the second Queen was placed in my care, I managed to fuck that up, too, didn't I?"

"You can't help whom you love. Or don't want to love," I muttered.

"I loved Kiarra for centuries, yet it was Adam, who had no idea who she was, who got to her first. Punishment, I believe, for my past mistakes. He was made Saa Thalarr first too, for those same reasons." Merrill heaved a frustrated sigh.

He was a handsome man—I'd always thought that. He'd only treated me as a child, though. That's what I'd been to him. To hear that he'd callously destroyed what could have been between us, well, that was a pain in my heart and one he could never repair. I didn't want anything from him that he wasn't willing to give. Love was one of those things.

"Now it's too late, for so many things," Merrill said, his voice filled with regret.

"Well, Merrill, I hope you got everything you wanted," I said. He had Kiarra; she was what he wanted. Isn't that the way things happened? Some people got everything, leaving the rest of us to scrabble and scrounge.

"What do you want, Lissa?" Merrill raised his eyes to mine.

"I can't answer that," I said, "because I would be asking for the impossible."

"At least tell me something," Merrill said.

I sighed and rubbed my forehead. "I want to feel safe, even if it's only for a little while," I began. "I want someone to love me. Someone who loves me completely, just as I am," I continued. "I want someone I can trust with my life. Somebody who doesn't think I'm young and stupid, Merrill, or who treats me with contempt because I haven't lived as long as they have. Somebody who isn't going to use me for what I can accomplish for them. Point out that person to me."

"Lissa, I want all those things for you, too." He disappeared, right in front of me.

"Fuck," I mumbled, wiping tears off my cheeks.

I was finally satisfied with the boulder, after misting it a few feet back and forth and turning it on its side more than once. It had stood on a corner of Merrill's property before, but there was a big hole there, now.

Merrill could find another fucking rock to replace it if he wanted. This one was a memorial to René. It covered the spot where I'd held his hand as he breathed his last. Now I settled on the damp ground before it, staring up at it with a sigh. At least a dozen feet high, it was oblong in shape and moss and lichen grew on parts of it.

"What am I supposed to do, René?" I asked the question a second time, wiping tears away. Things were spiraling out of control. I had a husband who didn't remember me. Three others who wanted to be husbands. One who'd refused me, sight unseen, with help from my own father. And that didn't include Kifirin, whom I hadn't seen since I left the High Demon's planet.

Truly, if it hadn't been for the Flakkar attacking worlds, I might have gone looking for a way out. As it was, I was the one who could destroy the monsters, so I was the self-appointed rescue committee.

I don't know how long he'd been sitting beside me; I was so involved with my misery. Nonetheless, he was there—tall, blue-skinned, with dark blond hair. I stared up at him—I didn't know this Larentii.

"I know you," he smiled down at me, and his smile stopped my heart. "My mother is Conner, who is also the Guardian. You have met my father—he is Barrigar, Graegar's Protector. They are both mated to my mother."

"She's so lucky," I sniffled, turning away so he wouldn't see the tears falling.

"Little rose," he turned my face back to him with a large, blue finger. "The bloom is on your cheeks, my pretty one. I thought you would never come to me."

CHAPTER 12

"Other races can be reborn as Larentii, although it seldom happens." Conner set a cup of hot tea before me. Connegar, her very tall Larentii son, sat beside me at the island in Conner's kitchen, a large blue hand on my back to steady me.

Conner's southern accent belied what I'd heard of her before, but then I hadn't seen the Guardian, either. She was beautiful, with long, pale-blonde hair clipped back from her face and blue eyes that studied me with a worried frown.

I'd fainted when Connegar repeated René's final words to me, so he'd taken me immediately to his mother. Together, they'd gotten me conscious again and Conner made tea for me.

"Mother can see who anyone was before, in their former lives. But I, having many of her talents, can also see this," Connegar smiled gently at me. "I held back from coming to you before, as you were upset and confused about the others. They only want your love and attention, and fail to see it is overwhelming you."

"I told Merrill he should have kept his mouth shut," Conner grumbled, sitting next to me with her own cup of tea. I almost smiled —Conner had a soft, southern accent, and it was such a contradiction to the Power clouding about her.

184

"I was born in Atlanta," Conner laughed at my thoughts. "Shane was my best friend and next door neighbor. When I was made Saa Thalarr, I couldn't leave him behind, so he came along as my healer. And then Franklin showed up, and well, you can guess the rest." Conner sipped her tea. I was beginning to like her—very much.

"Connegar and I have been swapping mindspeech ever since you came back from the dead," Conner grinned. "And he named himself after me. Most Larentii do that—name themselves after their mothers. Renegar, well, Kiarra's name was Renée, before she came over. So Ren took that name. The other would have been a nightmare to pronounce if you stuck gar on the end of it." Conner snorted delicately.

I laughed. I couldn't help it. Conner smiled into her cup of tea. Connegar rumbled a laugh beside me.

"Now, why didn't you send mindspeech and tell us you were here?" Franklin, Shane and Tomas folded into the kitchen. Shane, in true, old-style Greg fashion, had his hands on his hips and lifted an eyebrow at me. "Conner Louella Francis, you could have said something."

"Don't you three-name me, Shane Patrick Taylor," Conner shook a finger at Shane. I slapped a hand over my mouth to stop the giggles.

"Look who's here." Russell and Will walked in. "Lissa, it's been a while." Russell leaned in between Conner and me and pecked me on the cheek. Then he gave Conner a huge kiss.

"Lissa's responsible for that print of dogs playing pool in my billiard room," Russell rubbed noses with Conner before pulling away.

"Well, now I know who to blame," Conner swatted at Russell.

"He deserved it—Russell gave a perfectly good Monet to Wlodek because he didn't like it," I said in my defense.

"Is that what happened? Russell William Farleigh, your ass is in trouble now."

"Oh, she's using three names. I'm leaving," Will teased. I was now laughing out loud.

This happens often, Connegar whispered in my mind. *It is quite amusing.*

I like it, I sent back.

I am happy to hear your laugh, little rose.

"Connegar, why don't you take Lissa somewhere while I have a talk with Russell about expensive artwork," Conner smiled. "Lissa, don't let those old vampires bother you. Or, just kick their asses. They'll learn fast enough not to mess with you."

"I'll consider it," I nodded to Conner. She surprised me by giving me a hug, and then Connegar folded me away.

"Where is this?" I stared about us—we stood in a high meadow somewhere, while grazing animals bleated all around us.

"The Larentii homeworld," Connegar sat down in the grass and pulled me onto his lap. "These are Falaca," he nodded toward the animals.

They were wooly creatures, resembling a melding of sheep and llama. They also came in many colors, from black to white to a blue gray. "We make much of our clothing from their wool," Connegar wrapped long blue arms around me, and rested his chin atop my head. "We only use natural fibers, and no dye. We kill nothing in the manufacturing of our garb. It is the way it has always been with the Larentii."

"Really?" I leaned aside to look up at him. His sky-blue eyes were amused at my question.

"Little rose, you have no idea how much I love you. So I must show you. Larentii seldom do this, but in this case it is warranted and deserved." I was about to ask him what was warranted and deserved, when it hit me.

There isn't any way to describe it to someone who's never felt it. Light formed around us and I was drowning in love. That's the closest I can come to a decent description. I not only breathed love in; it soaked into every pore. Then the trilling came. Kyler explained to me later that the trilling is something the Larentii do for their mates. It is the most restful, intrinsically resonant sound in the universe, and soothes the soul. And, just as it was intended to do, it put me right to sleep.

"Come on, lazybones," Drake and Drew were sitting on the side of my bed, trying to wake me. Drake was rubbing the base of my thumb gently with his. "Connegar sent mindspeech last night to tell us you were with him, and to let you sleep late this morning."

"I want to sleep some more," I mumbled, turning over on my side to face the twins. I had to; Drake still had my hand.

"No, little firefly. You have to wake, now. We'll dress you if you're not up to it. You need breakfast. We finished sparring with Dad and Uncle Crane two hours ago."

"Firefly?" I opened one of my eyes to stare skeptically at Drake.

"Karzac's good at handing out nicknames. He's calling you firefly."

"Uh-huh." I slapped my free hand over my face.

"He calls Mom ladybug."

"What's with the insect names?" I flopped over on my back and pulled my hand away to stare at the ceiling. It was slowly coming into focus.

"Karzac says you're the one nobody can see unless you flash your light and power briefly and when you do that, everybody has to sit back and stare in amazement."

"Great. I'm a utility company," I grumped, sitting up.

"What's wrong with our girl?" Drake pulled me against him, stroking fingers against the back of my neck. I let my head droop against his shoulder. "That's right, just relax," he kept stroking my neck, letting his fingers slide through my hair at times. I heaved a shaky sigh.

Two gates were my objective that day—after I had breakfast and convinced the twins I had things to do. They were disappointed, I could tell. I took out forty nesting pairs of Flakkar. Their numbers were getting smaller, but their attacks were just as destructive.

Both worlds were in their industrial infancy and had no

explanation for the disappearances among the population and no way to combat the Flakkar, even if they'd known the monsters were there. I gated back to Earth when I was finished, feeling weary.

Misting inside my bathroom, I managed a quick shower before walking into my bedroom while I toweled off. Drake was there in my bed, waiting for me. "We flipped a coin. I won," he said. He was completely naked, totally unembarrassed about it and was stroking himself as he watched me walk around the room wrapped only in a towel.

"I don't know what to do with you," I said, sounding frustrated. Plus, I was having a difficult time taking my eyes off him. I'd read erotic romance novels that didn't get me this heated up.

"Come here and I'll show you," he purred, amusement lighting his dark eyes. "Come on, baby. I'll take good care of you, I promise."

What was I supposed to do? There was a very handsome man in my bed, offering to take care of me. I ended up at the side of the bed and he reached out, carefully taking my towel away with gentle fingers. Drake coaxed me into bed, put his hands on every inch of me and made me forget my doubts and troubles for a while.

"Anthony, what is taking so long?" Gavin always woke before Tony did, and he was eager to begin the hunt for three reported rogues in Amsterdam.

"Coming," Tony walked out of his bedroom, clean, dressed and ready to go. Both he and Gavin jumped when someone appeared in the tiny, safe house kitchen. Both relaxed when they saw who it was.

"I told you we'd see each other again," the tall male offered a smile.

"You look so much older," Gavin sighed, shaking his head.

"Hazards of the trade." A wry grin was offered. "Can't be helped."

"Why are you here? Is there a problem?" Tony asked with a frown. This one never came unless there was a problem somewhere. Neither he nor Gavin had seen him in more than two centuries.

"I came to give back what was taken from you," their guest replied.

"What?" Tony asked. Gavin's mask fell into place.

"Very important memories," their guest replied. Light formed around him while his eyes went dark as midnight, with stars shining through.

"What do you have, child?" Flavio looked up from his desk computer when Charles walked into his study, carrying a large file box. Flavio was puzzled—they no longer kept records on paper. Everything was electronic.

"I was asked to bring this to you, Father. It's important." Charles vibrated with excitement, and Flavio couldn't fathom the reason.

"Who asked you to bring it?" Flavio searched his only living child's face for answers.

"An old friend. He says this will give back what you lost. You and the Council," Charles grinned. "And when my friend says something like that, you can take it to the bank."

"Charles, no metaphors, please," Flavio stared at the box as Charles plopped it over the computer screen covering the center of his desk. Gone was the antique that Wlodek used so long—Flavio still had it, in his private suite. He used this desk instead, because the computer covered the surface.

"Go on, open it," Charles hid a grin.

"Child, if this is a trick," Flavio lifted the lid and light bloomed from the box.

"What do you mean, they all remembered? Is this some kind of joke? Belen says none of his kind had anything to do with it." Kiarra paced in her library, while Merrill, Adam and Pheligar watched.

"Flavio says Charles found an old box with all her information inside, and the memory triggered. Five minutes later, he received calls from the Council—they all remembered. We have no explanation for it. Flavio contacted Wlodek with mindspeech; Wlodek went to investigate. This box is what he brought from Flavio's office."

Merrill jerked his head toward the box sitting on the low table between sofas. It contained records, photographs and legal documents. "The entire Council wants a meeting with her, now. They all want her back. There's no way she'll consent to that. Lissa informed me plainly that she wasn't willing to answer to anyone, ever again." Merrill's voice held guilt as well as pain.

"I don't blame her," Kiarra snapped. "Merrill, if you'd bothered to tell me you were going to her alone; I would have told you it was a mistake. You should have taken Pheligar or Renegar with you. Preferably both of them, as she doesn't seem to despise the Larentii."

"Connegar is hers." Pheligar hadn't spoken until then.

"You're kidding? Why haven't I heard this before?" Kiarra stared at her Larentii mate.

"How can I get her back?" Gavin paced before Flavio's desk. Flavio watched Gavin's restless wandering before him, attempting to remain dispassionate over the entire thing when he wanted exactly the same —for Lissa to come back to him, the Council and the vampire race as a whole.

She could do so many things; things they didn't have the talent or the resources to do. They still had their misters and mindspeakers, but no new talent had been discovered since Anthony's turning.

Flavio didn't know what to do. He wanted to approach Lissa and beg her to help him and the Council when needed. She was protected however, and Merrill and Wlodek informed him that two Spawn Hunters for the Saa Thalarr, one of the giant Larentii and even a powerful wizard were all courting her. He didn't know how to break that news to Gavin.

"I have removed his jealousy," a dark-haired male appeared suddenly in the room. Gavin recognized him immediately.

"Kifirin," Gavin begged, "help me win Lissa back."

"That choice is hers," Kifirin lifted a gold ingot from Flavio's desk —Flavio once used it as a paperweight. Now it sat on a corner of his desk, mostly forgotten. "Bear in mind," Kifirin set the gold bar down, "that others now hold a place in her heart. You will not be alone there, vampire. The Queen's Inner Circle is forming. You must use your imagination if you wish to be included in their number."

"Inner Circle?" Gavin stopped pacing and stared at Kifirin.

"The governing body upon Le-Ath Veronis. Only the comesuli upon the High Demons' world are now calling it Le-Ath Veronis Imperea, which means Heart of the Vampire Queen. The rumors are flying among them, now, that they were saved by our Lissa. They are asking for the return to their ancient home. They wish to live and work among vampires once again. How would you answer their plea, Gaius Livius Montanus?" Kifirin spoke Gavin's original Roman name.

"What will it mean for Lissa?" Gavin answered Kifirin's question with one of his own.

"It means Lissa must choose whether to accept the throne—and the rule—of Le-Ath Veronis, and then work to bring in vampires from the worlds where they are now scattered. Some will not be eligible for that journey, as they will not be of sufficient character. Those whom she leaves behind will die. It is my promise to her and to the worlds of light where they now reside."

"Are you saying our days on Earth are numbered?" Flavio rose from his seat, staring at Kifirin.

"Do not fear, Sanguis Rex. There will be many cities upon Le-Ath Veronis. I believe Lissa will be more than happy to place you in a position of power. Imagine all the vampires on Earth occupying an entire city; one created solely for them? That is what awaits you if Lissa takes the rule. All hinges upon her, you know."

"Does she know this?" Gavin watched Kifirin, speculation in his eyes.

"Not yet. I will tell her soon if she does not discover it for herself."

"Tell me about this world," Flavio sat down again.

"It spins on its side," Kifirin gestured with his hands. "The southern half of the planet is in constant twilight. Think of what this means, vampire. You will be able to wake and sleep as you choose instead of having to deal with the sun's dictation of those events. Comesuli would provide blood to the vampires—at least in part. I believe their numbers would have to be subsidized with blood substitute; there aren't enough comesuli to cover the demands. Fresh blood would be available often, regardless. The comesuli, when they are turned, become male or female as their temperament dictates. On Le-Ath Veronis of old, the numbers of males and females were nearly equal."

"There would be more females?" Flavio had hope in his eyes. He had mates and the sun's rising and setting no longer held sway over him. This, however, would be a true blessing for the vampire race as a whole.

"Yes, as the comesuli were turned when deserving."

"This sounds too good to be true," Flavio lowered his eyes but not before Kifirin saw the glimmer of hope in them.

"There may be a period of adjustment—so many vampires coming together to live upon a single world instead of many. That is why each world's vampires will have a city to themselves. Earth's population is one of the largest."

Flavio knew they had Wlodek, Weldon and Merrill to thank for that fact, and for their willingness to forge peace with the werewolves when they did. And they had Lissa to thank as well, for keeping the peace when it was threatened.

There was now an official count of two hundred fifteen thousand vampires on Earth. An entire city where they could live appealed greatly to Flavio. With no need to hide, they could walk freely as they willed, no longer needing to conceal what they were. Their race would belong.

"Your race will belong," Kifirin drew the thought from Flavio's mind. "Your Council here could be the governing body in your city and you could help draw up the new laws governing the planet."

"The Queen's Inner Circle?" Gavin asked, forming the question.

"All her devoted lovers," Kifirin answered before Gavin could finish his question. "Find a way to bring her back to you, vampire. You would serve well with her." Kifirin folded away.

"Honored One," Gavin turned to Flavio, "I wish to contact Wlodek as quickly as possible."

~

"How is little Toff?" Glinda rocked Roff's child in her arms and cooed to him. He grinned at her, showing most of his teeth. Comesuli were born with a full set of teeth, which they lost at age eight or thereabouts, growing a new set rapidly. They ate animal protein from birth, hence the need for teeth. Their parent had no way to suckle them, having no breasts.

"Glindarok, Gardevik and I must speak with you," Jayd stalked into the room, looking a bit rumpled. Glinda was worried the moment she saw Jayd's face.

"What is it?" she asked, handing Toff over to Giff—Roff was away, getting their midday meal from the kitchens.

"Come with me; your meal can be delivered in the meeting hall," Jayd said. Glinda knew it was serious if they were calling a meeting in the meeting hall. Jayd lifted Glinda in his arms and walked out of her suite amid protests from his mate that she could get herself to the meeting hall just fine.

Glinda was settled at the table fronting the room, between Jayd and Garde. She breathed a worried sigh; the Captains of the Guard were all present, as were the heads of all the High Demon Houses including what was left of Croth and Drith.

The Croth and Drith who were present had been carefully questioned and vetted before they were allowed to take up their Houses once more. There was a scant handful who'd proven to be honest.

"We made a second journey to the Southern Continent," Garde began, "taking only High Demons with us so we could skip in and out, avoiding the ash that covers a great deal of the area. We found, quite far south, evidence that many of our enemy High Demons sheltered there, avoiding capture. There were fallen tents, debris and rotting food when we arrived. We estimate there are as many as eight hundreds."

"Where are they now?" Yurevik Weth asked.

"We asked for help and thankfully received it to determine that," Jayd spoke. "My sources tell me they have skipped off the planet—for the time being. It is my worry that they will find other allies as they did before and come against us a second time."

"What can they hope to gain? Kifirin is awake now; surely even they know this."

"Perhaps they are counting on his vow of noninterference," Glinda snorted.

"What about the Vampire Queen?" Lord Nedevik Weth rose. He was patriarch of the House of Weth and oldest among all High Demons.

"We cannot count on that help again," Jayd stared at the tabletop.

"Will she not come to protect her commons?" Lord Aldavik Foth stood. His words caused Jayd to glance sharply at Garde over Glinda's head.

I got three gates that day. The numbers of Flakkar were getting smaller, thank goodness. I was eating a late lunch after returning to the villa when the twins came to find me. "Come ski with us," they said. Yeah, they were asking me to ski. Visions of tall pines I would have to mist through to avoid mutilation came to mind.

"Come on, you won't know until you try it," Drake lifted me and tossed me over his shoulder. Feather, Mack's daughter, came to get us, folding us to another world where skiing and winter were both present.

I had to be outfitted at a shop there and felt terrible that the twins were spending so much money on me. The whole thing seemed to be a wasted effort. Feather, with her mates Christi and Kerry, all watched as Drake and Drew haggled with the shopkeeper over my outfit plus skis, poles and goggles.

"Baby, I don't think you know how to have fun," Drew said, rubbing my shoulders at one point. I wondered if he was right. Eventually I was fixed up, the twins paid and somebody folded us to the slopes.

"You're just going to push me down the side of the mountain?" I gulped, staring down the steep incline. Immediate misting came to mind as I contemplated my fate otherwise.

"Watch us," Drake grinned, pushing himself off the top. He was making short, sweeping turns with his skis, going down quickly and skillfully. Kerry went next, closely followed by his two ladies, Christi and Feather. They also skied very well and I started sweating.

"You go first; I'll come along and pick up the pieces," Drew teased.

"Oh, sure, laugh why don't you?" I swatted at him. "I end up with a broken leg and you'll just tell me to turn away from the tree next time."

"Lissa, baby, you'll do fine. Show me those vampire reflexes."

"Uh-huh," I eyed him skeptically. "My vampire reflexes are for getting me out of trouble, not getting into it in the first place."

"You're not afraid are you?" He was still grinning.

"Are you kidding? My knees are knocking. I don't know why I let you two convince me this was a good idea," I snipped.

"Come on, Lissa-love, just try it." Drew coaxed.

"Okay, but on my tombstone I want you to put that I thought this was a bad idea." I shoved myself onto the slope. I learned quickly that going down in a straight line is a terrible idea. My shrieks could be heard for miles and probably caused an avalanche or two as I hurtled down the steep side of the snowy mountain.

"Turn, baby!" Drew shouted as he made his way down behind me. I was shocked I could hear him over the sound of my own screaming. "Turn your body, Lissa!" Drew yelled. He'd seen the pile of rocks, just as I had, and I was skiing straight toward it.

I turned—skidding for yards and flinging snow up in cascades as I slid down the slope. Then, like an afterthought, I flopped over in the snow after coming to an eventual stop. I lay there in cold, powdery snow, panting and shivering.

I'd get myself up off the snow.

I would.

Someday.

Drew came to a neat stop beside me.

"Need a hand?" he asked, pushing his goggles up and leaning down to get a look at my face.

"I need a stick," I said tartly.

"A stick?"

"To beat you and your brother with," I snapped.

"But you did pretty well for your first time. The turn was almost classic when you made it."

"Yeah? A classic lapse of good sense," I grumbled. "It ranks right up there with sticking forks in toasters and taking baths with hair dryers." Drew snickered. I started laughing.

"Come on, you," he lifted me up, dusted most of the snow off me and we started again. "Turn your body from side to side," he was trying to get me to do things properly.

Sometimes that worked. Sometimes. At other times, I went hurtling down the mountain in a straight line, shrieking, turning and falling. Thankfully, no trees were involved by the time I reached bottom.

"You think this is funny?" I lifted an eyebrow at Drake, who was waiting at the bottom with the others, trying not to snicker. He bellowed with laughter. "You could have started me on the bunny slopes but nooo, we had to prove our point, didn't we?" I glared at him.

He laughed harder and the others were laughing, too. "Unbelievable," I grumped. Ignoring all of them, I turned myself to mist and went flying straight back up the mountain. It was better the second time, and by the sixth time I almost had the hang of it. I paid no attention to the others; they were going up and down with the greatest of ease. I had catching up to do.

"If I can't move tomorrow, it will be your fault," I pointed an accusing finger at the twins as we were folded home later.

"Come on, Lissy baby, you can't be mad at us forever," Drake hauled me over his shoulder and folded us to the hot tub. He removed our clothing with a thought and dumped me into bubbling water. I huddled between Drake and Drew when Crane, Dragon, Devin, Grace and Karzac all showed up later, getting in with us. Drake grinned. Maybe he was used to parading around naked in front of his parents and everybody else—I wasn't. I intended to mist out of the hot tub and see if they could track me down later.

"Lissa learned to ski today," Drew grinned.

"I did not learn to ski today; I learned not to kill myself while those contraptions were strapped to my feet," I said sarcastically. Devin laughed.

"She doesn't know how to have fun," Drake observed.

"You could have taken me bowling," I grumped. Grace laughed out loud. Karzac turned his head but I heard the snicker. "Don't laugh, you may have to fix my bruises later," I informed him. That did make him laugh—something that didn't happen very often.

"I'm going to bed, I'm tired," I announced a few minutes later.

"I can fold you to bed," Drew offered.

"I can mist myself to bed," I counter-offered.

"I'd prefer we both folded you to bed," Drake threw in a third option. He didn't wait for a reply; he went ahead and did it. He landed us in the floor instead of in the bed while we were still wet.

"My baby's tired." Drew *Pulled* in a huge towel and started working it over my body. I was tired—and achy, too—if I were honest. Killing Flakkar had worn me out and I didn't get my nap afterward before going to the ski slope.

"Come on, you just need to sleep," Drake said, pulling me toward the bed. "Karzac will beat our heads in if we try anything else. He's still sending me mindspeech, telling me how tired you look."

"Let me get my PJs," I said, going toward my closet.

"No," Drew said. "Don't put anything on, baby. I want the feel of your skin against me in the night." He had his arms around me, nuzzling my neck. Drake disappeared and Drew crawled under the sheet with me. "Go to sleep, love," Drew murmured against my temple. I fell asleep in his arms.

~

Anybody with mindspeech would have been tossed out of bed that night when *Spawn* was shouted mentally. Drew was out of bed like a shot, *Pulling* leathers and blades in with barely a thought. He was going off to battle Ra'Ak spawn, and he was leaving me behind.

I shouted as he disappeared. Well, it was time to see what I was made of. I threw on clothing as quickly as I could, *Looked* to see where Drew went and then working up the nerve, I folded for the first time ever. I landed in an open field on a world I couldn't name. I saw Drake, Drew, Charles and a multitude of Saa Thalarr, waiting for the approaching army of spawn.

Before, Dragon and I had only battled a few dozen. These numbered in the thousands. "What the fuck?" I muttered to myself as I stared in disbelief.

"An entire planet deemed not worth saving, taken by the Ra'Ak and a good number of them turned," Radomir settled beside me, with Devin at his side. "The Ra'Ak find this amusing, transporting armies of their spawn to innocent worlds to wage war against us, hoping to injure or kill any one of us," he added. "We cannot allow a single one to escape, as even one can destroy the population."

"They've hidden Ra'Ak warriors in their midst at times, too," Devin sighed, shaking her head at the approaching spawn. They were a quarter mile away, and the fields around us were seething with their mass. We were being surrounded.

"They hope to take us unawares, and they've nearly succeeded, many times," Devin added.

"Fuckers," I mumbled. Two huge birds flew over our heads—one a dark gray, the other white with black-tipped feathers.

"Crane and Gracie," Radomir nodded toward the birds. "They'll pop heads from spawn using their claws."

"Sounds good," I nodded grimly. "I'm going to mist. See ya." I misted away.

It was only seconds before the spawn attacked. The giant birds screamed overhead as they swooped in, taking heads. Drake, Drew,

Dragon and three other Falchani warriors unsheathed blades and began lopping heads. A giant Snow Leopard snarled and leapt. A Black Gryphon screeched and attacked. A nine-foot Unicorn ran her deadly horn through anything that came close. I, claws forming only, swept through the advancing army, removing heads and leaving spawn to dust behind me.

❧

"Baby, how did you get here?" Drew ran hands over me while Drake looked on, waiting for his brother to say whether I was injured. It had taken four hours to destroy the spawn army.

"Hey, I tried folding. It worked. I'm okay," I did my best to reassure my Falchani.

"Young Falchani, take your mate home," Karzac growled beside us. "She needs rest."

"We're going, then." Drake must have folded us; Drew lifted me up and I didn't argue—I was tired, just as Karzac said. I fell asleep in the shower while the twins cleaned me up—I couldn't keep my eyes open. And I slept most of the next day, too, before Drew woke me with a kiss.

"Dad says we're getting leathers for you and a tattoo if you want one," Drew gave me a lazy smile and kissed me again.

"No on the tattoo," I mumbled, thinking I probably looked like hell.

"You look beautiful. Now, unless you tell me no, I'm about to fuck you until you scream my name," Drew nuzzled my neck before kissing me again.

"You think so?" I mumbled between kisses.

"Oh, yeah," he murmured, his mouth settling on a nipple. He did. Twice, at least.

❧

Drake and Drew were off sparring with their father and the other Falchani when I slid off the bed the following morning. It was the best

I could do; I was a little stiff. A hot shower helped and I dressed in walking shorts and a tank top before pulling socks and athletic shoes onto my feet.

It was Friday, I discovered, and I forced myself out my bedroom door, down a flight of stairs and through the maze of hallways that led to the kitchen. I was almost limbered up by the time I got there.

"Coffee?" Mike was there, puttering around the kitchen.

"Hi, hon," I said, sitting down at the island. "Coffee would be very nice." Jamie walked in while I sipped my coffee laced with cream and sugar. "Today is laundry day," Jamie grinned at me.

"You guys don't have to wait on me hand and foot," I said, looking at him and Mike. Jamie had an arm draped around Mike's shoulders.

"It's our job, and we like it," Mike informed me. "Do not thwart us in our mission to feed, clothe and clean." He had a fist in the air, like a superhero. That made me laugh.

"Besides, you wouldn't believe how much we get paid or the health benefits attached or the vacation time we get," Jamie added. "Plus, we get to see shit that even sci-fi fans never get to see. I've even been folded here and there, a couple of times. You should see the beach house on their private planet."

"Uh-huh," I said. "And you now know that vampires and werewolves are real, too, I suppose."

"Oh, yeah," Mike sighed happily. He fixed breakfast for me while Jamie went off to collect laundry from all the bedrooms, including mine.

Five gates were taken care of that Friday. The Flakkar were nesting close together on those five worlds—large populations lived near them and were suffering losses, though the Flakkar nests were smaller in number than what I'd dealt with earlier. Seventy nesting pairs spaced across five worlds. I was exhausted by the time I finished.

A three-hour nap helped, but I was still groggy when someone tapped on my bedroom door. I got up to answer and was quite shocked to find Fox standing there.

"You know, I'm still coming to grips with the fact that Wlodek and Weldon ended up with the same woman," I said, inviting her inside.

She sat down on a chair in the corner across from my bed while I dressed. She looked so cute, perky and young. I wondered how Wlodek felt about that.

"Weldon tells me you almost died saving his life, once. And Wlodek says you saved him several times."

"Yeah, well, Wlodek needs to learn when to hand out important information," I grumbled.

"He knows that now," Fox replied brightly. "He's worried you won't ever forgive him for that."

"Like Wlodek ever worried about those things," I said. "You ever stand in front of him while your life is hanging in the balance?"

"No. He scared me a few times while he still held the position as Head of the Council, though. He can be a little intense."

"Hmmph," I snorted. Fox smiled.

"He regrets those things, Lissa. Very much. He still considers himself your second vampire sire."

"Yeah, well, I've already gotten the visit from Merrill, my surrogate sire. And I'm sure my actual sire wants to weigh in on all this as well." I hadn't thought about Griffin lately. Should I feel bad about that? My parting with Merrill, too, had been far from amicable.

"They care about you." Fox's words were simple.

"They have a funny way of showing it," I said.

Jamie had placed a pile of clean clothing on the end of my king-sized bed and I was now putting all of it away in drawers and on shelves in my closet. I'd napped with it sitting on my bed. I know—how lazy was I?

"I didn't come to upset you, honest," Fox said. "I feel like I need to know you better. How about going with me to do some shopping? Kiarra's birthday party is coming up and I wanted to look for a gift."

"All right," I said. "Am I dressed properly?" I held out my arms—I'd put gray slacks and a black tank top on, with sandals.

"It might be too cool in London for the tank," Fox said, looking me over critically. "Same with the sandals." That sent me back to the closet and I pulled out a short-sleeved blouse in pink with low-heeled black pumps. "Very nice," I got Fox's approval when I came out again.

She folded us to a huge mall just outside London. Malls were back in and this one could fit the Vatican inside it, plus a few small villages.

"She has so much jewelry already," Fox sighed as we passed a jewelry store.

I shrugged. I didn't know Kiarra at all and had no idea what she might like. We looked at clothing next, but again Fox said that Kiarra was kept fully stocked. We looked at electronics. Gadgets, knick-knacks, doo-dads, gizmos, everything. We ended up in an art gallery where all sorts of artwork and sculpture were for sale. We wandered through that.

"I don't see a single thing that might appeal to her," Fox grumbled.

"Well, she's the Unicorn—can we look for something in that direction?"

"Yeah." Fox smiled.

"I was fascinated by unicorns in my early years," I admitted. "I once painted a unicorn for my graduate thesis exhibition. It was huge, like four feet by four feet. I even had some offers on it but I kept it for myself. It was hanging in the house when I was turned vampire."

"Can we go see it?" Fox asked, dimpling slightly.

"Can you get us back there?" I asked. "I mean, the best time to see it was probably the night I was attacked. I doubt anybody was in the house then."

"Sure," Fox breathed. "Let's go take a look."

Bending time is easy, I suppose, if you have the ability. It only took a blink or two and we were there; inside my house on the same night I was being attacked outside a bar fifteen miles away.

I remembered the scent of the house as we landed inside it. It's funny, I know, that you don't really notice things like that so much when you're human. Now, scents were everywhere, telling me things I needed to know as often as not.

"It's in the bedroom," I told Fox, who'd landed us inside the kitchen. We walked down the hall I knew so well, then into the bedroom and past the bed I'd made up early that morning so I could get to the hospital. I sent up a quick mental *I love you* to Don—he hadn't been gone that long from where I was at the moment.

"This is it? This is incredible," Fox said, examining the painting. I'd always liked it, although my graduate committee had grumbled over it. The rest of my exhibition was more abstract—and in their eyes more acceptable—but I couldn't help myself on this one.

The unicorn was white, of course, standing in three-quarter view and gazing off to the side as if it were on guard and watchful. The mane and tail rippled in an unseen breeze as twilight was falling, with the barest hint of stars over mountains off in the distance. The gold horn was long and sharp; I'd always seen it as a weapon. Otherwise, why have it at all?

"Does it have a title?" Fox asked. She was still staring at the painting.

"Vigilance," I replied.

"Right now, this is still yours," Fox turned to me. "Take it, Lissa."

"If I take it, then I'll give it to Kiarra. I'm not the Unicorn, she is. This represents a part of my life when I still had idealistic dreams. That's what this painting is. May as well give it away."

I hadn't had any idealistic dreams in a very long time. They'd all been stolen or beaten out of me. I lifted the heavy painting off the wall —I'd had it framed nicely in a dark wood. Fox folded me back to my suite at the villa and I set the painting against the wall inside my closet. There was still plenty of empty space inside it, after all.

"I'm getting mindspeech from my mates," Fox smiled. "Time for dinner. Why don't you come with me? You haven't met Steve or Gilfraith, yet." She named two of her five mates.

"Fine," I muttered and Fox folded us again.

CHAPTER 13

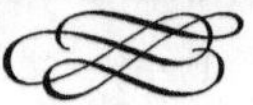

"*L*ook who I invited to dinner," Fox announced brightly as we landed in a very pretty kitchen with a huge, arched window on one side. Several people were there, Wlodek and Weldon among them.

There were two I didn't know and one had me drawing in a huge breath; I'm sure the shock must have been plain on my face. He was Ra'Ak. Or had been Ra'Ak—he had the scent, still, but it was overlaid with other things.

"That's Gilfraith," Fox patted my shoulder, smiling at the male with pale-brown hair and golden-brown eyes. He wasn't tall—perhaps five-nine or so, but that didn't matter. If he turned to Ra'Ak, he'd be formidable.

"I'm an expatriate," he nodded politely and offered his hand. "And I don't manufacture poison or turn much. I've helped train the spawn hunters and some of the Saa Thalarr." I could see how that might be helpful—Gilfraith probably knew all the Ra'Ak tricks.

"And I can't tell you how happy I am to hear it," I said, shaking his hand. He smiled.

"And this is Steve, Conner's oldest son," another man came forward as Fox introduced him.

"I hear you're mated to my half-brother, Connegar," Steve said, shaking my hand.

"Yeah, that's the current rumor," I said, feeling embarrassed.

"Hey, what's this? You didn't tell us where you were again; we had to send out blanket mindspeech," the twins showed up with Shadow.

"Do I have to tell you everything?" I asked, my hands on my hips as I stared at all three of them.

"You do not, but we would like it very much if you did," Connegar folded in, too. Weldon, the schmuck, snickered off to the side.

"Hey, keep your furry ass out of this," I leaned around Drake to point a finger at Weldon.

"I'll keep my furry ass out of it if you'll bake cookies," Weldon was still laughing.

Everybody ended up having dinner with Fox. I offered to help cook and a mountain of food was prepared. I baked a truckload of cookies. Three kinds, in fact—oatmeal, chocolate chip and peanut butter. I did get help—Fox, Grace, Devin and Mike all pitched in.

"I remember these," Weldon bit into a peanut butter cookie with a satisfied sigh.

"I remember you could eat a dozen by yourself," I said, handing him a glass of milk.

"Why is everyone getting cookies and I'm just now hearing about it?" Kiarra folded in with Adam, Merrill, Griffin and Amara.

"Baby, may I hug you?" Griffin came over and looked at me with the saddest expression on his face. What was I supposed to do? Refuse and embarrass both of us in front of all those people?

"I guess," I said. Griffin hugged me tightly.

"I'm so sorry, baby," he whispered against my ear. "Just believe me when I say I love you." He kissed my temple and was wiping his cheeks when he stepped away from me.

"It's not worth crying over," I said, handing him a napkin.

"Sweetheart, you have no idea what you're worth," he said.

Amara came over and hugged me, too. I know she wanted me to call her Mom. I just couldn't. Maybe someday but not that day, and she hadn't done anything to deserve otherwise. I was going to have to get comfortable with the idea, first.

"Cookies!" My nieces appeared, bringing Flavio, Dalroy and Rhett with them. I was worried we'd have to make more.

"This is the first time I ever got to eat anything Lissa cooked," Wlodek was very happy with the oatmeal cookies.

"You, maybe," I said. "Merrill there was drinking coffee and eating barbecue at least once a week the whole time I stayed with him." I wanted to call Merrill names. Tell him how awful he was. I couldn't. Kiarra was right there, and everybody else was watching. The vampire mask slid into place.

"You knew that?" Merrill looked shocked.

"You came in smelling like barbecue or some other thing all the time," I said, hugging myself and turning away. "I knew you weren't just vampire the first time I met you. Those sunglasses in the Range Rover weren't Franklin's either. You think I'd let that cat out of the bag and risk my life doing it? Jerk," I muttered.

"Lissa, we treated you like a baby vampire and that was perhaps our greatest failing," Wlodek admitted.

"Yeah, well, you can't undo it now," I mumbled, deliberately refusing to look at him.

"Go forward with us, instead," Adam offered. He and I had never really talked, but he was there in front of me suddenly, lifting my chin with his fingers. "Leave the past in the past, pretty girl. There's a world of light in front of you now; all you have to do is walk in it."

"I'm not sure I can," the tears dripped down my cheeks.

"Let it go," Adam whispered. Connegar was beside me, suddenly.

"You will try, won't you, little rose?" Connegar lifted me in a warm embrace and never said a word when I wrapped my arms around his neck and sobbed.

~

"Mother, Lissa needed to get away for a while." Connegar set me down at yet another large, granite island—the one in Conner's kitchen.

Conner was there having a late dinner with Russell, Will and Martin. Franklin, his mates Shane and Tomas were also there.

"Hi, honey," I walked over to give Franklin a hug as soon as Connegar let me go. "Hi, other honey," I gave Shane a hug, too. "Third honey," I hugged Tomas.

"Lissa, why have you been crying?" Franklin pulled me against him and wiped my cheeks gently with a thumb.

"Long story," I sniffled, wiping my own cheeks. "Do I look like shit, now?"

"No, sweetheart," Franklin pulled me against him. "You need to come over and see us more often," he scolded gently.

"I would not object if I were notified more often of the Queen's movements. I have attempted to see her many times," Erland Morphis folded in. I stared—I know I did. I'd seen him once before, in the arboretum above the High Demon's palace.

"He's mated to some of ours," Frank said softly. "That's how he found out you were with us."

"Do you remember meeting me?" I asked Erland, leaning against Franklin and putting my head on his shoulder. Yeah, I missed Franklin. A lot.

"When did we meet?" He didn't remember. Well, Kifirin had taken me to the future, so this Erland had no recollection of meeting me.

"Forty years in the future," I sighed. "Kifirin took me to Veshtul. We met in the palace arboretum. You told me you were a Karathian Warlock, and never cast dark spells."

"Fascinating. Did I also inform you that you are one of two women I would like to have in my bed?"

"Uh, no. And that's not embarrassing or anything. I thought you were attracted to males."

"I am currently attracted to males, but I would beg if it would get me into your bed."

"Uh-huh," I said, snuggling against Franklin. Maybe this conversation didn't embarrass Erland Morphis, but it sure as hell embarrassed me.

"See, I am forever to be rebuffed by the two females I would enjoy making love with," Erland declared, tossing up a hand. It made me wonder who the other woman was—after all, he was the second most beautiful male I'd ever seen.

"And the other is?" I asked, mildly curious.

"Glindarok. Only she treats me exactly the same," Erland grumbled. "My Lissa thinks I am the second most beautiful man she knows. My Glinda thinks I am the most beautiful." Well, he'd just plucked the thoughts right from my head. The schmuck.

"She hasn't met Kifirin, has she?" I asked. She couldn't think Erland was more beautiful than that.

"Avilepha, did you call my name?" The most beautiful man I'd ever met showed up right then, as if he were listening for his name to be called. *Nexus Echo*. I couldn't decide if that was a good or a bad thing.

"I did mention your name," I admitted. Everybody in Conner's kitchen was now staring at Kifirin with their mouths open. He had an angel's face. I always thought that, anyway.

"M'hala, you are too kind to me," Kifirin smiled.

"I am not, stop fibbing," I pulled away from Franklin and went to swat Kifirin lightly on the arm. "I missed you, you schmuck."

"I live for the day you call me darling or any other endearment," Kifirin sighed.

"Don't count your chickens, honey," I said. Conner snickered.

"I came to take you away for a bit, love. You appear to need a break." Kifirin reached out and touched my face gently. It was probably still blotchy from crying. At least the guys were all too polite to mention it.

"Where are we going?" I asked, wishing I had a mirror.

"You look beautiful," Kifirin informed me. "And I was going to take you to see Roff and Giff."

"Really?" I wanted to jump up and down with happiness. "They're still alive?" I missed Roff. Loved Roff. Really wanted to see Roff. And Giff, too.

"Of course. I see I chose the right thing," Kifirin flashed his perfect smile. "Come avilepha, we will go." Connegar nodded and smiled at me when I glanced his way, so Kifirin lifted me up and we were gone.

We were back in the High Demons' palace, only it wasn't in the future. I'm not sure how I knew that, I just did. Kifirin set me down, took my hand, kissed it lightly and then led me down a wide hall tiled in the beautiful marble I'd seen before.

The occasional sculpture lined this hall depicting High Demons, both humanoid and in their Thifilathi. That wasn't scary or anything. Those Thifilathi sculptures were life-sized and around sixteen to eighteen feet tall, which meant the hall itself was much taller than that.

We stopped at a door carved in ornate patterns and inlaid with gold, silver and semiprecious stones. The knob was also a carved oval in gold. Kifirin knocked out of politeness and then blew the door inward with Power.

Gardevik stood there with his brother Jaydevik and a woman was held behind King Jayd. Jayd looked as if he were about to explode or go Thifilathi. Garde breathed a sigh of relief when he saw it was Kifirin and me. Honestly, I wasn't looking forward to a battle between Kifirin and Jayd and was glad Jayd backed down.

"We wish to see Roff and Giff," Kifirin announced, as the woman elbowed Jayd aside and then stepped around him.

"Wait," she said. "I haven't been introduced to the person who saved us." She came forward and held out her hand. "I am Glindarok," she said. "Queen of the High Demons."

There wasn't any way around it, she was gorgeous. Long, white hair hung down to her waist and she had blue eyes and beautiful skin. She wasn't much taller than I was, either. I took her hand. "I wanted to meet you as soon as I found out you still lived," she said.

"Well, here I am," I replied. "I'm Lissa, but then you already know that. Erland Morphis just told me that you were the first woman he ever wanted to go to bed with."

"Why did that idiot tell you that?" she asked, smiling and releasing my hand.

"Because he informed Lissa that she's the other female he wishes to take to his bed," Kifirin announced. I wanted to elbow him in the ribs for that.

"As if he has time for a female," I snipped. "His first love is Erland Morphis, and any woman would stand behind a long line of males on the rest of his list."

"Exactly what I always thought," Glinda laughed.

Roff walked into the room at that moment, followed by Giff, who was carrying a baby. "Roff," I whimpered, wanting to run to him. I held myself back.

"Is this our Queen?" Roff asked, coming forward. This Roff didn't know me. Had never met me, or kissed me or held me. I missed the Roff who'd done all those things.

"Honey, I've missed you," I said, afraid to touch him.

"You call me an endearment?" Roff was surprised, I could tell.

"Do you not want that?" I asked, worried.

"I should be kneeling at your feet," he said, shocking me.

"Honey, don't you ever do that," I said. "Ever." I couldn't help it; I went to him and hugged him.

"The Queen loves you, Roff," Kifirin said softly. Roff's arms went around me.

"Would you like to offer your blood, Roff?" Kifirin asked; his head suddenly next to Roff's ear. I wasn't about to take much, just enough to give him satisfaction.

Roff couldn't speak, but he was eager. I held him away from me. "I won't hurt you," I said, leaning in to kiss him. Roff was ready now, and Giff watched in wonder as I leaned in, placed another kiss on Roff's neck and bit him as gently as I could.

Roff cried out in ecstasy; I held him while his body convulsed against mine. He was now holding onto me as hard as I was holding onto him. The High Demons were watching all of this, I noticed, when I licked Roff's neck to heal it and leaned away from him.

"Did you like that?" I asked.

"Very much," Roff's voice was hoarse, his brown eyes still clouded with pleasure. "I would like to do it again."

"I didn't take much from you, but you still don't need to do this again for a few days. Is that little Toff back there with Giff? You need your strength to take care of him."

"Yes," Roff was still trying to gather his wits as he motioned Giff forward.

"Hey, baby," I played with Toff's little hands. He was adorable and the proud owner of a full set of teeth—I saw that right away when he yawned in Giff's arms.

"They eat animal protein, straight from the birthing sac," Kifirin informed me.

"Because you made them that way," I looked up at Kifirin, who shrugged.

"What would your first law be, if you were Queen on Le-Ath Veronis?" Kifirin said instead.

"That it would be a death sentence if anyone drank from a child," I replied instantly. "The rights of the comesuli should be considered first, don't you think?" Kifirin's eyes lit up as he smiled at me.

"I will bring you a copy of the old laws," he said. "The first of which levied a death sentence upon anyone who drank from a child." Roff and Giff were listening to us, their eyes shining.

"Their rights first?" Jayd asked as he, Glinda and Garde moved closer.

"You are looking at potential vampires. They are vampire young in that respect and I have it on good authority that Roff and Giff are winged Infilathi and will make winged vampires. I want to see that for myself. How would you treat your children, Raoni?" I gave Jayd a hard look.

"We have laws protecting our children," Glinda said. "We should have understood what the commons meant to your race."

"Avilepha, we should go," Kifirin said. I nodded. No sense getting the High Demon King all riled up—it could affect the way Roff, Giff and the others were treated.

"Sorry we barged in on you like this," I apologized. "Kifirin offered me the chance to see Roff and I couldn't turn it down."

"You came only to see me?" Roff asked.

"I came mostly to see you. And Giff, and little Toff. I hope I get to see you again soon." I gave Roff another kiss before Kifirin folded me away.

"Roff, I think you're special to the Vampire Queen," Glinda gave him a hug.

"I cannot believe it," Roff said. "Why did she pick me?"

"Why wouldn't she pick you?" Garde patted Roff on the shoulder.

"Perhaps we should take Toff to the kitchens, he looks hungry," Giff said.

"Do you think so?" Roff lifted his youngest child out of his oldest child's arms. "Let us go feed Toff, then," Roff agreed, smiling as they walked out of Glinda's suite.

"In less than half a click, this story is going to be all over Veshtul," Jayd moaned.

"Stop whining," Glinda slapped Jayd's stomach with the back of her hand.

~

"The Queen gave the rapture? Truly?" Those words were spoken from one comesula to the next until it was all over Veshtul, just as Jayd said.

~

Kifirin spent the night with me, but left early in the morning after kissing me while I was still asleep. Just as well, I had things to do. More gates waited and I got another five, for a total of fifty-four nesting pairs.

Flakkar were just filthy and foul and if I'd had more time and energy, I'd have *Looked* to find where they came from and what their natural enemies were. I might have also gone *Looking* to find how they'd gotten there to begin with, but that would have to wait. People were dying in the meantime and I could only do so many things at once.

My nap came next and when I came out of my suite later to find a snack, Karzac was sitting at the island having a cup of tea.

"Hey, Karzac, I haven't seen you in a while," I said, unable to resist rubbing his back.

"I have been giving inoculations on Ooblerik," Karzac sighed. "Jeff and I volunteered to help the indigent population there. This does not violate the noninterference rules since we only use normal abilities for this."

"How's it going, then?" I poured some juice and sat beside him with my glass.

"We are currently in the middle of what should be classified as a jungle," Karzac replied. "Conditions are deplorable and many children are ill already. A border war is also threatening, so time may be short."

"That sounds awful," I said. "Why are they trying to wage war if people are sick? That makes no sense at all. Seems to me they're putting their life and the lives of their soldiers in danger if they send them into an epidemic."

"I think this as well, but often dictators and despots only think of the ground to be gained, the revenge to be had or the notoriety to be earned. They care nothing for the lives of the people." His words made me think of the High Demons who made a pact with the Ra'Ak, but I didn't voice those thoughts aloud.

"When are you going back?" I asked.

"When I finish my tea," he said and emptied his cup.

"Please be careful," I said, patting his shoulder as he stood.

"I will," he replied and folded away.

I was still sitting there sipping my juice when something happened, and if I'd thought my skin itched before when something terrible was about to happen, well, it was on fire now and all I could think about was Karzac.

I didn't even take time to *Look* or worry about folding where I wanted to go, I just did it. I flung myself out and found myself in the middle of the jungle Karzac had described, with an army advancing toward a village and firing weapons as they marched in.

The village was in chaos while people screamed and ran away from the encroaching troops. Children wept as parents shouted their names—the adults were frantically attempting to get the young and the old ones away while others fought off the invaders. Karzac was there, too—I just knew it. I had a choice to make and I made it quickly.

People are frightened when they're turned to mist and they don't know what is happening or how it happened, but it couldn't be helped. I'd chosen to take them out of harm's way instead of gathering up the enemy forces right then. Karzac and Jeff were both in the group I gathered, with sixty villagers, including their children. I dropped them off two miles away, and they were still screaming and crying when they materialized. *I'll be back*; I sent to Karzac and headed toward the advancing army.

Weapons misted out of hands and I dropped them into the nearby river before going back for the soldiers. I figured I could find where they came from easily; I had the resources, now.

It didn't take long to gather them up, although a few had scattered in fear. There was one more thing I collected before heading toward their village and the schmuck who'd sent them.

The soldiers were dropped (not gently) in front of the despot's home, all screaming and shouting. When the despot himself came out to see what had happened, I left the last gift with him.

The young man's body dropped right on the despot's head after I released it. The body had been ravaged by the disease and hadn't been dead long. The despot went down under the dropped weight and he was cursing and flinging the body away as I misted over his head, flying toward Karzac and the others.

The medical personnel were still trying to calm the villagers when I arrived. I did my best to appear behind a stand of trees before going to help if I could.

"Lissa, if you can place compulsion, now would be a good time," Karzac was desperate when I reached his and Jeff's side. I nodded; Karzac, Jeff and the others were dealing with mass hysteria.

"All will be well," I said to the small group they were tending. Cries and screams ceased immediately. I went to the next group, doing the same thing until everyone had been calmed. I turned to the volunteers next and told them they'd gotten advanced warning and managed to get the people to safety. They all nodded at the suggestion.

"Is it safe to take them back?" Karzac asked when I was done.

"For now; I dumped weapons in the river and then dumped soldiers in the despot's village," I said. "And I dumped a dead body on top of the despot. I hope it was still contagious."

"Did he touch it?" Karzac asked.

"He had to—I dropped it right on him," I replied.

"Good," Karzac nodded. "It takes two weeks for the virus to incubate and he hasn't been immunized. He thinks the gods are sending the disease."

"Maybe they did—for him, anyway," I grinned at Karzac. "Do you need help getting everybody back home?"

"We have it covered," Jeff came over to talk. "It's better if they don't remember you." He was definitely Merrill's son, but he didn't look as much like Merrill as Franklin did. I sighed.

"You're probably right," I agreed and folded away. I did a victory dance when I reached the villa again—I could fold without even thinking about it! How cool was that?

~

"Radomir, I haven't seen you lately," I said when I went back to the kitchen after my little side-trip. I wanted a glass of water; Radomir was sitting at the island having a sandwich.

"Lissa, I have been with Mack and Justin at the beach house on Kiarra's private planet. It is quite nice there at the moment. Warm, sunny days with little rain. You should go there sometime."

"Mike said something about that," I hedged. I sure didn't want to go if Merrill was going to be there.

~

Radomir watched Lissa closely. He'd spoken with Flavio and Wlodek.

He'd heard all the stories, now, about the Council, as well as Gavin and Tony. Somehow, they'd all remembered Lissa.

An unseen hand had delivered the memories, and now all were clamoring to see the little Queen. Wlodek had warned him, however. He'd said Lissa might bolt if she learned the Council was asking to see her. Radomir didn't know what to do.

~

"Is this what you wanted?" Flavio handed the small card to Gavin.

"Thank you, Honored One," Gavin reached out to take the card—it was an old driver's license, something made obsolete by the introduction of ID chips. Specifically, it was Lissa's driver's license; the forged one she'd gotten when she'd first been made vampire.

Gavin had kept it in his wallet since he'd taken her to the Council; hadn't been able to part with it until it, like his memories of Lissa, had disappeared. The photograph of Lissa was a good one; she'd been smiling in it. More than likely, the one who'd created the ID had said something to amuse her. Gavin had so seldom accomplished that.

"We're trying to get her to a Council meeting; I could use her help," Flavio muttered. "We have those two we're holding and if she knows who sired them," Flavio didn't finish his statement. So many times over the years, that talent would have helped them in their decisions. Now they had her back—but would she consent to come?

"The meeting is tomorrow night, Honored One," Gavin pointed out.

"And I'm working on this," Flavio rubbed his forehead. Gone were the days when they could command that she come. Not only was she a Queen that they could no longer threaten, she was protected. Flavio didn't want to think what the Larentii alone would do to them if they tried to coerce Lissa. Wlodek worried that Lissa would simply disappear if she heard the Council was seeking her.

"This is a quagmire," Flavio rubbed his forehead.

"I was told she died. And then was brought back, somehow. Is that true?" Gavin heard that rumor from Will—he and Tony had found the former vampire in a London pub. Will had probably tracked them down, but Gavin didn't object; Will had provided information when asked.

"Yes. Wlodek says that is true. I fail to understand the how or why of it, but we are all grateful." Wisely, Gavin didn't inform Flavio of the visit he and Anthony had gotten. Gavin imagined Lissa's life might be tied up with that one somehow, but was afraid to speculate over it.

"If she consents to come, I wish to be there. Only I wish to come in later, before the meeting ends."

"I have a better idea," Flavio said. "And if Anthony weren't in Barcelona, now, I'd include him as well."

"He can wait," Gavin muttered. "What do you have in mind?"

"Lissa, you got away last night before I could talk to you," Wlodek was suddenly beside me as Radomir and I were talking.

"Wlodek," I gave him a slight nod.

"Child, you once called me father."

"Is that what you wanted to talk to me about?" I asked, searching his nearly-black eyes for an answer.

"No. Flavio has two prisoners who have killed humans, and he needs help that only you might provide. There are two others he suspects of siring the criminals, but he cannot be sure and has no desire to bring charges against the wrong one. He worries that the prisoners' sire instructed them in the killing of humans, but they were taught never to reveal their sire's name. As both were never properly registered with the Council, you see how this might turn out."

He was right—I could definitely see how this might turn out. "And the laws have changed, daughter," Wlodek added. "If a vampire is not formally charged with a crime, he cannot be placed under compulsion by the Council. The two suspected sires will only be questioned."

"Are the prisoners really criminals or were they just turned and allowed to roam free?" I asked. If they'd killed accidentally while feeding themselves, there was no easy answers on this.

"Lissa, they have been questioned under compulsion and both have admitted to killing donors. It gave them pleasure to do so. However, as they were instructed not to reveal the name of their sire, Flavio cannot get around that. I can obtain copies of the records; Charles will be happy to bring them to you if you wish. Flavio only wishes to get to the bottom of this before sentencing. I told him you could give him the necessary information."

"When is the meeting, father?" I sighed, resting my head on my arms at the island.

"It is tomorrow night, child," Wlodek rubbed my back gently. "Gavin always said you carried stress in your neck and shoulders." He rubbed my neck carefully before moving to my shoulders.

"Merrill and I will take you to the meeting and ensure you remain safe there." I stiffened when he mentioned Merrill's name, but nodded while his hands carefully worked the kinks from my shoulders. Once upon a time, I'd have scoffed at the mere suggestion that any gentleness existed in the Head of the Council.

Flakkar were waiting for me the following morning. I got four gates that day, but they were very far apart and difficult to reach. Nevertheless, the Flakkar died as quickly as I could make it happen. Two of the worlds were preindustrial, which made it worse.

"Baby, where have you been?" Drake and Drew were both in my bedroom when I returned to the villa.

"Cleaning up a mess," I yawned. Either the gating or the killing of the Flakkar always tired me out. Or perhaps it was both, how did I know? "I could ask you the same thing." I gave the twins a weary smile.

"All you have to do is call our name and we'll be right there," Drake said. He sounded disappointed that I hadn't done so.

"I really need a shower and a nap," I pointed out.

"Then we'll help," Drew slid off the bed and came to me. I laid my head against his chest and wrapped my arms around his waist. He pulled his arms around me and they were warm, thick with muscle and the best thing in the world right then.

I got my shower without any extracurricular activity. Drake did tell me I wasn't eating enough—he said I wasn't gaining my weight back as quickly as I should.

"If Karzac takes the time to check on you, baby, he might be upset," Drake breathed against my ear as he covered me up later with a light blanket. I was left to take my nap but got the impression they'd be waiting when I got up.

Dinner was waiting when I woke and shuffled into the kitchen. Grace and Devin cooked since it was Sunday and one of Mike and Jamie's days off. Somebody asked for turkey and dressing. Who knew that somebody would cook it outside the normal holidays? I was glad to get it—hadn't had anything like it in a long time and I stuffed myself.

"She's eating a decent meal," Drew hugged me as I had more dressing. Before, food like that would have made me blow up like a balloon.

I changed into a nicer outfit later; black slacks with a cranberry blouse. Then I brushed my teeth and braided my hair for the Council meeting. Wlodek and Merrill did come to get me just as Wlodek said.

Drake and Drew would have come along too if they'd been allowed. Merrill had to promise them I'd come back in one piece before they stopped grumbling.

The Council was now meeting beneath an old church they'd bought and renovated. The church itself was open during the day for tourists and public tours. It was only at night—on certain nights—that vampires came and the grounds were guarded and off-limits to anyone else.

A door behind the pulpit led downward to the meeting cellar, and it was not only hidden, but built better than a bank vault. Henri and Gervais were guarding the door when we arrived. Both stood straight and tall as I passed them.

I recalled how we'd worked together to improve their misting time. I wanted to hug both of them, but that wouldn't do. Sighing, I passed them by and walked down steps leading to the Council chamber, flanked by Wlodek and Merrill.

Someone had recreated the horseshoe-shaped table in carved stone, but there were comfortable chairs placed around it now and the Council was already seated. Charles was there, not only as Flavio's Chief of Staff, but also as a Council member, along with Dalroy and Rhett. Finally, American vampires had broken into the European Aristocracy; Council members were automatic members.

What shocked me, however, was what happened as soon as Wlodek, Merrill and I walked into the large, underground room— every Council member, including Flavio, rose from their seat.

I figured it was out of respect for Wlodek. He was Flavio's sire after all, and had held the Head position for a very long time. Merrill steered me to a spot at the left where there were seats waiting for us. We sat and the Council sat.

"Bring the prisoners forward, as well as our two guests," Flavio ordered as soon as the Council was seated and comfortable. Two vampires in cuffs much like those I'd seen on Refizan were brought forward.

I recognized Trevor; he was still an Assassin and tonight he was in charge of the prisoners. He was still around, at least. The two who were missing from this meeting were Gavin and Tony. I sighed as quietly as I could.

Baxter and Dmitri, two Enforcers I recognized from before, brought both vampire witnesses forward. There were several other faces around the room I didn't recognize—vampires who'd taken the spots vacated by Radomir and the others. I'd know their scents next time, though.

"I must beg the indulgence of our Queen," Flavio said inside the dim interior of the Council Hall. That caught my attention. He was addressing me as Queen? That was unexpected. Wlodek must have convinced him, somehow.

I knew Flavio wanted me to discern the paternity of the two prisoners standing before him. I rose from my seat. Baxter and Dmitri were waiting next to the two unfettered vampires. I already knew what Flavio desired to know before I approached.

"Your name?" I asked the first of the unfettered ones.

"Samuel," he replied, watching me with wonder in his eyes. He'd never seen a female vampire before; I would have bet on it. Now he was seeing two—Susila was still on the Council.

"And you?" I asked the second one.

"Petrus," he replied.

"Honored One," I turned to Flavio. "Petrus sired both these vampires; Samuel did not make them." I jerked my head toward the prisoners. All three—Petrus and his two turns—held taint. All were guilty in some way.

Petrus attempted to get away but Trevor, Dmitri and Baxter had him subdued and cuffed after a very brief struggle. Samuel had gone to his knees and was thanking me, I discovered, just as soon as the scuffle with Petrus was over. Baxter pulled Samuel up and escorted him from the hall.

"Now, Petrus," Flavio placed compulsion, "tell me why you implicated Samuel as the sire for these two."

I was escorted to my seat by Dmitri; we all sat and listened while Petrus explained under compulsion that he wanted to draw attention away from himself. He'd turned his two murdering children in and implicated Samuel as their sire because he and Samuel had once been friends but had a falling out over the years. Samuel didn't agree with Petrus' views on blood substitute, it seemed.

Petrus, who'd been turned after blood substitute was created, had never been taught to take blood from a donor by his sire, who wished to prevent Petrus from taking from a donor to begin with. Petrus had taught himself—with the occasional mistake, here and there. That alone would have earned him a death sentence. He was barely a hundred years of age and had created and then taught the other two now on trial.

I knew how this was going to end; Trevor beheaded all three of them when the sentences were passed.

"Lissa, this is Montrose," Wlodek introduced me to the Council members afterward. I nodded to him and took his hand when he smiled and offered it. Jarl, the one remaining member who'd voted for my death in the beginning was next.

There was another new member I hadn't met; he'd taken Flavio's place when Flavio took over Wlodek's position. His name was Friedrich and he was nearly as old as Flavio. I shook hands with him; Susila and Oluwa smiled widely when I was introduced to them. Rhett and Dalroy offered their hands right away; Charles gave me a hug and a kiss on the cheek.

"Bubba, you look good as a Member of the Council," I patted Charles on the back when he let me go.

"Do I?" He grinned at me.

"Yeah, that outfit says it all," I told him. The 1930s weren't in only for women. He looked good in his double-breasted, pinstripe suit.

"We're going over to Flavio's for a drink," Charles said. "Why don't you come? Merrill and Wlodek have been invited and both want to go."

"Now, you know I can't hold my liquor," I said. I wasn't sure about sitting down for a glass of wine with Flavio, Merrill and Wlodek. Charles would be fine—in fact, I wouldn't mind going to a bar in London with him, for old time's sake.

"Nah, come to Flavio's. I promise to keep you from getting blitzed."

"We'll come," Wlodek was there beside me, placing an arm around my shoulders.

"Good," Charles grinned. "Give us half an hour to drive." I followed Merrill and Wlodek up the stairs and out of the church where hovercars were waiting to take everyone home.

We folded away, landing on the doorstep of what was once Wlodek's mansion. Flavio had it now. Rolfe answered the door just as he always did and I couldn't help myself, I was hugging him and crying happy tears.

"I was so afraid you'd be gone," I brushed away tears when I looked up at Rolfe. He would have been a welcome addition to any basketball team with his height and agility. I'd seen him fight.

"Little Queen," Rolfe smiled down at me. I blinked at him. How did he know? Perhaps Flavio had informed him, or he'd overheard it. Rolfe heard everything, after all.

"Rolfe knew I was a Queen before anyone else did," I hugged his waist again before Wlodek moved me away from the door.

"We should listen to Rolfe more often, then," Merrill observed.

"I think you should, too," I told him, causing an eyebrow to rise.

Flavio, Charles, Rhett and Dalroy came in later. Wlodek led me to the library in the house instead of the study where I'd always been taken before. I'd never been in the library, I realized.

Merrill *Pulled* in several bottles of wine—white and red—and uncorked them. Charles handed out glasses as Merrill poured. "Thank you for your help, Lissa," Flavio said, raising his wineglass to me. "You made this so much simpler for us since the Council now knows you can scent the blood. Charles and I already guessed at the truth, but we couldn't tip our hand. We have carefully hidden the fact that we aren't completely vampire, now."

"So you already knew Samuel was innocent," I said.

"I did. But how do you explain this to the Council without them learning you aren't one hundred percent vampire any longer? Merrill hid his from us, even from father. We never knew until after he became Saa Thalarr."

"I can't believe you didn't smell the barbecue," I muttered, sipping my wine.

"Lissa, you must have smelled it through my pores—I always took care to change and clean up," Merrill chuckled. Well, somebody was in a good mood.

"Her nose is better than any I've ever seen," Dalroy hauled out mixed nuts and pretzels. Rhett and Dalroy were having a beer. Well, my nieces' blood had worked wonders for those two. Flavio, too; he was dipping into the pretzels.

"Lissa, will you come with me to the kitchen? I need help getting ice and cookies." Charles grinned at me.

"You have cookies? What kind?" I was interested.

"I don't know, Kyler brought them earlier," Charles said. "Come on." He motioned for me to follow. I followed. We made it to the bottom of the grand staircase when Radomir folded in, and Gavin was with him. I squared my shoulders and looked away. Gavin didn't want me. Didn't recognize me. Somebody had done that to me. I almost misted away. I never got the chance.

Gavin can move very, very fast. I'd seen him do it in the past, after all. He'd been Wlodek's elite Assassin for a reason—very few could stand against him. Now, I was crushed in his arms, and he was crying amber tears and calling me every endearment he knew, in every language he knew.

CHAPTER 14

"**I** don't believe we were ever on Wlodek's roof before," Gavin said later. I was still held as tightly against him as he could manage without crushing me. "We were on Merrill's roof many times, as well as a few hotel roofs, at least one in Oklahoma City and another in Corpus Christi. I remember the one in Corpus Christi fondly." He leaned down and nuzzled my cheek.

"How do you remember?" I asked. I was still recovering from the shock of it.

"Cara, we all did—Anthony, I, the Council. All at once, the memories arrived. I cannot believe how we were made to forget."

"Winkler's gone," I mumbled, hanging my head.

"I know," Gavin said softly. "Do not weep again, I beg you." I'd been crying, right along with Gavin, when he'd swept me up.

"I'm doing my best," I told him while sniffling.

"Lissa, will you come home with me?" Gavin asked.

"Honey, I don't even know where you live," I replied.

"Anthony and I live at René's old home," Gavin informed me softly.

I'm going home with Gavin, I sent to Charles.

I will inform the others, came the reply. I hoped the others included my twins. Yeah, I thought of them as mine. I hoped they still thought of me as theirs when I didn't come home tonight.

"I know there are others," it was as if Gavin were reading my mind. "I do not care, love. Take as many as you like as long as I am included in that number. Something can be worked out among us, surely."

"I hope so, too," I said. "Wait until you meet Connegar," I said, more brightly. "You should get along with him, for sure." I folded us to René's old home.

"Anthony is on assignment," Gavin said as soon as we settled in the dining room. The floor to ceiling windows were still there, I noticed, although the table and chairs were different. "We donated much of the furniture to a museum," Gavin explained, hugging me. "There is an entire exhibit of period furniture now, and it is referred to as the de la Roque exhibit."

"René would have liked that," I nodded. I wondered if Connegar had been to see it.

"Lissa, is it too much to ask for you to come to bed with me?"

"I want to," I said. "But there's something I have to do first."

"And that would be?" Gavin thought he was going to have to wait and there was disappointment in his face and his voice.

"I have to give permission before you take my blood. Are you ready?" I looked up into his face and those beautiful brown eyes.

"I am," he nodded.

"My blood is a gift to you, Gavin," I said, placing my hands on his face. "You will take no harm from it. There are no bindings or conditions—it is freely given."

"I can bite you now?" he was smiling.

"You can bite me now. I was hoping we'd be in bed when you did it, though."

"Then I will show you my bed." He lifted me up and carried me halfway through the house just as fast as he could.

Did I expect Gavin to pass out the minute he got my blood? No. He did, though. He was snoring softly, too, instead of going into the rejuvenating sleep. Well, I didn't know that would happen. Eventually, I curled up beside him and went to sleep, too.

~

"Lissa?" Someone was shaking my shoulder, trying to wake me.

"Huh?" I mumbled, keeping my eyes tightly shut.

"Lissa, will you explain to me, please, why I am awake in daylight?"

Uh-oh.

Fuck.

Fuck cubed.

That was Gavin's voice. What had I done?

"What time is it?" I opened my eyes to find Gavin's worried face leaning over mine.

"It is after eight, the sun has been up for more than two hours and I am awake. Explain this, please."

"Uh, Gavin, I didn't know this would happen. Honest. Ever since I came back to myself after the big bang, so to speak, I knew I had to give permission if anybody wanted to take my blood. I just thought it would keep you alive. I didn't know this would happen."

"I still have my fangs and claws, and can still drink blood—I have done so already," Gavin said, sounding miffed and mystified all at once.

"Well, now you know how I felt after Griffin gave me his blood. At least you know what happened—I didn't—not for a while, anyway."

"I can still operate as a vampire, as you did?" Gavin asked.

"Yes. The only thing that's changed is your ability to walk in daylight. You get to choose when you want to sleep, now."

"The Honored One will ask for my resignation," Gavin flopped onto his back beside me.

"The Honored One might surprise you," I said tartly. "Come on, we'll go see him right now."

"He will be sleeping," Gavin muttered.

"Let's find out." I sent mindspeech—Flavio was still awake. *I'll be there in a minute, I sent.* Flavio sounded sleepy but said he'd be waiting. Gavin and I had to dress first and he grumbled the entire time. It was worth it, though, to see his and Flavio's faces when we folded in.

"Lissa Beth, does this mean what I think it means?" Flavio was wide-awake now, I noticed.

"I guess. I didn't know it was going to happen—honest."

"Honored One, why are you awake long past sunrise?" Gavin asked, folding his arms over his chest.

"The same reason you're awake," Flavio snapped. "And if you want further proof, go see Charles, Rhett and Dalroy right now. All will be awake or able to rise for exactly the same reasons."

"Your blood did this?" Gavin stared at me.

"Those guys bit somebody else with the talent, not me," I said, smacking him lightly on the arm. "But on the brighter side, you can have pancakes for breakfast with me."

"Pancakes?" Flavio was interested, I could tell.

"Come on." I folded both of them to the villa. Mike was fine with me fixing pancakes for breakfast and Radomir wandered in while I was mixing batter and broiling bacon. He got breakfast, too.

"Want to try coffee?" I asked Gavin, who frowned at me—he was very much into his syrup-covered pancakes, thank you. The bacon disappeared, too, I noticed. I had my short stack and slice of bacon with coffee while I listened to Gavin, Flavio and Radomir discussing current vampire politics and events. They were having a great time, just having breakfast together.

"See, I told you the Honored One wouldn't be upset," I made a face at Gavin.

"You are so beautiful, cara," Gavin mumbled, kissing my hand.

"My nieces are more beautiful," I said.

"You have nieces?" Gavin stared at me.

"I didn't know either," I said. "But they're twins. Kyler and Cleo."

"I have seen Kyler," Gavin nodded. "With the Honored One, here. She is quite beautiful, but to me, you are lovelier. Will you spend the day with me, cara mia?"

"I have some work to do, or I would," I replied. "I'll get you and Flavio home, first."

"I'll take them home," Radomir offered.

"Thanks," I told him, gave Gavin a quick kiss and took off. Gavin had changed—I could see it from a mile away. The edge had been removed from his temper, from the moment I'd offered him blood. Who knew?

Now, I had four more gates to get and I wasn't dressed to go after Flakkar. I went to my bedroom first, dressed quickly in jeans and a pullover then went after ugly, smelly things. I got all four remaining gates before coming back. I didn't expect to find Gavin asleep in my bed, though. I didn't bother him, just changed into my swimsuit and went to get in the hot tub.

"Now, see, you didn't tell us again," Drake and Drew were there—naked, of course—and sitting right beside me in a blink.

"I have been waiting for you as well," Connegar appeared, undressed with a thought and climbed into the water. He had to make himself smaller so the water wouldn't come to his waist.

"Hey, thanks for calling me," Shadow slapped Drake on the back and climbed in too. All of them were naked—had they no shame?

"Uh, Gavin's asleep in my bed," I muttered, sinking into the hot water.

"All right," the twins gave each other a high five.

"What was that about?" I asked.

"We had a bet going with Dad and Uncle Crane on how long it would take him to come to his senses," Drake laughed. "We just won."

"I'm gonna pull both your braids," I grumped.

"Sounds good," Drake said, scooting closer.

"Gavin received Lissa's blood and is now capable of walking in daylight," Connegar observed.

"Even better!" Drew laughed. "We'll sick him on Dad and Uncle Crane. We'll see how a vampire Assassin stacks up to the Falchani."

"I don't believe this," I felt a headache coming on.

"You did not have a midday meal," Connegar leaned around Drew and placed fingers against my forehead. "You should eat something."

"How about pizza?" Shadow suggested. "They never make it at Grey House."

That was how we all ended up eating pizza while soaking in the hot tub ten minutes later. Mack and Justin came in, bent time and came back with enough pizzas to feed an army. They also got into the hot tub and didn't mind a bit that they were naked, either. Grace and Devin had to be proud.

"Lissa Beth, what is going on?" That was Gavin and he was now awake and looking for me.

"Gavin, I'm eating pizza and soaking in the hot tub with a bunch of naked men," I answered honestly, looking up at him—he was standing over me on the flagstone floor.

"Are all these yours?" He had hands on his hips.

"Those two aren't," I pointed out Mack and Justin. "But they brought pizza so I'm not complaining." That made Justin snicker.

We had to do introductions after Gavin removed his clothing and climbed in nude. He'd been right all along—it was impossible to embarrass an old vampire. He didn't have a thing to be ashamed of, but then nobody else did, either.

Gavin was shocked when Connegar pulled himself to his full height so he could see. He'd seen Pheligar once but Connegar was a full foot taller. Gavin was duly impressed, even for a vampire.

"This is Shadow Grey, a Master Wizard of Grey House," I introduced him. Shadow offered his hand and grinned. Gavin shook. "And these are Drake and Drew—they're Falchani," I explained. Gavin shook with them as well.

"We want you to come and spar with Dad and Uncle Crane," Drake informed Gavin.

"Drake, I'm not sure they want to see what a grumpy vampire is like," I intervened.

"Cara, I am not that bad," Gavin defended himself.

"Like I said," I gave Gavin a pointed look. "Do you want pizza?" There were still a few slices left. Gavin tried it, liked it, and ate three slices.

Gavin spent the night, and we stayed up late talking. Eventually he convinced me to sleep—I was tired and he was used to staying up all night. While he was sleeping after dawn arrived, I rose to do some sleuthing. I wanted to know who'd sent Flakkar to unsuspecting and ill-prepared worlds and why.

I revisited several gates, discovering the local populations were trying to put their lives back together after the devastation. It wasn't easy; so many deaths had come with no bodies found to bury.

A couple of worlds had found bones inside nests, but that's all they found. Most were desperately trying to make sense out of the whole thing. I wasn't having much luck either, until I caught a scent at one gate and it was so slight it was almost non-existent.

Had they stepped a toe across the gate entrance while they held both sides of the gate open? That's the only conclusion I could draw, but the scent was there—Dark Elemaiya.

I *Looked*, too and determined that it would take two to hold a gate open. One could travel through alone, but to hold it open for longer than a second or two? That took more than one. My Dark Elemaiya had help. Whether it was another Dark Elemaiya or not, I intended to find out.

～

"Where can I find wrapping paper?" I asked later. Grace and Devin were swimming in the huge pool near the hot tub. I realized I hadn't even gotten into the pool, yet.

"What kind of wrapping paper?" Grace asked, coming over to the side of the pool to look up at me.

"Really big wrapping paper?" I held my arms out as wide as they'd go.

"Get some regular wrapping paper and ask Connegar to enlarge it for you," Devin suggested.

"I hate to ask him to waste his talents on something like that," I said. "Oooh—fabric. Maybe I can get fabric." I was off like a shot.

～

"You know, if we could get her to sit still long enough, we might have a good conversation," Devin laughed.

"I like her," Grace said. "She's not going to sit around and wait for the guys to come save her. She'll kick ass first, herself."

"My boys sure love her," Devin agreed. "I don't think Dragon would have appreciated any other woman where they're concerned. Lissa, though, the minute those boys said they wanted her, Dragon was okay with it."

"How many mothers can say their sons are mated to the Vampire Queen?" Grace laughed.

"Well, there's me, Conner, who is Connegar's mother, and Shannon, Shadow's mother. I think that's it," Devin floated away on her back.

"Mother would like you to come for a visit," Connegar helped me wrap the unicorn painting in drapery fabric. It was wide enough and I'd gotten a floral pattern with wide ribbon to match. I was tying the bow on the package when Connegar mentioned his mother.

"I love your mother," I said, straightening the bow I'd just tied. "Did she say why she wants me to visit?" I gave the bow a critical look and straightened it again.

"She just wants to give you information," Connegar smiled. He was on his knees in my closet, holding up the fabric-wrapped painting while I worked on the bow.

"All right, we'll go now," I said, letting him settle the painting against the closet wall. "Am I dressed okay?" I looked down at my linen slacks and sandals. I had on a royal blue silk blouse with pearl buttons.

"You look very nice. We will go." Connegar folded me away before I could change my mind.

"We are here, Mother," Connegar folded us into a beautiful study. Conner was there, typing on what was now an archaic computer. It even had a printer for paper copies—also something currently archaic.

"Hi, baby," she smiled at Connegar. "Shane is bringing us iced tea," Conner told me, turning her smile on me as well.

"Thanks," I said. "I haven't had iced tea in a long time." Shane did bring us iced tea, winked at me slyly and took off again after leaving petits fours with the tea. I love petits fours. There were two on little saucers with forks and pretty cloth napkins. Conner let me take mine first, and it was good.

The iced tea was good, too, and mine was unsweetened, just the way I liked it. I got up to examine the huge Richard Estes painting hanging on the wall in Conner's study. "I always loved his work," I said. Conner loved it, too, I could tell. We turned to other things after I sat down again.

"I wanted to talk to you about who you were before," Conner said after we'd finished our tea and tiny desserts. "Franklin and Greg wanted to be here for this, but I said no. It was difficult enough when I showed them their lives before."

"I'm just glad they found one another again," I said. "They were so close, before."

"They have a M'Fiyah," Conner nodded. "Those are generally set before birth by the recipients themselves. I know this; perhaps one or two others know, but that's it. They all think they're given to them. They're not. They choose. And all parties have to choose before the M'Fiyah is granted."

"Wow. This is really complicated," I said.

"I want to show you who you were before, Lissa. And there is a reason for this, you just have to trust me," Conner sighed. "It isn't to hurt you, or bring up old wounds. It's just to show you what you can be in the future. You need to see this."

"Is this gonna be awful?" I asked. "I've seen enough of awful, lately."

"It may be painful, but remember that you are here, now and not there, then. Does that make any sense?" Conner gave me a small smile.

"I'm not sure, but we'll skip over that part," I said, shivering. Connegar squeezed me gently, offering comfort.

"My son loves you and he'll be the one bending time. We'll be there with you, holding your hand, Lissa."

"What if I freak?" I was suddenly gripping Connegar's shirt in my fist. I was terrified, and thinking I must have been awful in my previous life to deserve what I'd gotten in the current version.

"Do not be afraid, little rose," Connegar said and bent time and folded space before I could object.

It was awful. As awful as it could be, and if Connegar hadn't been holding onto me, I would have misted away and gone somewhere else. Anywhere would have worked, just to get away from it.

We were on Le-Ath Veronis, and the Ra'Ak were there. The city was on fire and thick smoke billowed through the streets. Buildings exploded and collapsed, sending glass, cascades of bricks and bits of masonry flying everywhere.

It was similar to what I'd seen on the High Demons' world—with the screaming and noise of buildings and structures collapsing. The Ra'Ak were killing the few vampires and comesuli who remained, and there I was.

I knew it was me—the Vampire Queen—fighting them off as best she could. She didn't have the talents I had; she was using her speed, her claws and her will to slice into them. Her clothing was in tatters as she carved through necks and was blasted away more than once by Ra'Ak dust.

More vampires screamed and died from contact with the poisoned scales and teeth of the Ra'Ak. The Queen Vampire pulled herself up and started fighting again. Comesuli were swallowed up by feeding Ra'Ak and the Queen went after those monsters next. She was hit; a long gash down her arm and side and still she fought, trying to buy time for the fleeing comesuli.

"I don't want to see this," I buried my face against Connegar's neck.

"You need to see this." It wasn't Conner beside us any longer—it was the Guardian. Light and white flame shone around her, and I was compelled to look as the Queen—me, in my former existence—went after another Ra'Ak who was chasing comesuli. A vampire attempted to help her, but he was hit and crushed. The language the Queen spoke was one I'd never heard, but I understood it easily.

"I will take you all down, I swear it!" the Queen shouted as she sliced into another Ra'Ak who darted in, attempting to bite her in half. He shrieked and leapt back, while two more came to take his place.

It was those two that killed her; one got a bite in and flung the Queen onto the street while the other crushed her body beneath his weight. It was awful. The comesuli died and the remaining vampires died. They had no will left after their Queen fell. They'd died when she did.

When I was able to lift my head away from Connegar's shoulder, we were on the Larentii homeworld and Conner was no longer with us. "Little rose, that was long ago," Connegar soothed. Falaca grazed and bleated about us in their mountain meadow, while I sniffled and wiped my face with shaking fingers.

Connegar trilled for me and it helped, but I couldn't get the images out of my mind. If there had been Ra'Ak in front of me right then, they would have died. No matter what the cost to me, they would have died.

Out of all the Ra'Ak I'd seen, only one had set aside the murderous tendencies they all seemed to have. Gilfraith. I wondered what had made him different. It didn't matter, I suppose. He was far away from them and safe, I hoped.

∽

"My love, where are we going?" Gilfraith walked alongside Fox, who strode purposely through a narrow alley in London. Fox wore a stocking cap that hid most of her dark curls and her face held a grim, determined look.

"Gil, it's all right, I just need to pick something up," Fox replied absently. "They knew I'd know about it. It's here, somewhere."

The note lay atop an overturned rubbish bin. Gilfraith didn't like the scent about it, but he didn't argue—Fox would know whether it was dangerous. "What is it?" He turned worried eyes on his mate instead.

Nearly a century before, he'd attempted suicide—by offering himself to the Saa Thalarr. He hadn't manufactured poison, to keep from harming them. He'd remembered—after a time—just who he'd been while humanoid.

He found everything about the Ra'Ak (and himself) repugnant, and was searching for a way out. The Saa Thalarr sent to kill him was Fox. Instead of challenging him, Fox retained her humanoid shape and cautiously approached his Ra'Ak, placing gentle hands on his scales. He'd turned to Ra'Ak, hoping the end might be swift. Instead, the softest touch was offered and he was lost immediately. Now, he worried for his beloved mate.

"Gil, you have to trust me," Fox lifted the envelope. She was Ka'Mirai. The ones who'd written the note didn't understand her power. Yes, she could make things change. It just didn't happen all at once, as these believed. Fox was gifted with the ability to travel the time lines. And she could reason out which small events needed nudging in one direction or another, to create a cascade of events. Eventually, things would come out the way she wanted—had she not accepted the invitation to the Saa Thalarr. Now, she could not interfere and remain among them.

"Sometimes," Fox sighed, "I only have to place the information in the proper hands to make things come out right." She shook her head sadly and tapped the envelope. "So many people dead, just to get their point across." Gilfraith brushed away her tears.

When Connegar took me home after spending time on the Larentii homeworld, I discovered that Radomir had taken Gavin home. Flavio had a short assignment for him, but he left a note telling me he loved me and would be back as quickly as he could.

"Will you be all right, little rose?" Connegar asked before he left.

"I hope so," I said. He kissed me before folding away. I tried reading but that didn't work. I was too restless now and unable to get Le-Ath Veronis out of my head. Not only had the vampire planet fallen, but the werewolf planet and who knew how many others.

Surely, the Ra'Ak hadn't always been so bloodthirsty and evil. Or, perhaps it was because Kifirin was asleep at the time. Did his kind get tired? Maybe it was because he was the only one on the dark side while there seemed to be plenty on the light side.

Maybe I'd get to the bottom of it someday. Meanwhile, there was someone I wanted to visit, and chances are if it were night where he was, he might be awake and accepting visitors.

Refizan had a gate. I found that by *Looking*, so I gated in instead of folding. The gate wasn't far from where I'd seen the Ra'Ak appear the first time I'd seen them. Something bothered me about that fact, but I put it out of my head for the moment and turned to mist to find Gabron.

The brothels had moved; they were along the riverfront now, as the city had shifted and yawned while I'd been away. There was a beautiful view of the waters in front of Gabron's brothels—I'd found them by *Looking*.

Some things hadn't changed—women still wandered around the vestibule either naked or scantily clad when I walked inside. There were naked males there too, as well as some dressed suggestively. I tried not to blush, but wasn't sure how successful I was at it.

"May I help you?" A male vampire came forward to speak to me as I gawked at my surroundings like a tourist.

"Is Gabron here?" I asked. I could see in this one's eyes that he was just about to send me on my way when he drew in a deep breath. Yeah, that seems to get their attention every time.

"I will see if Gabron is available," he left so fast that papers and debris would have swirled in his wake—if any of those things had been present, that is. I waited less than two minutes before Gabron appeared at my side.

"Lissa, my Queen, what may I do for you?" Gabron looked as carefully groomed as he always did, his blond hair styled and brushed away from his forehead neatly while gray eyes examined me and a smile tugged at his lips.

He had my arm quickly and was ushering me down a long hall. Sounds of sexual activity came through several doors we passed. Gabron would never apologize for that. I'd come to accept it, I think.

"I just saw something horrible today and I wanted to get it out of my mind," I told him. He hid a smile as he led me through the door into his office and then through another door that scanned his fingers before allowing us through. We walked into his private quarters—I was sure that's what they were. Gabron closed the door quietly behind us.

"You said nearly those same words to me once before," he said, leading me down another hall until we came to a sitting room. Gabron seated me comfortably and then poured out two glasses of wine laced with blood. We sat there together in silence for a while, both of us sipping our wine and gathering our thoughts.

"I love you," Gabron said unexpectedly.

"What?" I asked, turning toward him.

"I loved you the moment I met you. Your scent overwhelmed me and shocked me at the same time; a female vampire, walking down a street in my city and I had no idea how she had come to be there."

"Gabron," I leaned my head on his shoulder and slid down farther into the sofa, "is Solar Red still out there somewhere?"

"If that foul religion is still alive, it is very well hidden," Gabron snorted. "It was outlawed across the Reth Alliance, and alliance troops were sent out to uproot it wherever it was. That was two hundred years ago, my love. I have not heard of it since."

"Yet the Ra'Ak are still around," I observed.

"We know that very well; I thought I lost you when the memory returned," Gabron sighed. "I was quite depressed. Erland Morphis came and demanded I come out of it. He said there was still hope—that he and I might work our way into your affections."

"Erland, Erland, Erland," I shook my head. I had no explanation for the Karathian Warlock. He was handsome, though, no doubt about that.

"He is holding off for the moment; he does not wish to overwhelm you," Gabron smiled at me before leaning in for a kiss.

"Gabron, something happened to the last vampire who took my blood," I said.

"What happened?" he asked, his mouth wandering across mine, and then over my jaw to my ear.

"They, uh, can walk in daylight, now," I said, beginning to breathe in gasps.

"You don't say," Gabron nuzzled and kissed my neck. I had to say the words and say them quickly before the bite came and I came right behind it, writhing in Gabron's arms.

Then Gabron was out—asleep while my blood wrought changes in his body. I sighed, kissed his forehead and misted away. When he woke, Gabron had a surprise coming. I just hoped he liked it.

"Sure, just go off and leave us behind," Drake grumped when I folded into the villa's kitchen later. He and Drew sat at the kitchen island, having tea. Not normal tea, either—the dark kind that would keep me awake for a week if I drank it.

"Drake, honey, don't be mad," I went to give him a hug.

"I will be mad—you need to tell us, next time. You scare me to death, Lissa, do you know that?" He held my face between two large hands, bumping his forehead against mine while looking straight into my eyes. Drew was beside him, waiting for his brother to be finished so he could do the same.

"Well," I quavered, "you can always send mindspeech. I'll answer if I can." Drake sighed at my words and pulled me onto his lap.

"Have you had breakfast?" he asked.

"No," I shook my head. Mike made breakfast for me while Drake and Drew fussed and teased. You couldn't keep a smile away from those two for long.

"We have a meeting at Gryphon Hall," Drew said when I finished eating. "Kiarra sent mindspeech. She wants you to be there."

"Why's that?" I emptied my coffee cup.

"She wants to discuss the Flakkar, and how they've been attacking worlds," Drew rumbled. He shook his head—that upset him, I could tell.

"We can't do a damn thing about it," Drake voiced his brother's thoughts. "As Spawn Hunters for the Saa Thalarr, we're not allowed to interfere. This is so frustrating."

I put a hand on Drake's cheek and leaned in to kiss him. They didn't know. None of them did. I wasn't Saa Thalarr. I didn't have their restrictions. As a result, I'd taken out every stinking Flakkar that somebody had dumped on numerous worlds.

Drake and Drew waited while I brushed my teeth, and then folded me to Gryphon Hall. "Lissa, thank you for coming," Merrill murmured as he led us to a sofa in Kiarra's library.

Extra seating had been brought in—looked like all the Saa Thalarr were coming. I was shocked when they began to fold in. Kifirin had told me once, when I'd been on Refizan, that there were seven, but that their numbers would increase.

They'd certainly increased. Their healers came, too; Franklin, Shane and Tomas grinned at me when they appeared with Conner, Russell, Will and Martin Walters. Radomir leaned in and pecked me on the cheek when he appeared with Devin, Grace, Dragon and Crane.

The library was crowded already, when the Larentii came. I learned that Pheligar, Renegar and three other Larentii all operated as Liaisons for the Saa Thalarr.

When everyone else had gathered, Wlodek and Weldon folded in, Fox held between them. Kiarra went to Fox and hugged her. Fox wiped tears away.

"We called all of you here, because Fox received this earlier." Kiarra *Pulled* an envelope into her hands. "It is a message," she looked around the room, "from the Elemaiya, Bright and Dark." My heart began thumping in my chest. I knew trouble was coming, and I knew what that trouble was likely to be. I waited for Kiarra's announcement anyway.

"It reads," Kiarra began, "To the Ka'Mirai, greetings."

I was furious when Kiarra finished reading the letter. It was a demand, couched in flowery language, for Fox to come to them. To take up her "intended duties," according to their message.

If she didn't, they pointed out maliciously, the Flakkar that were now devouring worlds were only the beginning of more terrible things. That pissed me off. Truly. And they were demanding that Fox meet them—on Kifirin. The High Demon's world. Well, things started falling into place for me, right then.

"Our hands are tied," Kiarra muttered angrily. "The Flakkar are still out there, killing twenty-seven worlds and there's nothing we can do about it. Fox cannot go; she is Saa Thalarr and prevented. These stupid fucks." Kiarra crumpled the letter in her hand.

Well, she'd just used my favorite word. And it was an appropriate one, too. But she didn't have information I did.

"The Flakkar are all dead," I announced. Yeah, the words just popped right out.

"What?" Kiarra jerked toward me.

"I killed them," I shrugged. "They're all gone, now." Pheligar was beside Kiarra in less than a blink, and his eyes unfocused—he was *Looking*.

"The devastation has ceased," he came back and lifted an eyebrow at me.

"Do you know how the Elemaiya got Flakkar to these worlds?" Kiarra was staring at me, now. "They don't have the talent to gather them—the Flakkar would just as soon eat them, like they do any other humanoid."

"They're asking Fox to come to Kifirin for a reason," I looked at Fox, who was biting her lip as she gazed back at me. "I know you can't lie, so I'll draft a message to the Elemaiya. I'll tell them Fox is coming. Only I'll be there—waiting for them when they show up. I have a feeling that when they do show up, they'll be bringing a bunch of friends with them."

I was angry. Very, very angry. And a showdown was in the works. Somebody was going down. Right then, though, I didn't know if it would be me or them.

❧

"Kifirin, I want to send the comesuli to Le'Ath Veronis. Just for a while," I said. "We need to make it look as if they've gone back to their own world, which I guess they will. We can put out the rumor that they insisted on it."

"It won't be a rumor—they are insisting on it," Kifirin leaned down to kiss me. I'd sent mindspeech and miraculously he'd heard me. We were standing on the lawn in front of the villa, and fireflies were winking here and there around us.

It was so beautiful there on that mid-May evening. The scent of the grass was sweet and the flower gardens surrounding the villa were all in bloom. "When should I take them?" Kifirin asked, a bit of smoke trailing from his nostrils as he nuzzled my collarbone.

"In two days," I said. "Do you think they can be ready by that time?"

"They are prepared to go now," Kifirin said, smiling and taking my hands to kiss them. "There is something you should know, avilepha. There are eight hundred Croth and Drith who have thrown in their lot with the others."

"I thought that might be the case," I nodded, watching his hands as they gently massaged mine. "I want to get the comesuli out quickly so they won't suffer losses like they did before. Hardly any High Demons died—the good ones, anyway, but the comesuli died in the thousands."

"I know this," Kifirin agreed, sighing. "We will do this, love. I will do this for you."

"Thank you," I smiled up at him.

~

"Can you get me to the Black Ra'Ak?" Kyler answered my mindspeech and now she considered my question.

"I can get you to the King of the Black Ra'Ak," Kyler said, dimpling. I'd stretched out with some of my newly discovered talents, and learned that Kyler was instrumental in bringing the Black Ra'Ak (the few that still lived, anyway) on board when the Copper Ra'Ak attacked Kifirin before. They'd helped fight off their Copper cousins.

"Good enough," I smiled at my niece. She took me to see Youon,

King of the Black Ra'Ak. He was in humanoid form and stood six feet tall, with light-brown hair and green eyes. He invited us into his library to talk.

I stared at shelf upon shelf of books—in languages I would have to translate to read. I didn't think his Copper cousins bothered to read; they were too busy causing trouble and eating people. I laid out my best offer to Youon. He thought about it.

"If we can continue to take from the worlds not worth saving as we do now, to feed ourselves," he nodded. "We are selective—we always have been. We do not take young. That has always been against our code. We are also selective in the ones we take to turn to Ra'Ak."

"Like the vampires do?" I asked.

"Similarly—yes. We look for those with redeeming qualities. We also feed upon animals, as you know. We take humanoids six times in every cycle, and those are always criminals."

"Six times a year," Kyler translated for me. "They raise their own animals, otherwise."

"I can live with that, as long as you keep to those rules," I agreed. "How often do you reproduce?"

"We keep our numbers at a constant," Youon informed me. "We lose some to punishment, or one is killed upon occasion. We are powerful as you know, but we can be killed." He smiled at me as he said that. He and I both knew what I could do.

"Lissa, I don't understand this at all," Gavin paced while I watched. Drake and Drew had come, along with Shadow and Connegar. Erland Morphis had brought Gabron for me on the condition that he be allowed to stay. Tony had also come; I almost cried when he showed up.

"Gavin, you don't have to understand it. You just have to stand behind me on this."

"I will support Lissa," Gabron said.

"I also support Lissa," Karzac walked in. I hadn't seen him since I'd hauled him around as mist in a jungle.

"I support Lissa," Kifirin folded in; he'd brought Roff with him.

"I support my Raona," Roff said.

"I support my little rose," Connegar said, causing Gavin to turn sharply in his direction.

"I also support Lissa," Erland Morphis declared. I wasn't sure he had a vote but he acted as if he did.

"Lissa, I don't like you going back into this," Shadow said.

"I know, honey, but right now this is the best plan we have."

"We are about to go into cardiac arrest," Drew said, pointing to himself and his brother.

"If this doesn't work then we'll all be gone soon," I said. "I don't think any of them are holding anything back this time."

"You mean every Copper Ra'Ak in existence is going to be there?" Shadow asked, sitting down hard on a barstool. We were holding our meeting in the kitchen at the villa. "How many of them are there?"

"Nearly thirty thousand," Connegar supplied the numbers.

"May the stars be merciful," Shadow whispered.

"Those numbers do not include the High Demons that have allied with the Ra'Ak or the Elemaiya, both Bright and Dark," Connegar added.

"Honey, you're not helping," I pointed out gently.

"Lissa, baby, are you sure you know what you're doing?" Griffin folded in. I heaved a huge sigh. I wasn't sure I appreciated my father showing up, but I didn't say anything, choosing to answer his question instead.

"I think I do. We'll know soon enough."

"Then I can't stop you, sweetheart. Just bear in mind I can't lose you a second time. Don't ask that of me."

"I hope I'm not asking that of any of you," I said. "But we'll just have to wait and see, won't we?"

"Lissy, tell me you know what you're doing," Tony begged.

"Tony, if I don't, it won't matter anyway," I informed him gently.

I was still up two hours later—after most of them had gone off to argue further among themselves. I just couldn't deal with it anymore. The only two left now were Karzac and Griffin.

"I took Karzac to see Belen yesterday," Griffin said, setting a cup of tea in front of me. I was zoned out, staring into space and not thinking about anything, mostly. My mind had gone into overload and I had just shut it off. Tomorrow would go as it would.

"Why did Karzac need to see Belen?" Griffin's statement brought me back to Earth.

"I, uh, asked him for a M'Fiyah," Karzac muttered.

"Can you ask for those things? Conner told me they were set in stone before we're born." I searched Karzac's face—he was usually so strong and sure, but now his face held a bit of uncertainty. I was about to get my heart broken again, I just knew it.

"They are," Griffin agreed, watching me carefully. I leaned my face into my arms at the island. "But as you know, Pheligar muted his for nearly fourteen thousand years before it manifested."

"True," I sat back up and sighed. I wasn't going to point out that Griffin had destroyed the one I'd had with Merrill. Griffin nodded anyway. He'd caught my thoughts. "What does Pheligar have to do with this?" I asked, steering the conversation away from shaky topics.

"You remember Thorsten?"

"I never met him, but I understand he was in charge when I helped Dragon on Refizan. I know it was a long time ago for both of you. For me, it has only been a little while. All those memories are still fresh."

"Thorsten interfered then, too. Just as he did so many other times," Griffin said, sitting beside me. "Thorsten was punished for some of his misdeeds; Belen sent him back to the beginning. Thorsten muted the M'Fiyah Karzac had with you, baby. Karzac felt a twinge anyway while he was with you on Refizan, but it wasn't full-blown as it should have been. Belen released the muting, Lissa. Karzac is yours if you want him."

I went numb. There were now so many new things chasing through my mind, and I couldn't grab onto any one of them and hold on for longer than a blink. "But what about Grace and Devin?" I almost choked on those words.

"They know already. They have already informed me that they are happy to share. You should have been my first love, Lissa," Karzac moved Griffin aside so he could stroke my hair. "Lissa, it still pierced my heart the first night you were with Dragon and me, and you asked me how much night was left before going out and treating Solar Red to some of their own medicine. You touched me first. I've never had a woman come to me. I liked it. And then you came haring after me and Jeff, just to pull us and many others out of a terrible situation. I had to ask Belen. I wanted you so badly by that time I couldn't handle it anymore. Say you want us, little firefly."

"Karzac, I wouldn't still be here if I didn't," I grumbled, putting my arm around his waist.

"That is all I need to know," he said and bent down to kiss me.

Karzac followed me to bed, placing me in a healing sleep before I could even argue with him about it. Fox was supposed to give herself over to the Elemaiya at noon the following day on the steps of the High Demons' palace. I needed my sleep for that, and Karzac made sure I got it.

Pheligar folded all of us, including every Saa Thalarr, every healer and every Spawn Hunter and a few extras—mates and such, to the palace in Veshtul the following morning. I dressed carefully and for effect. Fox was nearly jumping out of her skin at every little noise and Gilfraith, the expatriate Ra'Ak who loved her so much he couldn't stand it, was doing his best to calm her down.

"If this doesn't work," I quietly told Connegar in a corner of the suite we'd been given to prepare, "will you fold Fox to the Larentii homeworld? That's the only place I know where she'll be safe for as long as possible."

"I will do this for you if things go badly," Connegar promised. "The Larentii homeworld will be the last to fall as it was the first to be made."

I nodded mutely at his words. Kiarra was pacing off to the side. I looked around me—the suite was luxurious. The High Demons had spared no expense when the palace was built, and it was beautiful.

I remembered Kifirin once told me a vampire designed it. Not a High Demon—a vampire. That made me hold my head up. My Inner Circle—that's what Kifirin called them—were standing guard around me.

Karzac looked as fierce as any physician could; Drake and Drew were there in full battle gear—black leathers, head to toe, and two blades strapped across their backs. I could see either one of them as Warlord on Falchan at that moment. They were allowed to protect their mate—they were the only Saa Thalarr or Spawn Hunters standing with me.

Gabron was nearby, watching everything and everybody intently, although his body was as still and straight as a blade. Shadow was there, dressed in modified Wizard's robes. They wouldn't hinder him, and he wore the blue of his trade. Shadow was ready to put a spell on anything that moved.

Roff had come, although he wasn't prepared as well as the others. He'd insisted on being there; all other comesuli, including Giff and Toff, had been moved to Le-Ath Veronis by Kifirin.

Erland Morphis had come with Gabron, and he radiated with Power. I discovered Erland held a lot of Power, and wouldn't hesitate to use it if it were necessary. Gavin and Tony were also there, dressed comfortably for ease of movement. Someone had given Tony blood; he was standing there in daylight. I figured it had to be one of the twins. Last of all, and it came as a shock to me, Gardevik Rath came forward to stand with the others. I shook my head at his appearance, but I didn't say anything.

"Are you prepared?" Kifirin folded in at the last moment. I nodded.

"Then I will create the disguise," Connegar offered, placing his hands on my face.

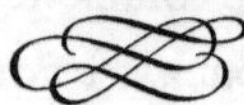

$\mathcal{I}$ looked exactly like Fox. For the moment, anyway, as I misted down the steps of the palace. I materialized on the third step from the bottom and surveyed the palace courtyard before me.

It was empty—for the moment. Jayd and Garde had warned everyone else away. Connegar was shielding the others from view; my posse—my Inner Circle, was standing at my back. I only had to wait a few seconds before the empty space in the palace courtyard began to fill.

Ra'Ak were folding in by the thousands, and all were in Ra'Ak form. None had come as humanoid. Somewhere amid that sea of Copper Ra'Ak, High Demons materialized in Full Thifilathi. They'd come for a lynching, it seems.

Then, when nearly all the Ra'Ak were present and all the High Demons were present, the last few Ra'Ak folded in with the Elemaiya. I was staring at the newly crowned Ra'Ak Prince, the Queen of the Bright Elemaiya and the King of the Dark Elemaiya. I'd seen both of the latter before.

"I see you made the wise decision," the Ra'Ak Prince growled around his serpent-like tongue and multitude of teeth.

"Perhaps. But before we go any farther, you should inform your allies of what it is, exactly, you intend to do afterward."

"That is of little consequence," the Ra'Ak Prince snapped. "Come to the Elemaiya. I care not what they do with you."

"Yes you do," I snarled. "You want the Ka'Mirai for yourself. You can cause a lot of trouble that way, can't you?" Elemaiya hissed at my words—they didn't believe. "You're here to take the planet," I pointed at the Ra'Ak Prince. "Your High Demon friends back there think you're going to hand it over to them, don't they? Only that's not the plan. You think to rule the Dark Realm yourself. You think you have that power, don't you?"

"We have the power. Stop this immediately and I may allow you to live." His words brought protests from both Elemaiyan camps. They were desperate to get their hands on Fox for some reason. The Ka'Mirai could turn back time for them—I knew that much—but hadn't gone into any of their reasons for wanting to do so.

The Ra'Ak, too, wanted something from the Ka'Mirai, and it was too terrible to contemplate. That had been a part of their agreement when they bargained with the Elemaiya, only they intended to take Fox for themselves and destroy the rest. I shoved those thoughts aside.

A voice now whispered in my mind. I'd heard it before, when it told me of the gates in my dream. It had explained to me then, just why I was still alive. It gave me a choice, too. That choice had been frightening at the time. Now, I was forced to make the choice, just as I'd done once before. I was choosing a path, so others might live.

It was time to act.

Time to see what I was made of.

Time.

"Then it may interest you to know," I said, flinging off Connegar's disguise, "that I am removing the rule of the Dark Realm from the High Demons." I held out my arms and *Pulled* Power to me. It answered so readily to my call, prepared to do anything I asked of it.

Light formed around me as I gathered energy, but I ignored it. My Inner Circle was pulling in to surround me, and I was only peripherally aware. More Power came and my light grew brighter.

Many of the Ra'Ak were now turning their heads—their eyes were the most sensitive and vulnerable thing about them. I'd learned that the first time I'd fought them.

"Who are you?" The Bright Queen demanded. Winds were picking up now, whipping and swirling around me. I'd left my hair loose intentionally. The Elemaiya knew I wasn't the Ka'Mirai—had known for several seconds.

The Bright Queen and Dark King both recalled seeing me before, with Kifirin. They were afraid to approach me. I pulled the last of the Power to me that I needed, holding it to me. I was shining as brightly as a star by that time. Connegar or someone shielded the eyes of my Inner Circle—they stood straight and strong, unblinking, behind me.

"You wish to know who I am?" My voice was thunder, echoing across the city of Veshtul. "I am Justice!" I roared and every Elemaiya, Bright and Dark, dropped to their knees.

"Take her!" The Ra'Ak Prince shouted, and I laughed. When several Ra'Ak attempted to fold in next to me, they discovered they were held back. I could do it—with only a thought. The planet now retained a shield around it for those attempting to flee. All who stood before me were rendered powerless.

"I will pass sentence first upon the High Demons who think to kill their brothers," I announced. "You are reduced to your humanoid status," I said, and all of them turned from their Thifilathi form, shrinking and screaming.

"You will no longer be High Demon," I announced. "Your power is removed and your lifespan is reduced to two hundred years. The remaining High Demons will determine your fate from now on." I heard shrieks and cries among the crowd—a few High Demons were being eaten by Ra'Ak. I ignored it.

"Now, for the Elemaiya." They were still on their knees and some were flat on the ground. "There are only a few of you who had no desire to participate in this takeover," I informed them, the power of my voice forcing them to cower. "Those I will send away with these words: You will never again be capable of gating between worlds— that ability is removed. You will also never reproduce with any others except yourselves. The days of procreating with humanoids are over. Be careful how you treat the others on the planet to which I send you. I will watch you carefully from this point forward."

Only sixteen Bright Elemaiya disappeared.

"Now, for the rest of you," I proclaimed. "You are also confined to a humanoid existence and will spend your days here, serving the High Demons. Your lifespan is reduced to two hundred years and you will only reproduce with your own kind. Your days of mistreating your quarter-blood children are over. It is my suggestion that you learn the laws of the High Demons swiftly, as they deal justice quickly if those laws are violated."

"You cannot do this; you do not have the power!" The Dark King shouted, rising up.

"Test me," I thundered. Black clouds boiled over our heads, and lightning split darkening skies. "Try your own power—I know you can shapeshift." He did try. And failed. He began to curse.

"Silence," I waved a hand and he dropped to the ground.

"Now, to the Copper Ra'Ak," I turned my attention to the Ra'Ak Prince.

"You cannot do anything to us—we balance the Larentii. Kill us and they die, too." He was so sure. So smug in his beliefs.

"That was true," I agreed. "Before."

"You cannot change that," the Ra'Ak Prince spat.

"I am changing it," I announced. "Your Black Ra'Ak cousins now hold the balance for the Larentii. They did not defy Kifirin as you did. Had you taken the rule, it would have been a hollow victory. You would have been Prince over the Dark Realm of dead worlds. Dead as you made them to die. You, also, are now reduced to the humanoids you were before becoming Ra'Ak. I decree this."

I blew my power and light outward, just as I often blew my mist outward. Each mote of light was charged with purpose and leapt to do my bidding. Ra'Ak screamed and writhed as they were flung on the ground and forced to change.

The Elemaiya were also screaming and crying as they scattered to flee the chaos. I still stood before them, no longer surrounded by light and power as they began to rise from the ground—human, frightened and unsure.

~

Jaydevik and his brother Gardevik now flanked me as I surveyed the thousands of powerless humanoids before me. "These are your replacements for the comesuli," I grumbled. "I don't think many of them know much about anything. You have a long road before you."

I looked up at Jayd. "If you want a safe place for Glindarok while she's pregnant, she's welcome on Le-Ath Veronis." I turned to walk up the steps to the palace. My Inner Circle pulled in and walked up with me.

~

"Where is the balance now—and the rule of the Dark Realms?" Garde asked me later. He, Jayd, a few High Demons, the Saa Thalarr, Spawn Hunters, healers, Kifirin and I were all in the meeting hall. The other High Demons were out herding former Ra'Ak, High Demons and Elemaiya around.

"It rests with my Lissa upon Le-Ath Veronis," Kifirin announced. "I made a promise not to interfere when I made the Dark Realms. That turned out to be a terrible mistake. My mate is now what I am and she made no such promise. You will all answer to her."

"You're one of the Nameless Ones?" Kiarra gasped.

"A sister to the Nameless Ones," I nodded. "Mate to Kifirin and Queen of Le-Ath Veronis," I replied. I was weary, too, but I wasn't going to show them that. I'd had a decision to make and once it was made—to accept what I had become—it was something that I couldn't forget or lay aside. It was forever.

The one who'd charged every particle of my mist with power and enabled it to come back together, had also allowed me time and the final decision. Time to work through the anger and betrayal, and then time to make the decision whether to accept what was offered or not.

The situation had been such that if I hadn't accepted, the worlds would now be dying while the Copper Ra'Ak danced their fatal victory upon the streets of Veshtul. I sighed.

"We can bring in artists, cooks and craftsmen to teach the rabble you now have," I offered. "Do not be lenient with them. They had no leniency for others." Jayd and Garde both agreed with me. Gilfraith came forward and knelt before me.

"Hey, don't ever do that," I said, pulling him up as gently as I could. Kneeling and bowing were just—embarrassing.

"I want to thank you," he said, looking into my eyes. "The Ra'Ak was always there inside me, and I had to control it every minute. It is now gone and I have not felt so happy since before I was turned."

"Then I'm happy with you," I said. Gilfraith smiled at me and backed away.

We spent the afternoon hammering out a few details, and I was exhausted when we finished.

"My Raona is tired," Roff announced as we left the meeting hall.

"Honey, you don't have to announce it to everybody," I whispered, putting my arm around him and leaning against his shoulder.

"If I am to be your mate and a member of your Inner Circle, it is my duty to make such announcements," he said, squeezing me tightly.

"Where are we going?" I asked. I was hungry, too, but I sure didn't intend to let that out.

"Le-Ath Veronis," Kifirin said, as if I should have taken that information from his mind. I could have, but that would be rude. I was in mid-yawn when we were all folded away, and the yawn turned to a squeak at what waited for me when we hit the ground on the vampire planet.

Well, ground wasn't the proper choice of words. We landed on marble floors, surrounded by marble walls with huge marble columns evenly spaced down a long marble hall.

"Tybus designed this palace as well; I only had to recreate it," Kifirin explained as I stared in awe. "He made the High Demon palace as a lesser version of this." He swept out an arm to indicate the

Queen's Palace on Le-Ath Veronis. Lights were everywhere, and the whole thing looked to be from a fairy tale.

"All solar-powered," Kifirin explained. "The power lines run from the light hemisphere. There are farms near the light half of the planet and the comesuli are already there and working them. Others are tending the flocks and herds and two cities of vampires are already here, avilepha. Gabron's vampires from Refizan are here in the southwestern part of this city—but there are only three thousand of them. The other city is twenty miles away. Do you wish for Earth's vampires to reside in the capital city with you?"

I was holding my breath as I looked around me. Gavin and Tony were nodding; Tony enthusiastically, Gavin's nod a bit more sedate. Drake and Drew were grinning; Karzac sent his agreement in mindspeech. Shadow shrugged, but it was Roff who made my decision for me.

"Giff will like it very much if Rolfe comes." I nodded and smiled wearily at Roff's statement.

"You're too tired to see your palace right now," Kifirin pointed out, once the decision was made. "Healer." Karzac came forward and I was out as soon as his fingers reached my forehead.

"I am King and Chief Advisor. The rest of you may sort everything else out," Kifirin waved an arm. He was sitting on the top step where Lissa's throne sat. He knew she wasn't going to appreciate having a throne, but it was expected.

"We will preside over security; both hers and that of the palace," Gavin pointed to himself and Tony.

"We will command the army," Drake and Drew grinned.

"I'll handle planning, construction, and the laws governing the infrastructure and utilities of the cities," Shadow said. "I have engineering degrees, after all. I want to inspect the water treatment facilities right away, and the desalination pipelines from the ocean."

"I will handle the courts and enforcement of the laws, which will require working closely with Drake, Drew, Gavin and Anthony," Gabron announced.

"I will handle the running of the palace," Roff declared.

"We still need somebody to handle the farming industry, plus we need to import fishing boats and other things to feed the comesuli," Shadow suggested. "And we need a chief of staff plus scribes, secretaries, whatever you want to call them," he added.

"I'd like the chief of staff job," Kyler folded in. "I'm not doing much of anything at the moment."

"I will handle the building of medical facilities for the comesuli and set up a proper training program for them," Karzac said. "As well as being personal physician to the Queen. I can't imagine the Saa Thalarr will need me much—Lissa just eliminated their job, after all." Drake grinned at Drew, giving him a high five.

"There will be other things to warrant their attention from time to time," Belen folded in. Kifirin rose and bowed slightly. Belen bowed back. "We also have an announcement to make," Belen nodded toward Kifirin. "We have permission to rebuild the dark worlds. That means the werewolf planet, as well as all the others, will be inhabited again one day. I wish to enlist the help of the Larentii on this." Belen smiled at Connegar.

"It is acceptable if the permission comes from you," Connegar rose and nodded respectfully to Belen. "Ferrigar will not refuse and many Larentii will be most enthusiastic over the project."

"What did I miss?" Erland Morphis folded in. He gasped when he saw Belen standing there, shining inside Lissa's throne room.

"Lord Morphis," Belen chuckled. "We cannot presume to leave you out, now can we? Perhaps you can oversee the business of the flocks and herds."

"Don't forget the fishing and mining," Shadow said.

"Mining?" Erland's ears perked up.

"We have a winner," Drake laughed.

"You mine it and I'll make jewelry out of it for the Queen," Shadow grinned.

"I don't want to go." Kiarra's birthday party was scheduled and my Falchani twins were dressed to attend. They were trying to convince me to come along. I wasn't in the mood.

Yes, Kiarra and I shared a birthday, but mine wasn't the one to be celebrated. I hadn't celebrated a birthday since Don's death. Well, this one would go uncelebrated, too. Kiarra and I would have shared Merrill, had he and Griffin not done what they had. I wasn't in the mood to see either of them. Two days had passed since the finale on Kifirin, and I was still tired. I had things to consider, too. Kifirin planned to bring Earth's vampires the following day, and I wasn't sure how some of them might react.

"Go on. Take this with you," I pulled the fabric-wrapped painted off the floor of my suite and handed it to Drew. He wore a sad look, as if I'd told him Christmas was canceled or something.

"Baby, come with us," he begged.

"No. Go on, now. I have things to think about." I shooed them out of my suite and shut the door. My suite. It was large enough to play football in—European or American. I hadn't slept well in it the past two nights, and refused advances from both Gabron and Shadow to spend the night in my bed. I sighed and shook my head before misting to the uppermost dome of the palace roof.

"You made the right choice." He was there beside me—the one whose voice I'd heard. We were connected, he and I. I shook my head at his words.

"If this body dies—this corporeal body—the only mate I can keep is Kifirin," I muttered, hugging myself uncomfortably.

"For now," he nodded. His eyes were filled with stars.

"How many thousands of years, though, in between?" My gaze fell upon the southwestern section of the city below the palace, where Gabron's Refizani vampires now lived.

A few lights twinkled there, and if I reached out with only a thought, I could see the vampires as they walked or worked or spoke with one another. They were no longer held by the sun. They could sleep and wake as they willed, now. But there'd been a price to be paid for that freedom.

I'd paid it.

When I made the choice offered to me, I'd consented to live forever—just as I was. The same memories would be mine. The same loves, hates, everything. There would be no rebirth and forgetting for me. Truly, there'd been no choice—if I hadn't done as I did, all would now be dying.

It might take some time for all the worlds to fall silent, but they would fall silent. It was the way they were made—the balance that they kept. Destroy the balance, and all would fall. Now, the balance was Le-Ath Veronis. Actually, the balance was me.

"I wondered when you'd realize that," he spoke again. "You managed to open the barrier between light and dark worlds, did you know that?"

"Yeah. I felt it fall when I made the choice," I muttered, leaning my chin on my knees. Before, only High Demons, Ra'Ak, and Karathian Warlocks and Witches held enough power to breach the barrier and travel between light and dark worlds. Now, that barrier was destroyed and all could come and go.

"Space travel will now be possible between the two." He chuckled at my thoughts. I sighed. "You know you can't do it again, don't you?" he added.

"Do what?" I lifted my head to stare at him.

"Hold that much power in your physical body. If you try, it'll explode and die."

"Yeah. I know that, all right." It was true. If he hadn't stood (invisibly) beside me on the palace steps in Veshtul, I would have exploded right then and there, after *Pulling* all that Power to me. He'd helped me hold my corporeal self together while I pronounced judgment against the Ra'Ak, rogue High Demons and the Elemaiya.

"If you're corporeal in the future, you can only employ what you had before. I can't help you. You can call some power to you if needed, but if you need real Power, you'll have to go to energy to use it."

"I guess that's okay," I sighed. "I'm pretty good with what I have."

"Yeah. I've seen that." He smiled, and just like that, his eyes were back to normal.

~

"Raona, tell me what you want and I will prepare it." Cheedas followed me around the kitchen as I searched for ingredients to make brownies. I wanted chocolate. And it was my birthday, so I was determined to have chocolate. One way or another.

Cheedas fretted the whole time I searched through his new domain—the massive kitchen inside my palace. I lifted my head at that thought. It was my palace. The whole, damn, stinking, huge behemoth. Mine. I slapped a hand over my face, and that's when they found me.

Roff walked into the kitchen, dressed in a tux. He was followed by Tony, Gabron, Shadow, Connegar, Drake, Drew, Karzac, Kifirin and Gavin. They were all dressed in tuxes, including Connegar, and I had no idea how that had been accomplished. He never wore clothing like that. I got the idea that whatever was about to go down with my posse, they hadn't planned to do it in a kitchen.

Roff knelt before me first, took my hand and slipped a thin band onto my right index finger. He smiled and told me he loved me before standing and moving aside. Tony was next; he selected a finger and did exactly the same. Gabron kissed me after placing his ring. Shadow's ring looked as if it were made of glittering diamonds. "Its Tiralian crystal," he said after kissing me. I had to *Look* to see what that meant. Tiralian crystal was extremely rare, glittered brighter than diamonds and the cost? I had a fortune on my hand, now. I also knew Shadow had made it himself and that it was a protection jewel.

"You're the best, honey," I smiled at him.

"Just don't forget it," he grinned.

"This is Larentii memory stone," Connegar slipped his nearly transparent ring onto a finger. "It holds the memory of what we saw upon Le-Ath Veronis in the past, and also what you did two days ago.

You kept your vow, little mate." He smiled at me, kissed my forehead and stood aside.

Drake and Drew came together—how could it be otherwise? They placed their rings onto my right ring finger. They were shaped as mirror images, and both held Tiralian crystal that fit together and looked like one band. Only they and I would know it was actually two rings. "My handsome Falchani," I had a hand on both their cheeks.

"I love you, baby," Drake whispered.

"I love you, too, Lissa," Drew said. "More than anything." They rose and joined the others who'd already given me rings. Karzac came then and placed his ring on my left index finger. It was wider than the other bands and carved in the likeness of fireflies in flight. Where each light would be there was a jewel that winked.

"Honey, that's beautiful," I said. He kissed me this time; I didn't have to kiss him.

Gavin came next and when he got down on his knee, he proposed. "Lissa, will you marry me and say yes to me, this time?"

"Yes," I couldn't keep the tears from sliding down my cheeks. He placed my old rings on my left ring finger, right where they belonged, kissed me several times and then moved away.

Kifirin was last, and I had no idea what he was going to do. He remained standing instead of kneeling before me. "This belonged to you before," he said, slipping a gold band onto the middle finger of my left hand. It was inscribed, only I couldn't see through my tears to read it. "It holds the Queen's promise to protect Le-Ath Veronis and her people," he said. "Your promise to them is a promise to me as it was before."

"Thank you," I said, as best I could.

"This finger will be ours," Erland Morphis and Gardevik Rath were both there quickly. They'd slipped in at the last. Erland was holding my right hand and stroking the ringless middle finger, offering a blinding smile.

"You need to take that up with the others over there," I nodded toward what was now my Inner Circle.

"Not many problems; we just have to deal with the current shortage of females," Flavio informed me as I was trying to fasten a bracelet on my wrist. That caused me to look up—Flavio, Kyler and Cleo were all in my suite, watching me dress for the stupid coronation that everybody insisted on having. "Get Gabron on that," I muttered. Well, he used to run brothels. Surely, there were women out there who wouldn't mind having intense orgasms along with a bite.

"I'll talk to him, then," Flavio smiled. He liked Le-Ath Veronis already. Nearly two hundred thousand of the two hundred fifteen thousand vampires had been brought to Le-Ath Veronis from Earth. Even Jarl made it, I was happy to see.

The ones who hadn't made it for various reasons had been euthanized. Kifirin was thorough and explained to me that the ones not making the transition were unsuitable. I didn't argue with him. We didn't need to hunt rogues right off the bat.

Flavio and the others had also come out of the closet regarding their modified status, and the vampires didn't seem to mind a bit. They were free now and didn't have to hide from anyone.

Flavio had the running of the city government and to my embarrassment, they'd named the damned capital Lissia. Was that awful or what? All the Council members were still Council members, seemed quite happy with that fact and loved their new homes.

Somehow, they'd managed to bring a large portion of their wealth with them, which made me sigh. Vampires tended to be old and wealthy. Banks were already going up and I had Kyler working on finding someone to oversee that. I asked her to approach Merrill, Charles and Adam soon and get them to help.

When I'd become what I now was, some of the hate and betrayal had been filtered out concerning Merrill and Griffin, but there was still an uphill climb for those two. They knew it. A wrapped package had been waiting inside my suite after I'd gone to bed on my birthday, and it held two paintings. One was mine—the Vermeer I'd kept long ago. The other was a Corot and beautiful—a scene of a single boater on a river.

That had come from Merrill and Kiarra, with a birthday card. Well, Merrill and I would never be. Being what I now was, Belen wasn't the only one who could mute or destroy M'Fiyahs. Merrill made his decision long ago. I was making my decision now, only I was muting it. Merrill had opted for destruction and for me, it was too much.

Cheedas, my new comesula chef, had taken over the palace kitchens and was hip-deep in cookbooks that Connegar translated for him. He was so happy he could barely contain himself and any night, almost, I could go down to the kitchen and find his latest cooking experiment baking or bubbling away. If he kept making brownies for me, I might gain some of my weight back.

I'd personally searched out Darvul, Orliff and Noff. Darvul wept at my feet when I found him on a farm on the bright half of the planet. Orliff and Noff were overjoyed that I'd remembered them, and shocked that they hadn't recognized the Queen when I was under their care. I gave each of them a kiss and told them I didn't know who I was, either, at the time.

All three were now learning from Karzac and Jeff, who'd come to teach modern medicine to the comesuli physicians. Franklin was designing a hospital for Karzac, and it would be built to his specifications.

Susila was often at the palace and looking for something she might do in addition to sitting on the city Council. Rolfe was chief of my personal guards, which pleased Giff very much. Someday, Giff was going to be a beautiful winged vampire and she and Rolfe were going to be very happy together.

Meanwhile, Kifirin and I were going among the oldest of the comesuli, determining which would make good turns and which would be female. We were also looking into potential sires for them. Being able to *Look*, with my other gifts, was a blessing. Many of the females would be placed with the vampires they would love. Someday, there would be equity in the male/female ratio.

"Are you ready, yet?" Charles poked his head inside the doorway. All the former vampires were here—this was a milestone for them as well. They were citizens of Le-Ath Veronis, just as the others were.

"I'm coming," I grumbled. The dress I wore was cloth-of-gold crusted with jewels and embroidery. I accused Erland of doing this to me deliberately—he, Gabron and Giff had gone to pick it out. Giff was now in charge of my closet and was busily stuffing it as quickly as she could. She also went to bed with Rolfe on his nights off. He seemed perfectly happy with that.

"Look regal," Flavio said softly as we walked down the long hall. I slowed my steps and did my best to look Queenly. My posse was waiting on the palace steps; they'd sent Kyler, Cleo and Flavio to get me. I still had no idea what was going to happen, and wished I were two light years away instead of heading to a stupid coronation.

The sea of vampires and comesuli that stood before the palace was frightening, and it was so quiet when I appeared you could have heard a feather fall. Erland Morphis was there, as was a film crew. How the hell had he managed that? Somehow, he'd gotten a newscaster (one who was famous, apparently), from a network that served the worlds that had space travel.

The journalist was making quiet commentary while the filming went on. Wlodek and Griffin stood nearby, and a microphone hovered above Wlodek's head. Who knew he could make a speech?

"We come here to crown a Queen," he announced, his voice echoing over the crowd. "A Queen for the faithful among the vampire race. A Queen to rule the Dark Realm and bring peace and justice to all who dwell there. Someday, too, the werewolves and many others will live again. The Dark Realm will be reborn through her."

Griffin came forward then, holding my crown on a pillow. It resembled a vampire's claws; ten long points rose from the gold circlet that fit on my head. I wanted to roll my eyes at all the fuss. Why did I need a freaking crown to start with? I had to keep my thoughts away from that; the cameras were trained on my face.

If the crowd wanted a show, however, they got one. Kifirin

appeared out of nowhere in a blaze of light. He was dressed as a King —crown and all.

"I am Kifirin, Lord of the Dark Realm," he announced as if he were used to being on camera every day. "I will crown my mate and Queen this day. If any choose to defy her, know now that they will have to deal with me."

He lifted the crown off the pillow, came to stand before me and carefully placed the crown on my head. It glittered with jewels around the wide band and was a bit on the heavy side.

"All hail Lissa Beth, Queen of Le-Ath Veronis," Griffin shouted, and the roar of the crowd below us was deafening.

The End